/3/72

The Vampires

BY THE SAME AUTHOR

City of Night
Numbers
This Day's Death

The Vampires
by
John Rechy

Grove Press, Inc.   New York

Copyright © 1971 by John Rechy
All Rights Reserved

No part of this book may be reproduced, for any reason, by any means, including any method of photographic reproduction, without the permission of the publisher.

Library of Congress Catalog Card Number: 70–155123

ISBN: 0–394–47585–2

Distributed by Random House, Inc., New York.

First Printing

Manufactured in the United States of America

For the Memory
of
My Mother

". . . a dead body which continues to live . . . sucking the blood of the living, whereby it is nourished and preserved in good condition, instead of becoming decomposed like other dead bodies."

—Georg Conrad Horst, about vampires

The following appear or are mentioned in this book:

RICHARD, the host.
TARAH, his first wife.
LIANNE, his second wife.
KAREN, his third wife.
JOJA, an actress; once his mistress.
MARK, Richard's son by Lianne.
GABLE, Richard's son by Tarah.
BLUE, a call-boy.
SAVANNAH, "the most beautiful woman in the world."
JEREMY, a Catholic priest.
BRAVO, an underground superstar; Karen's companion.
MALISSA, a "friend" of Richard's; she travels with a changing entourage of young companions:
    LA DUQUESA, a figure in mourning veils.
    TOR, a bodybuilder.
    REV, a hood.
    TOPAZE, a perfectly shaped midget.
ALBERT, Malissa's partner of vague relationship.
THE DUKE, la Duquesa's mourned lover.
THE MAMALOI, a voodoo highpriestess.
THE PAPALOI, a voodoo highpriest.
MR STUART, a male "madam."
PAUL and VALERIE, twin brother and sister.
HESTER, their mother.
DANIEL, her husband.
CAM, a youngman.
THE BLUE WOMAN, a drug goddess.

Part I

1

The two figures were silhouetted against the stark rectangle of sky framed by the wide window. Drapes thrashed savagely in a trapped wind dashing at the room. Rigid as if the blood had frozen it in that position, one figure knelt over the other. The long silver knife was poised ready to plunge again: *Now!* Swiftly it was thrust into the astonished flesh. Again! Again!—seeking the heart.

For moments, it was difficult to determine the origin of the scream, which had suddenly stifled other sounds of frenzy within the palatial house. A scream welling like a siren struck momentarily mute, only to rise grasping at all sound—did it come from the kneeling figure rocking back and forth over the slaughtered body in a rhythm which was almost sexual, the brutal knife buried in a savage ceremony? Or did it come from the body on the floor—a final severed protest against the silver object raiding it? Perhaps the scream, already fading into a chanted moan shrouding the others, was a fusion from victim and victimizer.

Suddenly the wind released the whirling drapes. Motion stopped. The two silhouettes were still and silent, dark statues.

Like uncaged birds, voices rushed to fill the silence as the others moved swiftly in an enclosing circle about the body drenched in blood:

"Is this the game?"

"No, God, nobody plays games like that!"

4 · The Vampires

"An exorcism!"

"Playing at God!"

"No—Satan!"

"No, no!"

"Your terrible experiment!"

"Exorcised!"

"Is this the game!"

That murder will happen tonight on a secluded island dominated by a huge mansion surrounded by coves and rotundas—an island embraced by water so clear it rejects reflections, revealing sand like pale-yellow sugar.

But that is not what Joja—red hair rumpled, purple eyes groggy—saw when she woke only moments ago. It was the angry sun clawing at her eyes through drawn drapes. She rolled to the other side of the bed to Escape the glare—and bumped into the body of a man, his head turned anonymously away from her, one naked leg curled over the black sheet.

A tattoo. There was an elaborately wrought tattoo on the man's ankle: A star enclosed in a swirl of curled vines. An inverted star. From times of dabbling at fashionable, not-quite-serious mystic rites, Joja remembered dimly: A sign of violence? . . . Who is he? she wondered—dismissing him quickly as one more in the army of nameless morningbodies.

Disoriented as to where she was, she rose naked from the crumpled bed. Her skin was as flawless as ivory. She staggered cursing across the plush rug (stretching furrily to the edges of the walls in which were exquisitely mosaicked figures in silhouette: gathered as if at an arcane invocation) toward the hostile windows, to pull the treacherous drapes.

Then she saw it on the fleecy rug: thin, delicately blue

like a piece of tissue paper. She bent over it. A prophylactic rubber, the lightest color of blue. A design was imprinted faintly on it. A cloverleaf. . . . No. The inverted star again among the viny swirls. A rubber used and slack—but nothing had been emitted into it.

She turned away from it. At the window, shimmering water flung darts at her eyes as she stood by the brocaded drapes. Thick vines with heart-shaped leaves, orange flowers with protruding slim tongues licked hungrily at the window. The naked sun commanded the green trees which rimmed the island like elaborately costumed sentinels. The island. . . .

Richard's island!

Joja turned eagerly toward the sleeping figure. Now she could see his face. Long ash-blond hair, sideburns a shade darker, thick eyebrows and eyelashes even darker, almost black—a startling contrast. A beautiful youngman. Perhaps twenty-three. Ten years younger than she, came the uninvited judgment. Yes, beautiful. A naked, depraved angel. But, of course, it was not Richard.

As if this would thwart the disturbing thoughts tugging insistently at the quivering edges of her mind, she began to draw the sheltering drapes.

The splashing of water demanded her attention.

Below the window, a pool looped in an extension of the curling sea. As if having been waiting for a signal from her window, a figure emerged quickly from the water and looked up.

Through sun-needled eyes, Joja had the flashing impression that the figure—a boy—was naked. In fascination she stared at him. But the figure dove back into the water, now a floating shadow beneath its surface.

Overhead, an insistent whirring gathered seeking to localize itself. Following the sound into the sky, azure and cloudless, a shield of blue silver, Joja saw a helicopter descending weightlessly on the island. Like a giant thin insect, it landed in a clearing. Swiftly a woman emerged from its belly.

Malissa! Joja knew. The diabolical woman who flaunted her courtship of evil. Unwelcome memories stirred like echoes: *"Burn me!" "Yes, darling, do!—she wants you to!" The odor of singed flesh.*

Now a man with enormous shoulders followed Malissa. Then a veiled figure in total, black mourning. And someone small—a child?—but was he carrying a cane? Then a man in shiny leather. Behind them all: a plump, older man, in a brown checkered suit.

Malissa—and Albert, still with her!—and this season's entourage collected as usual from the devil knows where!

What terrible games is Richard planning?

Joja pulled angrily at the drapes.

Why did I come back?

She returned to the bed. The foot with the tattooed star was stark on the black sheet. She heard again the beckoning splashing of water outside. Did she imagine it now? Because it was more like the echo of applause. Applause. (*A stage. "Louder, Joja!" Then the recognition: Her life a silent pantomime: "I had to kill her!"*)

To stop the pursuit of memories, she reached out to touch the youngman beside her. He did not react. The splashing of water faded, becoming now like the slow flapping of a bird's wings. Fiercely this time, she rose again. She looked out the window.

At the edge of the pool, the boy, now distinctly in trunks, looked up at her, capturing her eyes for a frozen moment.

Joja retreated quickly from the window.

Now the boy outside looked away and toward the

helicopter which had just descended from the sheet of blue onto his father's island.

Extravagantly shaped, backs like the spread tails of peacocks, grillwork chairs surrounded the pool. White statues stared without eyes at the blue jewel of shimmering water. On the vines, flowers sputtered like varicolored flames.

Facing the sun, Mark's eyes were shockingly green, rimmed by thick, long eyelashes—eyes astonishingly light in the deeply tanned face. His full lips parted only slightly in the barest ghost of an undefined smile. Dark hair, wet, clung to his forehead and, long, licked lovingly at the back of his neck almost touching his wide shoulders. Mature beyond his fourteen years, his body was perfectly shaped, bronze stomach ridged, legs sturdy, muscular, long—a fact emphasized by the brief black trunks cutting high into his thighs. A boy of unbelievable beauty and dark, cold sensuality.

As lithely as a panther through his jungle, Mark moved along the tangle of paved walks, toward the woman and the others who had descended from the helicopter a distance away. Along the paths, flowers grew like fragments of a shattered rainbow.

"Mark!" Malissa's hands were extended toward the boy. Her fingers, a fierce blaze of red rings, mimed the beginning of an embrace. But clearly they did not intend to touch the boy, nor did he move more closely toward her.

"Malissa," he said. The ambiguous smile did not yet fully touch his lips.

Her face resembled a mask, a handsome, stark mask; the skin was tightly stretched over high, dramatic cheekbones. It was a face, therefore, of indefinable age—she could have as easily been forty—or younger—as fifty, sixty, seventy. Her mouth was rendered more brutal by its dark lipstick. She wore a brown hat whose brim swerved in a diagonal "S" shading a side of her face. Even so, and despite blue-smoked bubble sunglasses, her eyes shone intense and cruel. Though she gave the appearance of height—because she was monumentally imposing, exuding the radiance of power—her body was actually small, and slim. Elegantly attired, she wore a tan dress—and rings, rubies, on all her fingers, rings as red as the scarf—red like fresh, young blood—about her neck. And one black coiled ring like an ebony snake.

Demonic powers were attributed to this woman. Her capacity for evil was legendary among occult groups throughout the world; she was reputed to be one of the most evil women in the world: a reputation enhanced by her vaunted proclamation of alliance with "the dark world." She carried that black reputation haughtily like an uncontested champion.

"Why isn't your father here to meet me?" she asked Mark.

"He went to the mainland," Mark said; that was their designation of the island city nearby. He spoke to her as a clear equal.

"Of course. He would be away," she said.

The others had remained in the background, behind her, like actors awaiting their cues, which were now being given in introduction: but it was, more, as if Malissa were exhibiting a carefully chosen collection, as inanimate as that: objects given names only for the purpose of reference:

"La Duquesa." Malissa extended a flashing-ringed hand toward the figure in mourning.

Dark black sunglasses stared from behind a black veil. The sheltered eyes seemed pasted on the pale-white face. Now one hand—fingernails lacquered black—drew the veil slightly apart, the other raised the black glasses, also slightly—to gaze at Mark for only an instant. But for that moment the sorrowful, black-painted eyes devoured the spectacle of the incredibly sexual boy. La Duquesa sighed, the veil quickly drawn, the glasses adjusted: a shield.

"Your grace," Mark acknowledged graciously, knowing la Duquesa was a man.

"Albert— . . ." Impatiently Malissa's fingers indicated a plump, past middle-aged, unattractive man in a brown checkered suit. He hovered deferentially about the woman, whose eyes avoided him entirely.

Mark knew him—Malissa's unlikely permanent companion, the only one who lasted from year to year: as she traveled like a high-class vagrant from country to country, collecting a new "entourage" of youngmen replaced each season: a source of constant speculation as to their purpose: Malissa was notorious for her hatred of sex.

The dumpy man smiled eagerly at Mark.

Malissa pulled away even the hint of attention from Albert. Her fingers shifted it—like a physical tide to be easily manipulated by her—to a youngman in leather. "Rev— . . ."

A diagonal scar from the edge of one eye to his lips sliced Rev's face into two distinct aspects: one hardened and savage, the other almost soft, the two fusing into a brutal, sensual face mounted on a slender body which instantly projected the tightly wound violence of a champion boxer. He wore black buckled boots, tight black pants, a leather vest open at the neck to reveal the growling face of an emerald-eyed panther tattooed menacingly on his chest.

Mark studied Malissa's companions, the smile on his face still not formed, objectless.

"Topaze!" Now Malissa's ruby fingers were reaching down as if to touch a very small man at her side. Again, they merely mimed the act of touching—as if, consummated, it might contaminate her. Inches from his head, the ringed fingers rose.

Slightly more than three feet tall, Topaze was a midget —rather, the miniature of a perfectly formed man, because there was nothing of deformity about him; his body was flawlessly proportioned. Strikingly handsome, about twenty-five, he was a dashing, haughty figure in a see-through flowered shirt with full sleeves, a bright neckerchief like a pirate's under his proud chin, a plumed cavalier's hat, and furled swashbuckler boots. He carried a studded cane.

"Tor." Malissa continued displaying her new entourage: Coolly: She could have been exhibiting her rubies. She had indicated a huge youngman with muscles like coconuts.

He wore a striped tank-top shirt which revealed deeply carved pectorals like armor plates and a small waist just this side of ridiculous over massively muscled, sculpted thighs; a body, not tall, astonishing in its muscularity, each muscle seemed to shock the others into competitive tension. For a moment, looking at Mark, the good-looking, squarejawed, blank face of the blond muscleman seemed to strain, unsuccessfully, to form an expression.

Mark shrugged his own broad shoulders. The floating smile had still not fully shaped on his face.

None of the entourage—nor Albert—had spoken, merely nodded in greeting—walkons on the stage of Malissa's life.

A goggled man waited silently in the helicopter for Mark's orders.

Given: "I'll send for their bags," Mark told him.

Malissa was looking at the house, Richard's house. It rose above the low cloud of trees like a temple.

Now Mark moved with her, the others following along the curling, mosaicked walks, the elaborate grottos, flowers like distorted stars, fountains jetting satiny ribbons of water. The sun gazed intensely, anxious to expose everything, yet emphasizing dark black shadows.

They reached the stairs leading to a wide semicircle of massive white columns choked by purple vines. Then they passed inside, into a giant hall with a high round ceiling like that of a cathedral.

Overhead, a clear glass dome captured a perfect circle of sky. In a graceful "Y," a swirl of balustered stairs swept to the upper stories of the palatial house: a luxurious cavern of ornate arches mounted on high, proud, elaborately wrought columns. Chandeliers hung like exquisite silver icicles: lighted despite the sun rushing through the dome: muted halos like burning moths in the brightness. The walls were a panorama of paneled tapestries and paintings: colors smothered: all depicting mute figures waiting somberly. Shadows of silhouettes. The floor was a gleaming vortex of whirling black and white patterns.

"Welcome to our house," Mark said with a proud toss of his head.

2

The motorboat cut the water into a frothy triangle which quickly disappeared behind them into a sea so calm that sand was visible like crushed crystals.

At the helm, Bravo faced Richard's island. A hostile world to be attacked. From this distance it was a cluster of green crowned by the luminous blue and gold dome of the house.

Dark-haired, amber-eyed, of angular, tall body, Bravo wore a cowboy hat thrust defiantly on her head, a vinyl blouse, brown bell pants, tight, emphasizing the extravagantly slim hips; and shiny boots to her knees. Even as she steered, she clung to a thickly woven whip, an integral part of the image she had molded on the screen, and, now, a part of her identity. Hard, fiercely feline, her androgynous beauty had made her an idolized superstar of underground films: Women admired the maleness, men desired her cold beauty.

"The boat may take longer, but it's better than being in that fucking helicopter with that bitch Malissa," she said. Two women sat behind her, one faced the island, the other turned her back to it.

"We could have waited for the helicopter to return for us," said Karen, the woman who faced the island. Her skin was so fair, so delicate that although she wore a wide hat she shielded her face with a hand. She had the frail, translucent beauty of women produced incestuously by generations of inbred kings and queens. Her eyes seemed still to be colored. There was a whisper of doom about her beauty.

"She would have left the odor of her rancid perfume," said Bravo. "She's a snake."

"More deadly than that," said the woman facing away from the island. She stared fiercely at the sea they left behind them, as if seeking something lost irretrievably within the mysterious depths each farther inch they advanced toward the house. This woman's beauty combined the vibrant sensuality of a whore with the cool elegance of a queen. In contrast to Karen, she—Tarah —exuded a ferocious, though cold, energy. "She's one of the most diabolical women in the world."

"Those youngmen she collects each season—why?" Karen asked.

"To torture Albert," Tarah said tersely.

"That pitiful man always with her," Karen understood. "And what happens to the others when the season ends?"

Bravo listened attentively as if plotting an assault.

The looming house. It was already a presence—even to Tarah, who had not yet faced it. Their words seemed at least in part meant to thwart their awareness of the island's approach.

"There's talk that she dazes them with drugs, pills—anything," Tarah said. "That she scorches their souls until they accompany her like zombies. When she's through, they just disappear."

Still forming words to diminish the awareness of the nearing island, Karen said, "Does Albert really support her? Why does he stay with her?"

"He's certainly not her lover," Bravo laughed derisively. "Malissa is sexless."

"Her black powers," Tarah said wryly.

"Bullshit!" Bravo spat. "All that Satanic crap—it's just her thing, man!"

"Some day they'll confront each other, Richard and Malissa—over the wreckage of the others," Karen said as if to herself.

"Maybe one of them won't be around for the confrontation," Bravo lashed.

Quickly, Tarah faced the island. The house. Like a mosque, looming. A bright apparition over trees mottled by patches of thick colored blossoms, its high dome crushed by the island's brooding verdure. Richard's house, his island: floating on the sea like a green shimmering oasis. "After so many years, I'm coming back," she sighed to herself.

"How many?" Karen asked, making Tarah realize only then that she had spoken the words aloud.

"Eighteen," Tarah said. "Though I've seen Richard in other places— . . . I was married to him for one year."

"The usual space of time," said Karen. "So was I." Then: "Why have you come back?" she asked abruptly.

"He invited me," Tarah said hurriedly. Yes, he had written her, asking her to come to the island again— that was true; but: "I'm not sure why," she said. "Perhaps that's the reason: To find out why." To define the void he carved! her mind cried, the void she tried to fill with youngmen: always with resignation like that of a person with an incurable malady, hoping for, but not rationally expecting, a miracle. The illness only manifested itself more deadly after each shadowy encounter. "And you—why have you come back?" she asked Karen.

"Because it's over," Karen said quickly. She spoke to Bravo's rigid back. "Because I'm free, now I can finally face him again." On his island, where he brought me to life only to "kill" me, she thought. (And remembered: *"There is your purity!"* And: *Two naked bodies groveling in a crushed bed. Faces astonished by the pouncing light. "Baby!" "I hate you!" "I'll kill— . . . !"*)

"And you, Bravo?" Tarah asked.

Bravo clutched her whip fiercely, a weapon. (*Two kneeling figures. The whip about their necks.*) "To be with Karen," she said.

The sound of the motor only emphasized the heavy silence demanding to be filled with the unasked question between the two wives: Why did he send for us?

"Will Gable be here?" Karen thwarted the silent question.

"My son? No!" Tarah blurted; it was a shout of protest. "I would kill him before I let Richard see him again!"

The boat had reached the shore. Bravo jumped out onto a sandy pierlike projection of the island. With untypical gentleness, she held her hand out carefully to Karen.

Tarah studied the island. Under the glaring sun it blazed with iridescent colors. Tropical trees and vines shrugged heavy with flowers. "Sometimes it seems alive," she said.

"Hello," Mark greeted them casually. He was moving along the shore toward them. Hearing the motorboat's approach, he had left the others in the house. "You're my two stepmothers," he said to Tarah and Karen. It was the first time he had seen them.

He was so much like his father they had recognized him immediately. "Mark," Karen said. Both women moved to touch him in greeting.

But he went quickly to the boat, fastening it easily to the dock. He smiled back at them. "My father's not here right now—he had to go to the mainland," he explained. "I'll send for your bags."

Bravo's eyes assaulted the boy—the son of the man, not yet met, whom she loathed.

Tarah was staring nakedly at the boy's body covered only briefly by the trunks. Quickly, she lifted dark sunglasses to her eyes.

The three women followed Mark along the path, thickly overlaid with luxurious nets of vines, veils of delicate lilac flowers shrouding arched trees. The path was inlaid with colored stones forming intricate designs —like all the others leading to the house: circuitously, to display the paradisiacal beauty of the island.

"There's a scorpion!" Mark said suddenly.

Karen stifled a scream.

Bravo raised her whip swiftly.

"They're fatal," Mark said. "But they strike only

when they're taunted. You've got to force them to sting." He glanced at Bravo's whip, ready to lash at the scorpion on a thick overhanging vine. "Can you really hit something that small with your whip?" he asked her.

"I'm an expert," Bravo said coldly.

"That vine," Mark indicated the one on which the scorpion was poised. "It's called *la malaspina.*" Its leaves were shaped like long hearts, yellowish green where they faced the sun—their unexposed sides were orange-veined, dark. Red flowers burned on it like dots of fire. "The black people on the mainland use it in their voodoo rites. It's supposed to be a powerful hallucinogen. They say it also induces confessions."

"What kind of confessions?" Bravo said abruptly.

Tarah frowned, a black memory smearing her mind: *Nameless bodies.*

"Whatever there is to confess," Mark said. "But it's just a legend."

Tarah paused before the house she had fled so long ago. (*A howling night. With Gable, a child.*)

Mark waited, as if for her decision whether to enter.

Quickly she walked up the white stairs, into the rotunda of columns.

"Some of the other guests are already here," Mark said. "An actress—Joja."

The two wives reacted tensely in recognition of the name. And so Joja too would be here.

A smile barely touched Mark's lips. "And Blue," he continued. "And Malissa and her companions. And a priest. And Savannah." He turned swiftly to Bravo for a reaction, as he had turned toward the others when he had mentioned Joja.

"Savannah!" Bravo said.

"You know her?" Mark asked slowly.

Bravo met his challenging look. "Yeah."

Clear, black-rimmed green eyes moving from one to the other, Mark faced the three women. Fully now, he smiled, a slow, sensual smile. "There will be other guests, of course," he said.

"Will your mother be here, too, Mark?" Tarah asked abruptly.

Mark moved into the house. Without looking back, he answered: "Lianne's in an insane asylum."

Captured by Mark's radiating sensuality, Tarah knew: I came back to kill Richard.

Joja leaned over the body beside her. The black sheet barely covered it. "Hey!" She allowed her nipples to brush his shoulder.

He opened dark, dark blue eyes.

Joja pushed her hair from her face. "Who are you? ... No—wait! *What* are you? I dig ... types." Her hand curled the dark brown hair on his chest. (There was something she must stifle: a fact to avoid facing.)

Without apparent source in any emotion, the smile on his face seemed attached. He lay back lazily, hands under his head: the gesture of a man used to being desired.

"You're— ... ." Her fingers floated down along the hair on his flat stomach, toward the thick triangle barely exposed by the sheet. (The insistent, avoided thought pulled at her mind, unwelcome. She thrust it away by focusing her total attention on the blond youngman:) "An awol marine!" She made love to the words with her full red lips. Her hair cascaded, orange, like an implied promise over his chest. Her hand paused in its exploration of his body.

"Yeah," he said, his voice a slow, lazy, deliberate

drawl—a put-on. "And my name is—uh . . . Mac! Yeah. And diggit: I'm an awol marine, a busted sergeant, man."

She threw her head back laughing, the red gorgeous mane of her hair cascading over her face. He was playing a role for her. (*A role. The curtain dropping like a symbol between her and the shouting audience: "Louder!"*) "With that long beautiful hair of yours you must have been awol for years!"

He threw his straight hair back with a careless toss of his head, a half-smile on his face, just slightly surly in the assurance of his desirability. He stretched his long legs so that the sheet fell away. He was obviously exhibiting himself to her. The hair on his body dark brown, it was thick on his chest, diminished to a thin trickle to his navel, then flared heavily again into a furry, inverted "V" at his groin. Only the tattooed ankle remained covered by the sheet now.

"Whatever you are, you're delicious. Ummm!" To prove it (and to cancel the ravenous thoughts gnawing even more insistently now at her mind to remember why she was with him), she licked his nipples. Then her head rose quickly, her mouth hovered over his, her breasts touched his chest. Now her left leg curled over his thighs, almost mounting him. Her lips opened wide, sucking his. Simultaneously her hand reached up, back, pulling at a remembered cord dangling to one side of the bed. Soundlessly, two round panels on the ceiling parted in a circle, revealing a mirror like a silver eye over the bed. It stared down at the two beautiful bodies doubly naked on the blackness of the sheets.

"You're not even hard!" Joja blurted. Instantly she slid off the youngman. Contemptuously, on his thigh, she dropped his cock, not even hardening.

The youngman sat up immediately. His deep-blue

eyes darkened violently on the woman. (*A face.* It invaded his mind. He saw: *A dark youngman.* Heard: *"You're not hard!" You're not hard you're not hard you're not hard!* Remembered: *Scarlet rage like an exploding flower. Blood!*)

"And you couldn't make it last night either!" Joja accused him. "You had a hard time getting into that weird blue rubber!"

His hand moved out menacingly as if to hit her; but, more, it was a motion of thrusting away a scarlet memory. Then the hand retreated, and he lay back: both bodies on the black sheet like corpses.

Suddenly Joja's anger funneled on Richard, and she allowed herself to face this: Richard had not met her last night at the airport. Now she tried to reshape the rest of last night. A complicated jigsaw puzzle, only the edges formed: Disappointment, indignation, rage. As the time of Richard's arrival stretched, she tried to wipe out the growing anxiety with liquor and pills, pills taken blindly, arbitrarily—"roulette," she called it—from small bottles always with her: the tiny powerful props of her barbiturate, amphetamine life. It was then that she picked up this blond youngman, also waiting for Richard. *Why did I come back?* To flee the city! Yes, already summer had threatened to collapse like a decaying body over the giant city. To flee that. And the memory of: *A child gasping*— . . . But even more— . . . To be with Richard again. After so many years: On a symbolic death row, she had learned of a reprieve—his invitation to return. An invitation. Yet she had felt . . . summoned. And then he didn't meet her at the airport, sent his mute pilot: tacitly allowing her and this beautiful, strange youngman— . . . The jagged pieces fitted, unwelcome, into an almost total recollection of last night: to the point of their arrival on the island: The warring pills had finally slaughtered her into momentary oblivion.

If he didn't want me, why did he send for me? The menacing question finally formed. "Did Richard— . . . Did he put us in the same room last night?" she verbalized the only remaining, harsh doubt. "*Was* Richard waiting for us?" she asked bluntly.

"I don't know Richard," the youngman said. He formed words: His mind still hovered on: *Naked bodies wallowing in blood. A woman's blue-painted body covered with feathers like squirming worms. Her voice trapped in a glassy trance: "A human sacrifice, a new king— . . ."*

"Then why are you here?" Joja asked him dully.

"He saw my picture— . . . He wrote me." (His mind exploded with the memory of headlines: "*MURDER!*") "My name is Blue," he asserted softly, as if that would explain everything about him.

The door opened.

Mark stood there.

Suddenly under the glass dome the youngman and girl studying the house were caught in the whirling vortex of the floor's black and white patterns. Gleaming vitreously, it created a reflected, inverted world of somber tapestries and dark paintings, of arches, pillars, icy chandeliers, gossamer halos about them.

The girl had an instant sensation of vertigo. To stop it, she reached for her brother's arm.

Eighteen, with dark brown hair, they were twins, remarkably alike except that what in her was feminine, delicate, lovely—she resembled a beautiful serene madonna—in him was masculine, strong, handsome. Only the dark eyes, too fierce, appeared incongruous on their faces.

"Look." Valerie pointed to an adjoining room.

"It's a theater," Paul said incredulously.

"Or an altar," Valerie said in astonishment.

They had moved from the domed hall and into a lavish room of gold, lofty arches, white paneled walls. Against one side was a round carpeted platform like a stage. On it were two black-draped forms—one large, elevated—it might have been a shrouded throne; the other tall, slender: props, perhaps, to be uncovered at the proper time. And an exposed, full-length mirror like a crystal trap. . . . Again, paneled paintings lined the walls: waiting figures; they conveyed the unfocused threat contained in tense dreams. About the large room, gilded divans, rococo chairs waited for an audience. One wall of the gold and white room was glass, allowing the island's torn spectrum of colors to invade its pristine harmony—but only within the invisible boundary of glass.

"Daniel mentioned Richard's elaborate entertainments. Maybe he's going to stage a play." Sensing his sister's sudden apprehension, Paul attempted to still it with mention of their father, whom they spoke of by his first name. He himself felt no threat. No: only an acute interest.

"I believe Richard will stage a play." The words had been spoken by Malissa. She was moving quickly toward Paul and Valerie, as if otherwise they might Escape. The blue-glassed stare enclosed them. Even now, without the shading hat, she appeared ageless. "You're the twins," she said. "You're very beautiful. Of course. Like all the people Richard— . . . Collects? Invites?"

Valerie averted the woman's blue gaze. "Thank you," she whispered.

"I'm not responsible for your beauty," Malissa rejected. At the entrance—somber silent figures like those depicted in the ubiquitous paintings along the walls—Tor, la Duquesa, Rev, Topaze waited. Albert lurked behind them. Valerie felt suddenly that they were blocking the door. She felt trapped within the woman's blue gaze. Now boldly, the plumed cavalier hat dashingly on his head, Topaze advanced into the room, inspecting the draped props on the stage.

"Your father," said Malissa, knowing immediately who they were. "Is he free?"

"Free? From—of what?" Valerie said tensely.

Malissa's jeweled hand made an arc before her, clearing invisible, obtrusive shapes between her and the girl. "From whatever!" she laughed. "It was just a question. One should always ask it. Free! So many are bound by something or other. Do you agree? . . . Your zodiacal signs!" she said peremptorily. Her hands indulged an arcane language of their own: They thrust, they parried, they sliced, gestures defined by flashing rubied arcs and lines, slashing. "Gemini is too obvious," she said. Her eyes adjusting carefully to their total intensity, she studied the twins closely like objects under a powerful microscope.

"We were born under different signs," Paul told the woman, apprehensive that she might guess it herself.

"Of course," Malissa said. "You're Virgo!" she tossed an ambiguous accusation at Valerie. "And you— . . ." Her finger was a jeweled stiletto pointed at Paul. "You're Leo." She did not wait for them to acknowledge her uncanny accuracy. Now she wove words hypnotically. Her mouth hardly moved. It was her hands, her eyes which seemed to speak: "Planets tossing through the sea of space—air, water, fire, earth. Planets rising and descending, choosing the shape of destiny: And yours!—separated by a mere speck of time in eternity. But a vast chasm between you, and a violent— . . ."

"You're wrong about violence," Valerie did not allow the woman to finish.

"Indeed." The stretched skin of Malissa's face eased into a smile.

On the elevated stage, Topaze was looking curiously at the tall, lean upright prop draped in black.

"Will he be here, your father?" Malissa interrogated Paul and Valerie.

"No," Paul said, awed by the strange woman.

"You've never met Richard," Malissa said. It was a statement.

La Duquesa drew her black veil to peer longingly at Paul.

"We've wanted to," Valerie said. She had a feeling that they were being led to a trap, but she did not know whether her words were pushing them into it or away. "But Daniel kept saying— . . ." She stopped. Words which had no significance suddenly became weighted with shadows. This was the trap, springing:

"That you weren't ready," Malissa finished for her.

Valerie touched her brother; a sudden, barely consummated contact.

"But now you are ready," Malissa's dark lips said.

3

Joja reached for the black sheet to cover her nakedness from Mark. Blue made no motion.

"Don't you knock before walking into someone else's room?" Joja said. Instantly she felt an iron fascination which obviated the tone of her voice.

Clearly unperturbed, "I'm sorry," Mark said. "The door was open, and sometimes I use this bedroom."

"You're Mark," Joja said. Of course she knew it: Richard's stunning, depthless eyes, the same perfect teeth, the same—already—sensual mouth: a glimpse of Richard as a boy. Her eyes glided from the boy's face to his body, to the film of sunbleached hair on his legs. It would feel like velvet, she knew. She turned away quickly.

Blue's eyes were clamped to the boy's face. He remembered another dark, young, sensual face. But, no, there was no real similarity; it was only that the obsessive image was constantly being projected by his memory on the screen of his mind.

"Yes, I'm Mark." The boy looked first at Joja, then at Blue. "And you're the famous actress," he said to the woman.

Does he know! (*Louder! The curtain falling like the sharp blade of a guillotine. The girl gasping for breath.*) No, he couldn't know. Joja reached for a nightgown among clothes spilled on the floor. Now covered in diaphanous blue, she stood up, showing her body.

"And you're Blue," Mark said to the youngman in bed. "I recognize you from— . . ." He paused, very long.

Blue's eyes deepened darkly. (*Like slides shifting rapidly: Black newspapers, black photographs, black type: "Notorious male prostitute— . . ." And his photographed face buried under the black tombstone of headlines.*)

". . . —from my father's description of you," Mark finished finally.

"Yeah, man, I'm Blue." Again the name was a definition of himself. He still lay defiantly naked before the unperturbed boy.

"Do you know much more about us?" Joja tried to assume the tone of someone parrying with a bright child, but she had not been able to withhold an edge of apprehension from her voice: The question was important. Her fascination with Mark grew; he was so poised, so cool.

"My father doesn't keep anything from me," Mark said. He sat on the bed, one bare leg propped before him, leaning his head on it over crossed arms. Then he saw the blue rubber on the floor. He seemed to study it as if it held a profound secret. Swiftly he looked at Blue's tattooed ankle, now exposed, and smiled.

The remembered face lunged again into Blue's mind.

"My two stepmothers are already here," Mark told Joja.

Joja felt a stab of bewilderment, resentment: Then: Fear. Richard's ex-wives. And she, once his mistress. Summoned? Why? "You were a little boy when I was here last," she heard herself saying to Mark, explaining away a suspicion vaguely forming.

"That was six years ago," Mark said. "I asked my father about you," he said.

Though spoken with typical casualness, his words startled her. Had they tried to convey a message from Richard? the thought formed involuntarily.

"I remember how you used to hold me," Mark said.

"You were a child," Joja answered. It was suddenly as if she must defend herself.

And then Mark's words were bullets: "I remember the man who burned you the night before you left."

(*I felt dead!*) Joja's eyes flashed angrily at the boy for evoking the ugly memory.

Suddenly for Blue the room pulsed with vibrations of violence which he must flee: The remembered face was a presence here, now. To stir his physical motion, he got up. He dressed in a pale-blue shirt, buttonless, open, and white pants. He remained barefoot, the tattoo like a signal.

Joja sat before a mirror near the window, searching the scorched scar on her breast. She touched a button on the wall. A halo of amber lights surrounded her image. Her face was livid suddenly, features erased, as if it were fading into a beautiful lifeless specter.

Blue moved wordlessly to the door, his hand on the knob. He waited there.

The pit inside Joja whirled. Richard! she thought. But it was his son she was looking at in the mirror. She held her breath. Then she began to rehearse, consciously—with difficulty—the words she must soon ask Mark: What do you want to tell me about me and Richard?

The door closed. Blue left the room. He walked soundlessly along the golden halls, down the swirl of steps. Tall, sensual, he moved stealthily, as if he were stalking someone, or being stalked. It was partly that which surrounded him in an aura of existing within a symbolic glass booth, remote yet visible, almost on display: allowing others to view him, yes, but not to touch him, or to enter his silent world. Though blond, he conveyed a sense of darkness.

He stood under the glass dome. He heard voices from another room, from within the cavern of lofty arches. "And so here we are waiting for Richard." The voice extricated itself from others. Blue moved toward it. He saw a woman standing before a youngman and a girl, their backs to him.

Now Malissa looked away from the twins and at the stage. The draped props stood like witnesses waiting to testify. Quickly, she moved out of the room, into an anteroom next to it, as beautiful as all the others: this one amber; that color warmed the striped chairs like frozen zebras.

Topaze moved alongside her. He walked with a flourish, a swagger; acutely aware of his stunning, miniature beauty. The rest of the entourage, and Albert, had followed her as if on cue.

Now she sat on one of the striped chairs. On a stool beside her, Topaze leaned thoughtfully on his cane, his chin propped.

"Yes," Malissa continued, "Richard would make sure we waited for him. But I don't mind. Great generals often wait for war!" Malissa savored each seasonal encounter with Richard. They were preparatory encounters, she knew: One day they would confront each other. It was inevitable. Each season, she watched Richard, studied him: waited for the exact time when she would assert her power.

"War?" Paul questioned her, he and his sister joining them. Emptied of the others, the propped stage had suddenly threatened him. "Why do you expect war? We're Richard's guests."

"Of course," Malissa said. Her eyes closed behind the smoked-blue glasses, as if she were receiving a message which her sight might dissipate.

Against a wide window: Staring intently at the complex of the gardens outside, paths like mazes: Incredible shoulders braced, Tor stood, a shadow waiting for its features to be assigned.

In a private revery, la Duquesa sighed: "Even now, without the Duke, the most beautiful thing in my life is the memory of his love."

Picking at his nails with a knife—a part of him—Rev, eyes shifting constantly as if he expected to be threatened, glanced at the queen as if each word provided a mounting challenge.

"You're very lucky to have known love, your grace," Albert said seriously.

Malissa's eyes opened on him, swallowing him with contempt. One hand spoke its violent language: It rose slowly, fingers spread; then it fell. Lifeless.

"My God! What a beautiful man!" la Duquesa gasped involuntarily. Through the door she had seen Blue. Restraining herself quickly, she sighed: "But I'm in mourning, I will be true to the memory of the Duke."

Blue stood at the entrance to the anteroom. Beyond it he saw the empty stage: the central black prop. (He remembered: *A black throne!*) He felt Malissa's eyes. The inverted star on his ankle—was it there that she stared? Now she seemed to be magnetizing his eyes, to pull them toward her. Turning his face, he broke their powerful wrest, for now. Paul. Blue's eyes glided toward the youngman. Was he to be haunted all his life by that other face, imprinted now on this youngman just as it had been on Mark's earlier? No, Blue told himself, again there was no real similarity. Between this youngman and Mark, yes—but not with— . . . Now again, like a powerful pulling current which had been allowed to ease only momentarily to exert its irresistible power, Malissa's gaze, even distilled by the blue glasses, commanded him to look at her. He did. Soundlessly on bare feet he walked toward her, accepting her challenge, to face her. The tattoo burned on his ankle. He stood defiantly before the seated woman. He saw: Her red rings, and the black coiled one. (Remembered: *An old man. Long ringed fingers. A fingernail outlining a star on his palm.*)

Malissa looked down quickly at the ornate tattoo, and then as quickly into his face as if she were staring through crystal ice. "Pisces!" she called his sign suddenly.

Blue nodded.

From behind the blue glasses, her gaze plunged like a nail of fire into his frozen façade. "With Aries rising!"

He nodded somberly again.

There was a sudden vicious snapping sound. Bravo's whip had sliced into the room, seeking no object except stunned attention.

"*My* sign—call it, Malissa!" Bravo challenged. Karen stood next to her.

Malissa's head spun toward Bravo. "Scorpio!" she tossed quickly. The smile on her face allowed no error. "Double scorpion!" she flung like a curse, one flashing, rubied hand thrust outward in a sudden motion as if the words were physical weapons. "Both sun and moon in Scorpio! Not the upper aspect of the eagle—but the lower path of the scorpion— . . ."

"The path of death," whispered Blue.

"And decay!" lashed Malissa. "Signs of decay and death!"

"Is she right?" Karen asked without looking at Bravo.

"She's *guessed* the *signs* right," Bravo said. She grasped the whip before her with both hands. "And *your* sign?" she attempted to flail at Malissa, seeking any wedge with which to pierce her cunning, sure triumph.

Malissa's face hardened like plaster. "I was born under the evil aspects of *all* the signs," she said. Then her laughter was a stake slaughtering the vibrant silence. "You have an admirer," she said suddenly to Blue. "La Duquesa— . . ." She motioned tauntingly, introducing the staring queen as if she were an object for ready scrutiny.

"Contessa— . . ." Blue realized she was a man.

"*Duquesa*," la Duquesa corrected him, huskily. "I was married to a Spanish duke."

"Your grace," said Blue.

"The Duke is dead," la Duquesa went on. "I'll be in

mourning forever." She drew the black veil which filtered her view of such beautiful men, whom she must not even see. The masculine beauty surrounding her constantly—it was like a conspiracy to assault her memory of perfect love. But she would not succumb. Deliberately she remembered: *A windy gray day. The grave. The wreath of flowers dyed black. The weight of her black veils. Her tears piercing the soil to bathe the beloved slaughtered corpse.*

"How unexpected to see you here, Malissa," Bravo said.

"Nonsense. You saw me at the airport," Malissa said.

"I preferred to believe you were going somewhere else."

A smile invaded Malissa's face: always something foreign. Her hands answered silently. They made two arcs before her.

"You look well," said Bravo, "for a woman of fifty . . . sixty? . . . seventy? Is it ninety?"

Malissa laughed. "As old as evil, which is always young," she refused the insult.

In a pale lavender dress, Karen appeared even more frail. Yet her beauty shone more translucent; frailty was its source.

Malissa acknowledged Richard's third wife with a nod. "Will *all* the wives be here? Richard is always startling!" Quickly: "What is your name?" she asked Blue. She spoke to youngmen always as if she were interviewing them for a position in her life.

"Blue." His parted lips seemed to kiss his name.

"And you carry the mark." She did not have to point to the tattoo.

Blue turned away from her coldly. Then he saw, through the door, a youngman standing in the main hall, on the vortex of black and white patterns on the floor. He was dressed in black. Now Blue saw the white collar.

Malissa followed the point of Blue's attention. "Oh, the priest," she said softly.

The young powerfully slender priest did not yet move toward them.

Malissa rose from her chair. She thrust her hand out abruptly, as if grasping at something unseen. Like a page, Topaze snapped rigidly beside her.

Now the priest entered the room. His hair was dark brown, the color of his eyes; his face was beautiful—it had the almost passionate, almost sexual look of martyrs. He scanned the people in the anteroom. "And Richard?" he asked.

"Making us wait!" said Malissa. "And you're Father— ...?"

"Jeremy," the priest said. "My name is Jeremy." He looked at the woman's ringed hands: like drops of frozen blood. (And remembered: *Blood coloring his world red.*)

"Father Jeremy," sighed la Duquesa, again uncovering her face, allowing just a glimpse of the priest. "The name fits. . . . A beautiful—pure—priest: as pure as the memory of love."

(The priest heard: *Laughter!* Saw: *Yellow-gray corridors. Bodies.*) He turned from the queen.

"You really believe in God, man?" Rev asked the priest lazily.

"How dare you!"

They all turned startled to Malissa, who had shouted the words. The mask of her face was white with rage. "How dare you question the existence of God!" There was no mockery in her voice, only a profound seriousness. The words issued furiously from the stark black mouth: "Without God there would be no force to vanquish! Without God you would deny the power of Satan!"

Topaze smiled victoriously at Malissa's attack on Rev. Her body still rigid with fury, Malissa turned from him.

The City of God, the City of Satan, the priest remembered St Augustine's designation of warring countries.

"Do you know Richard, Father?" Valerie asked the priest. The priest's affirmative answer might vanquish her growing fear, reassure her. Paul's firm hand on her shoulder already attempted to still the apprehension in her tone.

"Very slightly. He came to my church not long ago. I'm secretary to the archbishop," he explained. "The archbishop invited him to dinner. Richard asked me to visit him on his island—a vacation. The archbishop insisted."

"Richard is intrigued by beauty," said Malissa, softly now, the cool mask of her features intact again. Then: "And are you here to listen to confessions?" she asked the priest. Again she was using the tone she had used to interrogate Blue.

"Of course not," said Jeremy.

Blue stood near the priest. Again the imprint of that distant face. Did it spring from his suddenly febrile mind? No. This time distinctly: Cam's features, uncannily, on the young priest's.

"But *would* you?" Blue astonished himself with the abrupt question. "Would you hear confessions?"

Avoiding the intense, cold-blue—deep, deep darkblue—eyes, the priest looked down. He saw: the inverted star tattooed on the youngman's ankle. Quickly Blue covered it with the heel of one foot.

"Father, bless us quickly!" said Albert compulsively.

Malissa's look executed him.

Embarrassed, the priest raised his hand in a vague

gesture. The pudgy man before him bowed his head.

Impulsively Blue's hand reached for the priest's, and he kissed it lightly. (Remembered uncontrollably: *The woman, kissing the tattoo! White feathers on her nude blue body. "My king!" Then the others followed! "Prince Susej!" The dazed, smeared, drugged eyes!*) Withdrawing, regretting the gesture, "When I was a kid," Blue explained with a trace of anger, "I was taught to kiss all priests' hands. It was, uh, like an echo from another righteous time, man."

"I was taught that too," the priest eased Blue's resentment of his impulsive action.

Malissa seized their words. She eyed them as if through a powerful lens.

Suddenly there was a rustling in the room. A bird—black—was gliding across the arched ceiling, long wings flailing.

"I'll kill it!" Rev said. He poised his long knife to pinion the bird to the wall.

"Put that knife away!" Malissa yelled. *"I'll* tell you when to use it!"

Tor opened the glass door, allowing the bird to Escape, and stared at it until it had disappeared into the blue and green island.

"It looked like a bat," said Topaze, who had removed his cavalier's hat as if to lead the bird away—or trap it. "It had an ugly little face!"

To explain her untypical defense of life, Malissa said in a tone of mockery: "All life is sacred, isn't it, Father?"

"We have to think that," the priest said, "although there are times— . . ."

"When isn't it sacred, Father?" Malissa's eyes closed, to grasp the priest's words more totally. This time the rubied hands did not speak. They rested dormant.

"Always," the priest relented. (Remembering: *"Don't*

let me die!" The cold hand. Blood like a molten red jewel. "Let me go!") "All life is sacred. Always."

"Even the life of a murderer!" said Albert, like a child, aghast, glancing at Malissa. (He saw: *A youngman's body shattered on the street like a bloodied fallen star.*)

Malissa did not look at him.

The priest said, "Yes."

Blue removed his heel from the tattooed ankle, exposing it.

To block one violent memory with another less threatening, "I remember— . . . I drove the archbishop once into the desert," the priest recalled. "On the highway, ahead, I saw a dozen, perhaps more, terrible black creatures crossing from one side to the other. Tarantulas as big as my hand." He opened his hand, staring down at the open fingers; he closed them quickly, into a fist. "A deadly species in that part of the world. Their hairy legs floated over the asphalt. I sped the car to slaughter as many as possible. Then as the tires squashed the dark lives, I thought I heard their cries of protest. Only then did I feel remorse. Those terrible creatures would harm no one in their isolated world of the desert. . . . They seemed so lonely in their evil."

"Yet they carried poison!" Valerie said.

"Poison which they would use only if stirred," said the priest.

Blue opened his lips: *Father, forgive me, for I have sinned.* Only when there was no reaction from the priest, nor from anyone else, only then did Blue realize he had not spoken the words that begin a formal confession. They had merely thundered in his mind.

4

"What do you want to tell me about me and Richard?" Joja said the words. She saw: Her reflection in the haloed mirror, the luminous red hair, the purple, heavily eyelashed eyes, the mouth like a rose: Youth had extended its lease to her. But how much longer? *Time exists only on my face!*

"I remember the man who burned you," came Mark's cold words again.

An invisible fist pulled at Joja's skull. "How dare you!" she tried to challenge the boy.

"You reached for the man's cigarette, for his hand, and you brought it against your breast—right here— . . ." He touched her there. "And you laughed while you forced him to burn you in front of my father and the others," he went on rapidly.

I felt dead, I wanted to feel pain to know I was Alive! Joja's mind shrieked. Remembering: *Malissa was there, hissing, coaxing: "Burn her, darling, she wants to be burned!"* "I had been drinking. I was— . . ." Joja continued her ambiguous defense.

"Stoned," Mark finished. "On pills and everything else."

"Which your father provides in abundance!" Joja hurled. "And I was hysterical," she continued, compelled to explain. "Your father had just told me— . . . something."

"That he was marrying Karen—and not you," the boy finished.

Yes! Like that! Suddenly I was through! My period of strange probation was over! I had failed him mysteriously like all the others in his search for— ... *What!* Her mind screamed that. But in an irrational effort to erase the feeling of having been cornered, she shouted instead at Mark: "You weren't wearing those trunks earlier!"

"I wasn't wearing anything," he said easily.

She gazed at his body. The velvet down of hair thickened at the edge of his trunks.

"What's that scar on your neck?" he asked her abruptly. The halo of lights locked their reflections in an intimate circle.

She touched the scar, almost with affection. "Your father— ..." she said dreamily, the memory inducing a trance, "Richard, once—one time— ... he— ... bit me there! He called it a symbolic ritual of— ... our 'affection'!"

Mark touched the scar gently.

Joja lifted her head. The invisible fist that had clutched her skull relaxed magically at the boy's touch.

Outside, there was the whirring of the helicopter.

"Do you love my father?" Mark asked softly.

She could not form the words which her mind quickly supplied: He brought me to life, if only while I was with him. She remembered: *The only fulfilling interlude in the wailing emptiness of her life.* Love? No. But only because that word was not powerful enough to define her desire, her need—all sealed by the ritualistic initiation performed by his mouth on her neck: her blood in him. I need him! she knew.

"I asked him to invite you back," Mark flung the words into the roiling silence.

He's lying! she thought, the words stirring vague fears. Was there a rivalry between father and son?

Mark leaned over her. His bare thigh touched her arm.

Joja closed her eyes, raising her face to the boy.

It was uncanny, the resemblance between Paul and her son. That thought frightened Tarah. She had been ready to join the others in the anteroom. Now she stopped abruptly. *Why are they here?* . . . Richard's terrible experiments. No!

Paul was aware that the woman was staring at him. Without realizing it, she had moved to within a few feet of him. "I'm sorry," she apologized to him. "You remind me so much of— . . ."

"Someone you loved," sighed la Duquesa. The thought floated to the surface of her mind from the pool of her private reveries. "Someone who died, at the summit of his beautiful life—and loved you with all his heart— . . ."

"No," Tarah said quickly. "He isn't dead. He reminds me of my son."

"Will Gable be here?" The words formed like ice on Malissa's dark lips.

"You know I wouldn't allow it, Malissa!" Tarah said. Automatically her eyes scanned the beautiful youngmen in the room. She throttled the images. The fever— . . .

"But *you* are here," said Malissa. "And indeed so are we all—waiting for our host to surprise us, and, perhaps, to surprise our host!" Then her eyes sliced the room in an arc, gliding from a figure in the domed hall to Bravo for an important reaction to be studied. "Savannah is here," Malissa said casually.

"Shit," Bravo said. She brought her whip against her thigh with a *whack!*

In a haze of gold light, a woman of stunning beauty stood under the crystal dome. Often described as the most beautiful woman in the world, she moved toward the others now, slowly as if her beauty had an actual physical weight which must be borne with care. Dressed in sheer tan, the color of her body, she appeared almost naked. Eyes the color of honey in the warm sun, the same color as her hair; long eyelashes black and lush; full orange lips: a perfect, starkly sexual face rivaled a perfect body: tawny, lithe, slender, with full, firm, tight breasts. Savannah's beauty was utterly flawless, the reality of it surpassing even its legend.

As she entered the anteroom: With a hiss, the tip of Bravo's whip lashed outside through the window (before which Tor still stood vacantly in search of the Escaped bird). The whip choked the stem of a vermillion flower, and broke it with a snap. Bravo retrieved the blossom, marched toward Savannah; and—booted legs spread defiantly—she dropped the dead flower like a severed head at her feet. "The virgin whore!" she slashed at Savannah.

Savannah laughed: loudly. A derisive laughter meant to obviate whatever of triumph the gesture held for Bravo.

Malissa joined the other's laughter; then Topaze too; then Rev.

"A dramatic gesture, Bravo!" said Malissa.

"A scene from one of your unreleased movies?" Savannah said.

"What happened to your prince?" Bravo attacked Savannah.

"*Which* one?" said Savannah coolly.

"The one she pimped for you," Bravo spat, indicating Malissa.

Savannah brushed her long hair from her face, dismissing the memory evoked.

"Are you still a virgin!" Bravo continued the assault.

"Yes!" Savannah's eyes were like rare, blazing, amber jewels.

Tor stood next to her, flexing his giant muscles as if to challenge the woman's beauty.

"Boo," said Savannah. But no response from Tor. "Doesn't he speak?" she asked no one, anyone.

"He flexes," said Malissa.

"And performs feats—interesting feats," Albert volunteered excitedly. "Topaze performs . . . feats, too; we found him in a circus!"

Malissa's silent hands, barely rising, restrained Albert.

"Your entourage for this season?" Savannah asked Malissa.

"And la Duquesa— . . ." Malissa indicated the queen in mourning drag.

"Where the hell do you find them?" Bravo demanded.

"We found la Duquesa outside of a cemetery," Malissa answered easily.

"She was actually hitchhiking!" Albert blurted. Once again he retreated quickly.

Rev laughed, glancing from Albert to la Duquesa.

"We were on our way from somewhere," Malissa said. "A bleak day. We saw the figure in black. Waiting. She intrigued me, standing there in mourning, in the drizzle—looking like a figure expelled from the cemetery."

La Duquesa remembered: *The grave.*

"Doesn't he—she—speak either?" Savannah asked.

La Duquesa drew the black veil from her face. She enunciated slowly: "God is a transvestite! Created in the image of *both* man *and* woman. . . See, I *can* speak."

The priest averted la Duquesa's searching eyes.

"A cemetery . . . a circus. . . . Where did you find the others?" Bravo taunted.

"We found Tor on the beach, everyone was staring at his body!" Albert said breathlessly. "And Rev tried to rob me on the street—I was alone. Then Malissa came and laughed in his face. Now he's fiercely loyal to us."

Rev looked at Albert with undisguised contempt.

"To *me*," Malissa corrected him. "Rev is fiercely loyal to me. Show them what you can do, Rev!" she commanded the man in the leather vest.

"Toss it!" Rev barked at Topaze. The midget flung his cane quickly into the air like a baton. Rev's hurled knife buried itself into the tip of the spinning cane.

"Can you match that, Bravo?" Malissa challenged.

Bravo's whip lashed out like lightning. Its tip grasped the buried knife, pulling it out of the cane. Retrieving it, she pushed the knife contemptuously back to Rev with her foot. To cap her flashy triumph, she turned her head quickly, like a cobra ready to strike, toward Malissa: "But what do you *do* with them, Malissa, these people you collect? *You* have no sex. Do you just drain theirs vengefully because you have none? What happens to them?" Though she addressed Malissa, her eyes sought the current entourage, to stir rebellion.

"Terrible things happen to them sometimes!" Albert blurted. "The dancer last season—he jumped out of a window. Malissa just stood there. He thought he could fly, and she encouraged— . . ." His eyes glistened with tears at the memory. "His beautiful young body shattered on the street. He was . . . floating . . . in his own . . . blood!"

La Duquesa saw: *The Duke's body, crushed roses of blood on his chest.*

Blood like a torn, sheer, clinging red sheet on the naked bodies. . . . Blue's black-blue eyes sought the priest's.

"And the transfusions— . . . !" Albert gasped.

"What transfusions!" Bravo demanded.

Malissa's hands rose, the fingers spread. She could have been controlling an invisible current to crush Albert's words:

Suddenly he covered his mouth.

Valerie turned her head quickly; she and her brother had remained silent, witnessing the beginning of a struggle they did not understand. "I abhor violence and cruelty," she protested.

"I adore violence too," said Malissa.

"She said she abhorred— . . ." Paul corrected.

Malissa ignored the correction. "Poor Albert," her lips said; her face had no expression. "I've been considering committing him."

"No, Malissa!" Albert pled. "I was just making up stories!" he told the others frantically. "I swear I was! Everything I said is a lie!"

"He imagines things." The words formed about Malissa.

As if some key word had pried open her memories, la Duquesa said: "I allowed no one else to attend the funeral of the Duke, my husband, my lover." (*The body on the street. She placed her hand on the red spot, to stop the blood carrying out his life. "Get away! What are you looking at! He's my husband!"*) "I didn't even go back in the long black limousine. . . . When he was alive, we would drive along the deserted coast."

"In winter?" Rev asked abruptly.

"Yes, in winter," la Duquesa said. "He held my hand."

(*A hand. "Let me go!" Death.*) Retreating from the evoked memories, the priest met Blue's stare; it seemed to pull him instantly into its dark depths.

Looking back at the priest, Blue moved like a gliding shadow out of the amber room, through the gold and white hall in which the stage waited. The shadowed props. Into the domed hall: outside: into the rotunda of vine-choked columns: along the complex maze of gardens: soundlessly. Then he reached an alcove, the round hollow created by shrugging trees. Naked statues, frozen white shadows, guarded it blindly. Blue sat on a bench and waited.

Footsteps.

He didn't look up. "Hello, Father," he said.

"You surprised me," said the priest. "I didn't know you—anyone—was here," he explained pointedly.

The sun penetrated even the vine-veiled alcove. Shifting sequins of light needled the priest's eyes hypnotically.

"Father," Blue spoke the words that had begun to shape earlier. "There's something I need to tell you, man. About a black throne— . . ." He retreated quickly from the expelled words. "About a face, and the devil— . . ."

Immediately, the priest felt assaulted by a powerful force spiraling from the depths of this youngman's darkblue eyes: whirling vortexes funneling from the center of his convoluted soul. "You want to confess," he said.

"Confess?" The word itself seemed to confuse Blue. Confess. . . . An entity, seen before, but not recognized. "No, just rap, man." Then he blurted: "I saw the Lord Sa— . . . I saw Satan's face!" The expression on his face did not match the intensity of his voice: His face was impassive.

(*"Hurry, it's urgent! She's dying!"* No, it was not like that. The priest canceled that other memory.) "Did you invoke his spirit?" He looked down, to establish at least the superficial order of an impersonal confession, to render the thundering words more tolerable. He saw: The inverted star tattooed on Blue's ankle. He thought:

The ram's head; the ram's head is missing within the tattoo.

"No, uh. No— . . ." Blue twisted his foot, concealing the tattoo.

"By your actions— . . . ?"

"Diggit: This is how it happened: I worked through a contact service," Blue said; "a man got me clients, a male madam—Mr Stuart."

The priest remembered: *Arched bodies.* He turned toward the cold statues, searching cold, blind eyes. "This belongs in a confession," he said. In the cloistered booth of a church—its mosaicked windows so beautiful, its saints like dolls—the harshness of life was rendered less real: the purpose of the gray whispered ritual.

"No," Blue insisted. "Listen, man: He commanded me to— . . ." He shook his head, as if to shake those words away. Interrupted images: like a spliced movie in which a recurrently hinted scene is omitted.

"Who commanded?" The priest felt trapped in a clear shaft of light which Escaped suddenly past the huddled, conspiratorial trees.

"Commanded?" Blue asked vaguely, caught in a haze of memories. "Oh, uh, what? Oh, nothing, man. This is what I want to tell you. The face— . . . One day I had had four assignments—all insisted on me, even when Mr Stuart told them I was busy; they'd wait, they said—I was the most popular. I felt righteous loved," he spoke words.

Words which came too easily, with something of defiance, something of pride? Merely the words of an exhibitionist flaunting his life? Or was he truly anxious to tear a horrible blemish from his soul? The priest had this sudden feeling: of attempted confession of a lesser evil, of the deliberate use of horror to thwart a greater horror. He waited for the unmistakable tone of a wounded soul, the indication of a soul in cold fire. "You felt desired," he said.

"Loved, desired—the same thing, man," Blue said impatiently. "And I rushed to the mirror when I got to my pad, to groove on all that love showing on my face— . . . But— . . . But the face I saw, it was a distortion of my own—like— . . . *like it was turned inside out, man! Like the inside of me was reflected in the mirror!*"

Had there been, then, a clear note of genuine terror in the voice? The priest did not fill the suspended silence.

"Do you believe in Satan?" Blue asked the priest abruptly. A paradoxical smile touched his moody face.

Again, the priest did not answer.

"*Do* you!" Blue insisted. The vague smile was marooned in a twisting sea of dark, shifting expressions.

"The spirit of— . . . The mind is capable— . . ." the priest stumbled.

"Was that *his* face I saw in the mirror?"

"Sometimes guilt—. . ."

"Diggit, man, I don't feel guilty about anything!" Blue said defiantly. "I just want to know: Do you believe in Satan?"

"Yes," the priest answered finally.

"I was his prince," said Blue. "He commanded. She —the Blue Woman—and I, we sat naked on the black throne. The others knelt. *Listen to me!*"

Wings! Wings flapping! The black bird glided gracefully over the alcove. Now it seemed suspended weightlessly over them for moments. Then it soared away, up, toward the dome of the house. It seemed about to land on the ledge of Joja's window. Instead, it floated suddenly into the sky.

Mark saw it. He moved abruptly away from the actress. "I think other guests are here!" he said. "I heard the helicopter."

Joja opened her eyes. The world shattered in her face. Her arm felt cold where only moments earlier the touch of Mark's thigh had warmed it like a promise. Over her—her neck still stretched—the exposed round mirror in the ceiling seemed to spin; a glass maelstrom— . . . She heard the door close. Mark was gone.

She grabbed a purple robe. On a current of depression, anger, rage, frustration, anxiety, doubt, despair, she rushed out of the room and along the halls. Mirrors grasped at her image. She glided past the panels of vague, waiting figures, a panorama of tense, gold silhouettes like accusatory witnesses pursuing her reflections. Down the sweeping stairs. Over her, the exposed dome stared like a blank eye.

"*Richard!*" she yelled defiantly into the empty room. "Richard, where the hell are you? Watching us? Forcing us to wait? Already playing your demonic games?"

She saw a small, beautiful man staring quizzically at her. "Who the hell are you?" she demanded.

"Topaze," he answered.

"He belongs to me," Malissa called. Her voice floated along the tunnel of arches from the anteroom.

Still in a rage, Joja stormed in. "Where's Richard?"

"Keeping us waiting—as you observed earlier," Malissa said. "And we'll wait—for now."

"What a stunning robe!" la Duquesa sighed, looking at Joja, who stood like a royal queen facing the others. "The Duke always bought me the most gorgeous gowns, he selected them himself. Although he was all man, he had exquisite taste; he bought me only originals by Jacques-Valentine. When the Duke died— . . ." She glanced quickly at Rev, then as quickly away; she went on: "When he was killed, I dyed all my clothes . . . black."

Joja saw Richard's two wives. And so they were here. Only Lianne was missing. Joja and the two women recognized each other, without embarrassment, with—only—wonder at their having been brought together. Joja thought uncontrollably: We've come back to be resurrected by Richard, the only one who— . . . She stopped the sudden thought. Magnetized by it, her eyes shifted to the propped platform in the other room. A stage. (*Another stage. The racked sobs.*) Looking at the stage and the people here, suddenly she felt they were all characters in a drama still to be written.

The tension erupted, she laughed loudly, huskily. "What has he planned for us?"

"His games," said Tarah. (Her mind saw: *The dark stairway. The two men waiting to tear her apart.*)

"They've already begun," the mask of Malissa's face said.

"All I'm waiting for," said Bravo, guarding Karen, "is to see the bastard—and to have Karen face him again."

"Of course," said Malissa.

"If you hate him so much, why come at all?" Paul asked them suddenly.

"To pass the time," said Savannah.

"We like games," said Malissa.

"Doesn't *he* talk?" Savannah indicated Tor.

"Talk for her," Malissa told the bodybuilder. "Tell her about the contest."

"Mr America," said Tor. "I lost."

"I'm sorry," said la Duquesa. She glanced wistfully at Tor, a powerful wounded animal she might shelter. She grasped her black veil like an anchor.

"You're Gable," Joja said to Paul.

"No!" said Tarah. "Richard will never see my son again."

"Why not?" Paul challenged.

Tarah said softly to Paul: "Richard contaminates everything he touches. It's his life. To take what's pure —and sully it."

The words dug into Karen's mind, retrieving jagged memories, as sharp as shattered glass. (*Purple laughter gluing the bodies crushed intimately together. And her mind screaming: Mother, Mother, Mother, Mother!*) "Purity affronts Richard," she said.

Malissa closed her eyes. Her hands rested on the arms of the tall chair like guards, alert.

"You must not be speaking about the man we know of," Paul said staunchly. "The Richard we know about, my sister and I, he helped Daniel—our father— . . . when he lost everything. Without Richard's help— . . ."

Tarah remembered: *The twins' mother, Hester. Daniel. Daniel. A night. Richard. A trial.* Did they know? "Do you live with Daniel?" Tarah asked. The question was suddenly important.

"No. We see him as often as he can visit us," Valerie said.

Tarah persisted: "Do you go to school?"

"We live in the country," Paul said. "We have tutors."

"Nuns and priests," said Valerie.

"And Richard made it possible," Paul continued his defense of Richard, although it seemed to him, hearing his own words, that he was defending his own father.

"Richard made it possible for your father to shelter you from the corrupt world," Malissa spoke, as if she were uttering a verdict carefully arrived at.

Tarah felt fear like a cold wing. What did Malissa know about the twins? Why were they here? Her fear was augmented when she turned to face Mark. When had he entered the room? How much had he heard?

"I'm Mark," he introduced himself to those he had not yet greeted.

Valerie looked from her brother to the boy in trunks, noting the resemblance.

In another room, a lavish table was being set with food, wine—arranged on carved ice, ice like free sculpture. Servants moved as quietly and unobtrusively as shadows, like acolytes at a secret mass: mute figures like those in the dim paintings, the gold spectral silhouettes on the white panels.

5

Like a general resting before a crucial engagement Malissa retreated to her apartment in the east wing of the house, the same elaborate suite Richard reserved for her each season. Earlier in the anteroom undefined tension had brought them all too prematurely "close." A deliberate postponement, then, of confrontation was in order. And so Malissa withdrew. Now she sat on a gilded tall-backed state chair, like a queen granting an audience. To Albert.

"Please Malissa!" he exhorted her urgently.

Her eyes poured their contempt, drowning him. "What you said downstairs—..."

"I'm sorry! *Please!*"

La Duquesa stood by the window, gazing into the sky, a mirror image of the sea. Her black veil filtered the noon brightness.

Topaze sat on a chair next to Malissa's, lower than

hers; he listened attentively to Albert. In the adjoining room, Tor, in red trunks, was exercising his biceps with a pair of heavy dumbbells. Already flushed by the pumped blood, his arms strained like balloons.

"Which one?" Malissa said, her mouth a cruel, cold dark slash. Her hands curled like jeweled claws, tensely, on the chair's armrests. Hatred seemed a presence in the room—a dazzling, bejeweled presence waiting to be commanded by the woman.

As if to obviate—in any frantic manner—the scene she knew would follow, la Duquesa said: "When I first met the Duke, it was a day much like this."

"In spring?" asked Rev without looking up from the ubiquitous knife he was now carefully honing.

"Yes, in spring," sighed la Duquesa.

"Of course," Rev said.

"I had seen him once before, but we didn't speak until that afternoon," la Duquesa went on, turning to glance at Albert to see whether he had moved from the entreating position before Malissa; he had not. She went on: "The flowers were in bloom. He gathered a small bouquet for me and brought it over."

"In a park?" asked Rev.

"In a park," confirmed la Duquesa. "That beautiful giant of a man—six-feet-two in his stocking feet, weighing a muscular, lean 185 pounds, stripped—that man bent, gently, to present me a bouquet. The flowers would soon turn black. The weeks of our life together—..."

"You said years before." Rev still didn't look up.

"Of course it was years," said la Duquesa. "But they were seconds in the ocean of eternity; they evaporated into memories when he died— . . ."

La Duquesa's deliberate attempt to thwart the scene

she knew was developing had not been successful. Malissa had not removed her eyes from Albert, who was already answering her last question:

"Tor—Rev—Topaze— . . . Any of them! Please!" he pled like a child for candy.

Invisible destructive currents from Malissa's blue-shielded eyes vibrated powerfully toward Albert.

Poor little man, la Duquesa thought. Each time, he's sure she'll finally allow it. Why does he take it? And remembered: *Spittle on her face, smearing her lovely makeup. The white cum contemptuously tossed not into her eager mouth but on her carefully arranged breasts. . . . Love*— . . . "The Duke despised cruelty," she said emphatically, her back to Malissa, to avoid the already unraveling scene.

"Very well," Malissa said, like an executioner. "To pass the time." An empress about to witness the acts preliminary to a gory spectacle: "While we wait— . . ." she spat the words, "for Richard. . . . Tor!" she called peremptorily to the bodybuilder.

His muscles gleaming with perspiration so that he seemed to be sculpted out of diamond-hard ice, Tor approached Albert, but stopped a few feet away in response to Malissa's raised hand. (He saw: *Eyes! Gold-painted bodies!* Heard: *Dark commands.* And: *Screams!*)

Albert flung himself kneeling on the floor. His hands quickly encircled Tor's naked thighs.

"He touched him!" Topaze yelled.

Malissa was looking only at Albert. "Albert!" she warned.

"I promise, I promise not to touch him!" Albert held his hands locked tightly in back of him to restrain them. "I'll just . . . look at him. Please— . . ."

Malissa nodded toward Tor, allowing to proceed a

scene often enacted with only minor variations.

Upper arm parallel to the ground, forearm perpendicular, fist clenched inward so that the biceps bulged, the other arm raised higher, slightly over his head, that fist also clenched but pointing outward, lats spread and tensed so that they flared like bat wings, narrow waist held in tighter, ridges of the sculpted abdominals straining against the flesh, Tor posed before Albert.

Kneeling hardly a foot away, Albert gasped.

Malissa did not even glance at Tor. An invisible shield separated her from all that was sexual. Her eyes studied Albert relentlessly, carefully collecting the imprint of each hint of torture, frustration on his face.

"The trunks!" Albert begged. "Tell him to take them off. *Please!*"

The body allowed to relax, Tor's fingers looped about the edges of his trunks, lowering them slightly.

"He's going to take them off!" Topaze warned Malissa.

"That's enough!" Malissa ordered, still without looking at Tor.

Imperturbably, Tor returned to the other room, to the weights.

Topaze roared with laughter at Albert, who was trembling visibly.

"You pitiful, sad, poor man," Malissa whispered to Albert. From her those words were utterances of a merciless sentence. Her left fingers glided over the stones on the right knuckles, back and forth, hypnotically.

"I don't care what you call me—but let me, please—. . ." Albert supplicated.

La Duquesa closed her eyes. The only purpose of the entourage—to torture this man? And is it true he supports her, the elegant hobo? she wondered. Why?

"Do you want— . . ." Malissa feigned kindness in her voice. But the arcane language of her fingers—the one black ring like a gouged eye—continued relentlessly to spew contempt.

"Yes, yes—any of them, whomever you choose, Malissa!" Albert said eagerly.

"La Duquesa!" Malissa chose.

That convulsed Topaze. Rev smiled derisively.

Albert shook his head frantically.

"Not la Duquesa?" said Malissa in mock amazement. "Perhaps, though, you'd like to wear her clothes. . . . Lend him your veil, your grace!" she called to the queen in mourning drag. "We'll see how Albert looks in drag!"

"Be-yoo-ti-ful!" Topaze laughed.

"Your grace— . . ." Malissa repeated firmly. "Lend . . . Albert . . . Your . . . Veil." Uttered with deliberate slowness, each word contained a threat.

But la Duquesa did not move. The memory of the Duke would give her the strength to resist the powerful woman. She sighed: "On long rainy afternoons the Duke and I would merely lie together, touching, for hours. The day he was killed, I was going to meet him. I was wearing red, the color of his blood which would spill on me. The Duke— . . . The Duke despised cruelty."

Malissa's stare focused frozen blue on the queen. She could demand that she drape the veil over Albert, she could *make* her respond. Of course. But that would thwart the present game. Time enough for la Duquesa: a more interesting game, in reserve. She nodded instead to Rev, who understood.

Quickly he opened his black vest, revealing an almost solid, symmetrical tapestry of tattoos on his lean chest. Menacing snarling beasts, dripping knives, barebreasted women—all amid viny rosebuds which themselves seemed curiously menacing.

Albert rushed to him—but restrained himself, nevertheless so close that Rev, looking down at him with hard, mean eyes, could feel the pudgy man's breath on his flesh. Tongue gliding, Albert inched toward the tattoo of a bird swooping over Rev's left nipple. "The pants," Albert begged. "The pants—..."

"Show him," came Malissa's voice. Her eyes were nailed deeply into Albert, yet shut to Rev tantalizing him on her orders.

Slowly Rev opened his pants, one button at a time; the tapestry of tattoos continued along his lower torso. His open pants revealed the beginning of a tattooed snake, winding through the thick mat of black hairs. Lower on, it would coil about his groin. Only the upper part—the head ready to lash and emit its poison—was visible now.

Albert strained toward it.

"He's moved closer!" Topaze shouted.

"Enough!" said Malissa. Rev quickly raised his pants, closed the vest, turned his back to Albert.

Albert rushed frantically to Malissa. "Please, please, *please!*"

"Topaze!" Malissa called.

His hat rakishly on his head—a depraved musketeer—the midget smiled demoniacally, his even teeth bared, his eyes gleaming. He stood swiftly, that perfect miniature man, like an actor on the center of the stage.

On his knees, Albert faced the midget eagerly.

Standing with his hands on his hips, thrust forward slightly, Topaze removed his cavalier's hat, slicing the air with an audible *slash!* before Albert's neck.

La Duquesa drew the black veil more closely over her face, her back still turned on the scene of cruelty. She remembered: *The dress torn from her body, sequins on the floor like violated stars.* The veil clung to her cheeks, glued there by sudden tears.

Braced on his hands, Albert leaned on the floor toward Topaze—oblivious of all else, ruled by desire. Now the midget undid his own belt, allowing the buckled end to dangle tantalizingly before Albert's face, which stared fascinated, yet pained. A surly smile curling his lips, Topaze quickly dropped his pants and lewdly thrust his slim hips in simulated orgasm toward the man's face.

Albert moaned, staring in those fleeting instants at the midget's cock, which would have been gigantic on a tall man.

"Enough!" Malissa's words slaughtered the scene savagely. Her eyes were still buried into Albert.

Laughing tauntingly, Topaze raised his pants and moved back. Rev joined the derisive laughter. Face down on the floor, Albert whimpered like a wounded animal.

"You sniveling creature," Malissa said to Albert. "Have you learned yet? Have you? *Have you!"*

Drops of frozen blood, the rubies on her slashing fingers flashed a series of arcs shaping her convoluted rage. Propelled by the violent thrust of her anger, she stood up. Then wordlessly she left the room, moving swiftly along the corridors. Mirrors everywhere! Images must not Escape in Richard's mansion! Must be caught! Servants floated about the halls. She hurried down the stairs. In the domed hall, she met Bravo, with Karen. Bravo made a move as if to intercept Malissa. Malissa did not look back. She flung herself into the maze of gardens. Now she rushed past the wide glass wall of the house, on the other side of which Joja stood staring at:

Red orchids with velvety yellow hearts. They leaned toward the white sun.

And looking at them through the glass wall, Joja was aware of that which requires something more powerful than itself for survival. She thought of the ocean: its imprint on the sand after it withdraws, the debris left as a reminder.... She glanced at the stage. Finally she had entered the gold room to study it. The somber props. Another empty stage to be filled with artificial lives, roles which had swallowed her being. Would this stage witness the unraveling, finally, of her own withheld identity?

"How did Richard send you away?" Tarah asked Joja bluntly, like a prosecutor collecting only evidence he knows will damn the accused. She had followed the actress here. Only the two women, first wife and ex-mistress, were in the room now.

"By telling me he was marrying Karen," Joja said. "Just like that. Without warning or indication." Looking at the draped platform, she felt suddenly that they were all props on a stage erected by Richard. "How did it end with you?" she asked dully.

"I—... He led me—... I left him after he—..." Tarah's words stopped, the images flowed: *Bodies on hers like hungry animals, bodies entering her simultaneously, in front, in back.* "... —after I realized—... after he made me feel empty."

Joja knew: *The pit.* To be filled with substitutes, strangers like this morning's, the beautiful mysterious blond youngman who had failed her twice.... Strangers who left her empty. And guilty: As if *she*—and was it so with Tarah, too?—had failed Richard.

"But my son changed that," Tarah said firmly. "Gable purified me of that night—..." (*The long corridor she walked with Richard into the dark room of savage orgy.*) "I took him away from Richard."

"And Richard allowed it?" Joja asked.

"Yes." The strangeness of it had not occurred to Tarah: He had never fought for Gable. Quickly: "Why did you come back?" she assaulted Joja with the question she and Karen had asked each other earlier—a question important without discernible reason.

"Because— . . ." (*Because I need him? Because he summoned me? Because without him I'm dead?*) "Because I was bored with New York," she answered finally. (*The protesting voices beyond the finally lowered curtain had continued accusing her, judging her.*)

Then she saw Mark.

Still in trunks, he stood at the entrance to the room. Tarah's back was to him. And so Joja knew it was to her that he nodded slightly. Summoning her? She thought progressively in terms of a summons. Issued by Richard. And Mark? She *felt* her body advance toward the boy's —although she did not actually move.

Mark tilted his head, challenging her to look away.

Joja tried, but her eyes were scorched to his in that powerful moment.

Brought suddenly into the whirling spiral between the boy and the actress, Tarah looked back quickly at Richard's son. Then as quickly away. "Why did Richard bring us all together?" she asked the actress.

Finally wrested from Mark's, Joja's eyes saw Malissa beyond the glassed wall as if trapped within the maze of gardens.

Then the figure disappeared entirely: Malissa had entered a white rotunda: vine-cloaked pillars supporting a dome enclosing marble benches, statues, a fountain— a sheet of diamonds under the omnipotent sun.

Malissa despised being ruled by anything, even anger.

It was her burgeoning rage at Albert she had fled. She must command even her own savagery.

Her eyes widened: She saw the coiled thing moving: a snake almost touching her feet! No—it was Bravo's whip! Suddenly it was withdrawn with a crack like a bullet. Malissa faced Bravo.

"I didn't expect you," Malissa said coldly. "I saw you only moments earlier with Karen."

"She went to her room to rest, she's very weak," Bravo's words accused Malissa vaguely.

"Richard has an exhilarating effect on her; he'll . . . revive her," Malissa said cunningly.

"Karen doesn't need Richard," Bravo said.

"Doesn't she?" Malissa flashed. "I don't really see *you* replacing Richard."

By Bravo's look—which Malissa studied—and her silence, she knew what she had suspected: Bravo desired Karen, yes, that was obvious all along; but the desire was still to be consummated, if ever. The last words entered her mind like flung weapons to be honed for future use. Karen and Bravo. Bravo's notorious sadistic affairs. . . . But Karen? The beautiful young woman who had become Richard's third wife. Once she had glowed radiantly. Only for Richard? Karen and Bravo. Karen. Inconceivable. Could it be that Karen had mysteriously tapped in Bravo a pool of . . . gentleness? . . . If so, Bravo was infinitely vulnerable! Malissa's mind arranged these thoughts automatically, exploring for all its possible weaknesses a country soon to be assaulted.

The white hypnotic sun ruled the ocean of sky. The smell of wild roses was heavy and sweet.

Malissa's fingers prepared the words: "You followed me, Bravo. What do you want?" she asked.

Bravo stood before her. "The black ring," she said.

"Don't be foolish. Why should I give it to you?" The

ring coiled on Malissa's hand almost the length of her finger, a wound snake choking a black pearl.

"Because it's the ring you got from the prince for introducing him to Savannah when— . . ."

"When *you* wanted her!" Malissa recalled her deliberate triumph over Bravo.

Bravo said it casually, so that the horror, shaping slowly, was more intense; she said: "There's a scorpion on your shoulder, Malissa."

Malissa's body froze.

"Richard's son told us they're fatal," Bravo went on. "But they never strike unless they're taunted. You have to force them to sting. But you know all about that, Malissa; you've been here often before."

Malissa glanced at her shoulder. She saw it: its yellowish outline. She felt it there, quivering. Even now, threatened by deadly poison, her façade remained composed. It was her hands—still—which conveyed fear.

"I'll drive it away with my whip!" Bravo offered, moving back, her hand rising to lash with the whip.

"No," Malissa said, trying not to breathe.

"You're right, I might just succeed in aggravating it; and it would certainly sting and kill you. . . . How fitting, Malissa! A scorpion—perhaps like me a double scorpion. The lower path of death— . . ." she mocked.

Malissa's neck began to ache.

Bravo moved farther back, as if to abandon her. Suddenly, she spun around; and her whip snapped toward Malissa's shoulder. "Oh, I missed," she said smiling, "and I never do—unless I want to."

The yellowish thing trembled on Malissa's shoulder. "Don't taunt it." She felt it advancing lightly toward her neck. The yellowish form erect now, poised to strike, she knew.

"Why shouldn't I taunt it?—after how you pimped—..."

Malissa squeezed the words: "You . . . wouldn't . . . want . . . Savannah . . . she's . . . a . . . virgin."

"The legendary virgin. Exactly why I wanted her. . . . Now tell me about the transfusions, Malissa!" she barked. "What was it you stopped Albert from telling!"

"He lied. . . . The scorpion—remove it."

"Why don't *you* brush it off?"

"I can't see it any more."

Bravo leaned over Malissa's shoulder. Then she blew tauntingly, barely, on the thing. "I think it's becoming agitated! It's raised its tail! *It's ready to sting, Malissa!* . . . The ring!" she commanded.

"Brush the scorpion away!"

"The ring *now!*" Bravo demanded ferociously, the butt of her whip ready to prod the yellow thing.

Her shoulders rigid, Malissa removed the black ring. Bravo took it triumphantly.

She stepped back. She raised her whip. "I'll try it again," she said coldly. "If I miss again— . . ."

Malissa's hands were dead.

Bravo's arm came back, the whip uncoiled swiftly. *Crack!*

Malissa felt the sudden breath of the whip's tip. The thing on her shoulder was gone. She saw it pinioned to the tip of Bravo's whip.

Bravo was studying it. "It wasn't a scorpion at all," she said mockingly. "Just a small yellow leaf." She held the leaf toward Malissa. "Look, Malissa, it wasn't a scorpion at all."

"You knew it all along." Malissa tried to smile, to deny the other's victory.

Bravo dropped the black ring at Malissa's feet—and she laughed loudly in the woman's face.

60 · *The Vampires*

Behind the blue glasses, Malissa's eyes spilled with anger. But the mask continued to smile, containing the rage in order.

Bravo's laughter plunged into an ocean of hatred.

Blood, death. Blue remembered: *The black throne-bed. He lay naked with the Blue Woman. The others knelt, chanting, at their feet. The black rosary about his neck, the cross inverted. The star on the stretched blue rubber.* "I was tripping with Satan, man," he said to the priest, studying his reaction.

A shaft of crystal sun spilled into the alcove like something thrust there from heaven. Clinging like a lavender shroud over the trees, a vine cast a purple filigreed shadow at their feet.

"You know, man, dropping acid," Blue clarified. "L-S-D." He paused, ready to seize the priest's withheld reaction. "That stands for: Lord Save the Devil."

"You're deliberately being blasphemous!" the priest said angrily.

"Blasphemous! What the hell's that, man?" said Blue. His face was a vicissitude of reflections projected from within onto the surface of his face, like quickly changing slides.

"I won't listen if you persist— . . ." The priest made a motion to move.

"No!" Blue reached out urgently with his hand. "Wait. I have to tell you— . . ." The features of Cam's face, remembered, seemed suddenly superimposed on those of the handsome young priest. "Cam— . . ." Only when the priest responded did he realize he had spoken the name aloud.

"Who is Cam?" Jeremy asked.

"Who? . . . Oh, someone," said Blue.

The shadows darkened in the intense afternoon, like the gray screen that separates confessor and confessee, a secure boundary.

"The tattoo," Blue said. A disorientation?—the way his mind shifted as quickly as his moody expressions, without transition. Or was it rather a shifting clarity about himself?—not a blurred focus so much as a prismatic view of himself? "I went to a seer in the Hollywood hills, a client. That was before— . . . I had just begun to work for Mr Stuart. The man looked at my hand. He outlined an inverted star on it with his finger." (*Ringed, bony.*) "His fingernails were red."

Red fingernails clawing at a swollen stomach. In the priest's mind, that image faded into: *The white flesh of grasping fingers clinging to him, to be pulled from death.* He looked away from the dark-blue eyes and up at the sky, seeking its crystal purity, azure without a smear.

"The man said I carried death and violence: He saw the inverted star of Satan on my hand," Blue said softly.

"A superstition," the priest insisted quickly. "And the mark is incomplete without the ram's head." An echo of his own voice. Its tone. It was suddenly as if he had begun to defend Blue of a crime not yet charged.

"Yeah, the ram's head," Blue said. "What that man said—it freaked me out," he continued. "I went to a tattoo shop soon after. I heard myself tell the man, 'I want an elaborate inverted star tattooed on my cock.'" His eyes were blue magnets. "But I changed my mind: On my ankle, I told him. Diggit, man," he said slowly, as if trying to understand his own story, "I wanted the mark of Satan to show...."

"Like a warning—or a threat," the priest heard himself say.

"Yeah! I even started going barefoot. But I also like wanted to hide it—..."

"Like a confession," the priest said.

Blue covered the tattoo with his other foot. "No. Yes," he said vaguely. "Then it became like an added trademark: I already had the blue rubbers." The kaleidoscope of his mind shifted: "I started in a gas-station head; a man picked me up on a street, he blew me in a pay head, I let him for ten bucks." The navy-blue eyes glared accusingly at the priest.

"Now you feel guilty," Jeremy said. The words echoed, false sounds, in his ears: rehearsed, stock, artificial, borrowed from a world which had no relation to this one.

"Guilty! For *that?*" Blue laughed. "Man, you're putting me on!" The smile pounced on his face from somewhere outside of him; the rest of his face was somber. "I could tell you things—*black* things, man—..."

The priest's mind thundered with questions, but they remained unasked, although it was as if—and was this the reason he did not ask them?—Blue *wanted* to be questioned. About the ritual of evil? No. The real evil; and what was it?

"Diggit: Then I met Mr Stuart," Blue continued. "Right away I became his most popular—..."

"Prostitute," the priest contained a flowing anger.

"Whore," Blue said coldly. "Men, women.... I never wanted any of them, they wanted me. But I needed them to want me. That's what made me hard, someone else's righteous desire of me. I felt only contempt for them, man. Diggit: I could do anything I wanted, and they took it, that's how heavy they grooved on me. One dude —diggit—I wouldn't even let him touch me, and he paid— . . . Before I started tripping with— . . ." his voice faded. "But it was never enough," he mumbled, shaking his head.

"The drug?"

"What drug, man?"

"The acid."

"Acid? Oh—uh, acid. No, man. Sex. Diggit: It was never enough. Mr Stuart didn't know that I had begun to cruise the streets, the beaches. Nothing was enough."

"Your body was sated. But your soul was starved." Again the priest's words were like entities, pulled, ready —cold—from within him.

"No," Blue said peremptorily. "Diggit, man, I needed constantly to feel *loved*— . . ."

"Desired!" the priest heard himself shout.

The shadows in the alcove were like gray ice in the shaft of light.

"It's the same thing!" Blue shouted back. Then he said softly: "The blue rubbers. A client had them made for me, he grooved seeing them on me. They became my trademark. I'd leave them with my customers, that proved they'd been with me. Then—uh—then— . . . What? Oh, when I had the mark put on my ankle, I had it put on the blue rubbers, too." He paused, frowned. His mind darted: "The Blue Woman. Sometimes she called herself the dark virgin, but she was a nympho. She was beautiful— . . . She heard about me, she went looking for me in that crazy silver Packard of hers, asking about me. See, I carried the mark, and she knew. We'd sit naked on the black throne before the others. All I wore was— . . ." (*The black rosary and—* . . .) " . . . —the blue rubber."

"And so the tattoo ended up where you originally wanted it," Jeremy said with abrupt anger.

Blue reacted in surprise, jolted by the realization. "Yeah, it ended up on my cock," he said fiercely. "I fucked people, with death."

Footsteps. The priest saw Malissa moving toward the house along another path. Bravo's raucous laughter still pursued her.

Malissa did not glance back. The black ring was again on her finger. She entered the house, the domed hall.

In a light-blue dress—like that of a Greek goddess—Savannah was descending the stairway.

Synonymous with power, her beauty was her total identity. Her life was a series of seasons made possible by it. It was purchased like a precious stone, by the highest bidder. Rather, it was rented: Savannah belonged to no one but herself; to be otherwise would render her unfaithful to herself. But it was not only her legendary beauty that made her perhaps the most sought after and expensive woman in the world. It was, also, the enunciated cult of her purity: Her beauty was flawless *because* it was pure. That was her proclaimed doctrine. And purity was her vaunted virginity. No one could dispute it: not the rulers, millionaires, the most powerful men in the world—they purchased only the company of her beauty.

Facing Malissa, Savannah paused on the stairs.

Bravo had entered the house. Seeing Savannah, her laughter stopped.

Then: *Snap!*

Bravo's whip snaked expertly through the air, almost singeing Savannah's flesh.

Malissa knew: And so the wound, the longing to conquer Savannah, was still alive. Would it then be through

Savannah? Or through Karen? Finally through whom would she ultimately destroy Bravo?

Savannah's face registered no outrage. To do so might mar the perfection of its features. Calmly she continued her descent down the stairs.

Again Bravo brought her hand back. The whip lashed in a threatening "S."

Snap!

This time it almost kissed Savannah's bare shoulder. Still no reaction.

Snap!

The tip of the whip breathed against Savannah's breasts.

Snap!

The whip clutched the flimsy dress—and, pulled back, it split it along the front. The dress fell at Savannah's feet, a soft blue cloud. Savannah stood naked, exposed nipples like rouged circles on her breasts. Unperturbed, she walked to Bravo. She stood before her and smiled. Then she said huskily:

"Hello, Bravo."

"Superb theater!" Malissa passed judgment on the scene between the two women.

Calmly, Savannah turned from Bravo and walked back up the stairs, slowly.

Slapping her thigh with the coiled whip, Bravo rushed up the opposite flight; along the hall. Without knocking —softly—she opened a door into a shaded, pastel-hued bedroom.

The room seemed an extension of Karen, who stood with her back to the door. She stared down at fragile flowers, like powderpuffs, on a table. She touched one, it dissolved like a breath. She withdrew her hand in surprise.

"Once they're cut, you can't touch them," said the voice at the door.

"Oh, Bravo, you startled me."

"You left the door open," said Bravo.

"I hate locked doors." (*The key opened the locked door, the two women were not aware—until the scream.*)

"You're pensive," said Bravo.

"To face Richard, after so long— . . ."

Bravo slammed the door. Now she stood in back of Karen, the whip firmly against her own chest as if to protect the other woman from anything, even an invisible assault. "The first time I saw you—you were already married but you were alone, remember, Karen?— I wanted to protect you," Bravo confessed; her deep voice mellowed incongruously, forming foreign words. "You seemed so— . . . pure, so helpless in your purity."

Pure. Thoughts burst like a fragmented rocket in Karen's mind: *"There's your purity!" The woman's head was raised from between the other's spread legs. "Karen, baby! Baby Karen! Baby, baby— . . . Oh, God! You bastard!"* She said: "What is there to protect me from now?"

"Whatever threatens you," said Bravo. "I'd kill— . . ."

"You're too vengeful," Karen said.

"I'm like the scorpions on this island—deadly. I strike when taunted. . . . We can take the boat back now," she said with abrupt urgency. She longed to stroke the woman's hair.

"I have to see him," Karen insisted.

Bravo struck the table with her whip, a harsh period to the conversation. The flowers disintegrated into a film of white petals on the table. Still behind Karen, Bravo moved her hand over the other's head, as if finally to touch the beautiful hair. She withdrew it.

She had never yet touched Karen, that way. Toward her, Bravo experienced a new feeling which confused her. Not the familiar sadistic yearnings to conquer the most beautiful women—and she had always succeeded, except with Savannah. No, with Karen, there was a tenderness she dared not name.

She leaned forward. Still without touching her, she mimed the kissing of her hair.

The three were caught in an emotional pool: Tarah, Mark, Joja. A silent tense triangle before the lifeless stage, black figures on it like anonymous death. It was Mark who shattered the mood: He moved out of the room, the house. Moments later Joja turned from the empty stage. Nodding at Tarah, she left the room too.

Through the window, Tarah watched Mark. He stood by the pool now, poised to join his own image floating on the water's surface. Tarah thought of Gable. If she had not taken him away, from Richard, from this island, this world, Gable would be like— . . . There was something profoundly sinister about Mark, beautiful as he was. Now she saw him lying on a bench beside the pool, which lapped into the island like a tongue from the sea.

He faced the sun, his body stretched sensually. His eyes were closed.

Now Tarah saw Joja advancing toward the boy.

Joja stood over him, studying him. The hair on his legs. It shone like golden dust on the brown body.

He drew one leg up, lazily. His eyes remained closed.

"Mark!" Joja called rashly.

He sat up, propped on one elbow.

The lengthening silence demanded she fill it. But she did not know what to say, had forgotten the words of this strange role. Finally: "Why did your father bring us all here?" The words surprised her; she had merely reached into her mind, and the first coherent order of words available was the one she had formed, the question Tarah had asked her.

"My father likes interesting people," Mark said. Now he stood up. The bronze body. He had a stunning beauty that might yet rival his father's. He moved behind her. "You have beautiful red hair," he said. "Was my father a good lover?" he asked her abruptly.

Again, the jagged, sharp edge of fear; and again a suspicion of rivalry between father and son. She did not answer. She was aware of his body next to hers. Again. Innocent? Taunting her?

He moved away, again severing the contact abruptly.

Joja felt as if she had fallen from a great elevation into a pit of anger. Anger at this boy! Yes, a boy! she told herself. . . . Grabbing for release, any release, she laughed loudly.

Mark's face blackened with such intense fury that her laughter stopped as if severed by a cold knife—and she turned away from his rage.

The next words came at her like a fusillade of bullets, the voice so much like Richard's that, turning, she expected to see him. But Mark had spoken them. Darkly. Ominously. He said: "One of the guests is a murderer."

(*"I killed her!" The child in her arms. . . .*) Through the glass wall, Joja saw the waiting stage.

7

Their dark eyes were intense. Perhaps savage. Yet the rest of their faces expressed only wonder: Valerie and Paul returned to the room with the draped props on the waiting stage: watching, fascinated, the bare shadows of a world they had never even glimpsed before. Spectators, yet, now, potential players: A foreign world to be exhibited to them on that stage?

Indeed, theirs had been an enclosed world, of private tutors—nuns and priests: filtering agents allowing only parts of the vast world to seep in: A pantomime of living, Paul thought suddenly; he and his sister involved in a mute pavan while those carefully selected to witness it applauded silently: a rarefied life made possible by an invisible source of wealth. Even Daniel, their father, they saw only periodically; and then it was as if he were apprising himself of their . . . "progress." That thought came with sudden retrospective clarity to Valerie. Had they lived for eighteen sheltered years for some furious, stark, sudden revelation?

The stage stared back at them. It was as if from the moment of their arrival they had existed under the intense scrutiny of invisible eyes. Or was it since before their arrival? Acting out the preparation of a fateful ceremony still to be performed? It seemed suddenly to Valerie that they had been waiting to meet Richard all their lives.

"Paul, let's leave," she said.

"We haven't seen Richard."

"I know," she said quietly.

"What do you think this is?" Paul asked his sister. His face still serene, his eyes, devouring everything, blazed like gems.

"A throne," said Valerie, looking at the black-draped prop on the stage. "Or a bed. . . . A confessional booth."

"Or an altar," Paul said. "And this?"

Valerie stood before it—a tall, straight, black-draped object.

Paul's arm was on her shoulder.

She spun around, away from the upright prop. "Don't uncover it!" she protested.

Paul had stripped the black draping.

Valerie winced as if he were ripping away a secret part of herself.

"It's— . . . It's a wooden stake," Paul said incredulously. "No—it's a sheath—for a long knife— . . ." He stood eyeing the strange, long weapon buried into a wooden stakelike scabbard mounted on a small dais. It would be sharp and deadly. Flesh would melt like wax at its touch.

Urgently, Valerie covered the knife again with the black drape.

"I knew your mother," Tarah said to them. She had stood silently, unnoticed, observing them from the door. (She remembered: *Murder.*) Her eyes sought Paul's. (She remembered: *"I'll be gone for the weekend." "Where do you go?" "I'll be back Sunday night."* Then: *Bodies.*)

Valerie turned eagerly toward the woman. "Was she ever here?" she asked, to piece the shadow of an intimate stranger, her mother.

"Yes," said Tarah.

"She died just after we were born," Paul explained.

"I know," said Tarah. They know nothing about the horror, the trial, she knew.

Then they heard again the flapping of a bird's wings. The sound came from outside. Beyond the glass wall.

Again, the bird disappeared into the sky, a sheet of blue shattered shimmeringly by the spilled sun.

The bird floated weightlessly over the island, over trees closing in over an alcove, leaves creating an unfinished jigsaw puzzle with the jagged patch of sky.

Blue looked away from the bird. "After I saw the hideous face— . . ." he said.

"The demonic face in the mirror," Jeremy remembered. "Before your association with the woman you mentioned— . . . ?" The question formed involuntarily. He regretted it instantly. It committed his interest, which he wanted suddenly to withdraw. Because he felt threatened: Blue's words were assuming a curious physical shape about him. Strange images: like predatory birds clawing at him. He was aware of a struggle, unnamed, between him and the youngman. Only its style was being shaped now.

"No—before. I was terrified by that face, man. It lasted only a few moments. But I kept thinking it would come back," Blue said. "And the thought kept bumtripping me."

And did it come back? Jeremy wanted to ask, but this time he didn't.

Blue answered the unasked question: "It never came back. So far."

"Is that what you want to confess?" Jeremy asked. This time, the question was a challenge.

"I'm not *confessing*, man," Blue said, understanding the implied challenge. "Just rapping." His mind floated over the battlefield of sexual memories. "Diggit: A meek little man. He lay on the floor, man, I straddled him." His eyes demanded a reaction—shock, indignation, anger.

But the priest did not react. He could still hear the sound of the bird's flapping wings. Or did he merely grasp for it to thwart the sound of Blue's words?

"The little man pretended he was a urinal," Blue flung the words defiantly at the priest. "And I pissed on him through a hole he had just bitten at the tip of my blue rubber— . . ."

"What do you want from me!" Jeremy demanded suddenly. He stood up, Blue stood too.

With real panic, Blue yelled at the priest: "I want you to— . . . What I've told you, it's only— . . ." (*Blood!* The remembered spectacle of it seemed to smear the priest's fierce face.) "Listen, man! Listen to your fucking blasphemy! I called on the Lord Satan!" Blue shouted. "I became his disciple Susej! And he demanded a human sacrifice!"

Would he understand my confession? It was that sudden thought ripped uncontrollably from the priest's mind that made him move away from Blue, from Blue and his words. He walked away from the alcove quickly, as if those words would pursue him, capture him, assault him.

Before the house, he paused, undecided whether to enter. Suddenly he was aware of a somber figure staring down at him from an upstairs window. (*Painted fingernails on the swollen stomach.* He remembered that, and he heard: Echoes within the canyons of his mind: *Laughter, moans.* And: *A scream from another eternal moment.*) Before ascending the steps leading into the white rotunda, the priest turned away from the house, along another path.

Now the figure at the window in Malissa's suite looked beyond the beautiful priest and saw Blue walking toward the house. He moved weightlessly, like a cunning, sensual animal. La Duquesa sighed: "I'll always be true to the memory of the Duke."

"Always, huh?" said Rev.

"Always." La Duquesa drew the black veil protectively over her face, as if to hide even further from Rev.

Topaze was impatient for Malissa's return; he strained toward the door. Tor still worked out with the weights.

Without looking at her, Rev said to la Duquesa, "What is it like to wear a dress?"

Albert frowned for la Duquesa.

"What is it like to wear pants?" la Duquesa snapped haughtily.

"But a *dude* wearing a dress!" Rev attempted to taunt her.

"Then ask a *dude* who wears a dress!" la Duquesa rejected the taunt.

Albert laughed, approving la Duquesa's answer. "Well spoken, your grace!"

"Albert!" Malissa had entered the room. "Are you annoying them?" At the door her fingers reached out as if to claw at Albert from that distance.

Topaze stood instantly beside her like a tiny sentry.

La Duquesa drew the dark veil only enough to expose a gentle smile to Albert. "He's not bothering anyone," she defended him.

Albert looked at la Duquesa in flooding gratitude. His ally! His only ally!

It was that. Just that. As little as that. That smile—and the sudden thought of an ally. It was that which brought it about:

As if he had been seized totally by another being, suddenly Albert faced Malissa defiantly. Topaze was the first to notice that. Alerted to the possible violence of insurrection, the midget's eyes sparkled. He pointed at Albert.

With great dignity—attempting to stretch his dumpy body to greater size—Albert announced, enunciating clearly: "Rev, Tor—you, Topaze!" He did not have to include la Duquesa; she was his ally. "All of you, listen, I want to tell you something. Finally. I want to tell you that *I'm* the source of the limitless wealth, *I'm* the one who has the money to support you. Not Malissa." The finger he had intended pointing at her did not dare rise, not yet. "Without me," he went on in a firm voice, "the entourage wouldn't exist."

Malissa's extended hands dropped in a flash of rubies, a brutal pantomime of crushing.

"Without me," Albert went on as if reciting words silently rehearsed for years, "without me all of you would be back to— . . . Topaze, you'd have to return to the circus. Imitation, gaudy finery, Topaze! Not the tailored clothes that hug your body! Tor, you!"

Tor walked into the room. His blank face struggled for an expression.

Malissa had not moved.

"Tor," Albert continued, "think of the endless days on beaches, waiting. Think of the eternity of the afternoons when it rains, when it's cool—when there's no sun to warm your muscles. Think of that. And think, Rev— . . . Petty crime— . . ."

"Petty!" Rev objected.

"Yes, petty," Albert insisted. "Always hiding— . . . Do you want to go back to that—the circus, beaches, streets?" he asked the entourage. "*I'm* the one who keeps you from those lives." He swallowed. "Topaze! Come here!" he tested his new authority.

Topaze looked at Malissa.

Only her eyes sent commands: a vortex of funnels, spirals, currents: twisting.

"Topaze!" Albert repeated, trying to square his round frame, to force it to grow; but, already, a note of entreaty had crept into the imitation authority.

Topaze did not move.

Desperately Albert spun about toward Tor. "Tor!" Albert's voice assumed a hard tone. "Come here!"

Instinctively, Tor flexed. Malissa's blue-shielded gaze was on him like dry ice. Tor's body relaxed.

Frantically, Albert implored: "Tor . . . I command—
. . ."

Now the bodybuilder did not move.

Tears, perspiration, either or both covered Albert's face. An inept general, he had moved too quickly, too clumsily into a fatal ambush. To thwart total defeat, fighting for authority, he rushed at the midget: "Topaze, I command you— . . .!" He moved frenziedly now to Rev. "Rev!" He tried every possible exit out of the trap.

The cold-blue message of Malissa's eyes was a presence. It restrained the others almost physically, binding them to her.

"Rev!" Albert gasped. He pulled at the dark-young-man's vest. The exposed head of the tattooed panther, eyes glaring, menaced him. Rev looked quickly at Malissa. She nodded like an empress at a gory circus, calling for the slaughter. Rev pushed Albert violently back.

Albert fell panting to the floor near la Duquesa.

She looked down sadly at him. With dignity, smoothing her black veils, she knelt to help the quivering man. She held out her hand to him.

"Thank you, your grace," he whimpered gratefully, taking her hand.

"Albert!" Malissa buried the name into him like a fatal knife. The word released her body. The slashing motions of her fantastic hands resumed, spewing out their arcane curses. "Enough of your lies and your ridiculous poses! I may have to commit you if you continue to hallucinate!"

Albert reacted automatically like a private summoned to attention.

"Note this well, Albert!" Malissa whirled toward Topaze. "Topaze, choose!"

Topaze moved quickly to her side.

"Rev!"

The knife in his hand—an additional ally she could count on—Rev stood next to Malissa.

"Tor!"

He joined the others.

Malissa glanced at la Duquesa. The veiled eyes met the blue-shielded eyes. No. Not yet. Quickly Malissa said: "You're wrong, Albert. *I* have the power. Without *me,* you have nothing! *Repeat it, Albert!*"

"Without you, I have nothing," Albert whispered.

Tarah watched Paul and Valerie move away from her in the room where the draped props waited to be revealed. She saw: In the domed hall Mark stopped to speak to the blond youngman who moved like a stealthy cat.

She turned away swiftly. She had returned here to confront Richard. Nothing must thwart the impact of that confrontation. Yes, hatred bound her to him like love. That night, as she crossed into the dark room from the lighted hall—in retrospect, the tunnel of a nightmare—she had intersected the line of love and hate. She had also moved into the country of unfillable sexuality carved by Richard, she reminded herself firmly.

Her thoughts had seized her so intensely that until she saw her reflection in the water she did not realize she had actually walked outside of the house and now stood at the edge of the pool. The sun was an unshifting, glaring white eye. Tarah hid from its brightness behind dark sunglasses. Bending down, she thrust her hand into the water, destroying the reflected reality of her world. Then she saw the shattered reflection of someone beside her. The young priest.

"You startled me," she said, rising.

"I'm sorry," he apologized.

"Why are you here, Father?" she asked him.

For a moment he seemed not to know what to answer. Then he repeated the facts of Richard's invitation, the archbishop's insistence. "And Richard said he needed me."

"Richard? Needed you, Father?" she said in astonishment. "Richard doesn't need anyone." Over his white collar, the hair which must coat his chest heavily was visible. Tarah imagined the stark pattern, a solid "X" on his naked body. He was so young, so beautiful. So pure. Had he ever been with a woman?

Removing the sunglasses, she held them clenched in her teeth, the frame on one side pointing to the parting between her full breasts.

The priest followed the direction of the dangling frame. (*Flesh! Bodies mounted on bodies like animals!*) He tore his stare from the woman's breasts. "I'm sorry I startled you," he said.

As he moved away, she studied his broad shoulders, narrow hips. The nerve of her sensuality had been touched—a sensuality hidden from her son during the periodic trips when she was a sexual prowler. Now, here— . . .

Thoughts tumbled into a frenzied fantasy of bodies, sexual images like hungry eagles raiding her mind: Tor, she preferred lithe bodies, but his was so outrageously stunning, the bulging muscles pressed against her body, Rev, the hint of sex braced with violence, the exposed tattoos, Topaze, the perfect miniature man, Blue, the tawny, sensual, brown body, the curiously intriguing tattooed ankle, her mind swept with images, the priest, beautiful like those martyrs who burn in ecstasy with the passion of sexuality: all thrusting into her.

The fantasy erupted further. For an astonished instant before she rejected it, her mind caught the beautiful face of— ... A man, a youngman. Mark— ... Richard's features superimposed— ... Richard! No, Mark— ... Paul! Paul— ... Mark— ... No— ... !

With a sudden muffled cry of despair, fleeing a vicissitude of bodies and faces becoming one, just one, she ran frantically toward the house.

From his room upstairs, Blue saw the priest move away from Tarah. Now he looked at her as she rushed into the house.

Without his realizing it until now, Blue had been repeating the same words over and over since he had separated from the priest in the alcove:

Father, forgive me, for I have sinned.

Suddenly the origin of the unpronounced words was reversed: In Blue's mind it was the priest who knelt before him.

Savannah's room swam in mirrors. Still naked, she pulled the cord to one side of the bed on which she lay. Withdrawing panels over the bed revealed still another mirror, amber-tinted, round, gold-wreathed. Savannah stretched her glorious body, exposing it more fully to the golden pool of the mirror, offering it to its own reflection. Her auburn hair covered only one breast. The honey triangle at her legs was just lightly brushed with tawny hair, highlighted gold.

Untouched! Unsmeared! Unsullied!

Her mind repeated those words over and over, a litany to her perfect beauty.

Now her arms rose toward the mirror as if to bring

the reflection of herself on her: her body on her own magnificent body.

In that moment she appeared to herself a reflected "X" laid out in naked sacrifice.

(*Blood!*) Swiftly she shifted her body, destroying the reflection. (The memory persisted: *Her hand. Blood covering her fingers!*) To expel the unwelcome images, she dressed quickly. The room seemed to scream a buried secret. She left it, closing the door hurriedly as if to lock within it the savage vibrations.

Now completely composed, wearing very low-rise lavender pants, inches below her navel—her blouse exposing a major part of her breasts, the rim of the nipples lightly outlined under the sheer material which clung to her extravagant body as if wet—she descended the sweeping steps into the domed hall just as the priest entered the house, followed moments later by Tarah.

In the dining hall the elaborately set table of food was intact.

"Father!" Valerie rushed to the priest, as if for protection from something undefined.

The priest was holding a branch in his hand.

The girl looked at it.

"It's a branch of wild rose," he said, and gave it to her. "I found it outside." He moved closer to Valerie, and to her brother—as if they must begin to choose sides in a terrible game.

"There's a superstition about wild roses on the mainland," Tarah said. "They ward off vampires."

"There's no such thing," Paul said.

The priest smiled, deliberately to veil the harshness of his next words: "There's evil that procreates evil, it lives on the symbolic blood of others; as red as— . . ."

"Blood isn't red," said Blue. "After a while it becomes almost black." Soundlessly, he had entered the room. He brushed one unruly lock of hair from his forehead. He shrugged his shoulders. A smile assaulted the moody face.

"Blood is filthy," Savannah said.

"It's the color of old roses," Karen said. She leaned slightly on Bravo as they descended the stairs.

The priest thought: Blood can color a whole world.

"I hate even the thought of blood!" Valerie's mind burst in a shatter of red.

Paul studied each of the people here. Suddenly the world was on display. A kaleidoscope changing in flashes of violent colors, shapes.

Looking at her brother, Valerie saw the glimpse of a stranger.

"Blood will have no color," Tarah said ambiguously. She saw Mark upstairs looking down at them.

Now Tarah left the domed hall. As if to pry its meaning, she returned to the room where the stage waited.

"Why did you come back?"

Tarah froze at the question.

Mark had asked it.

She regained control immediately. "Because I have to discover again how utterly I hate your father."

Mark stood on the platform of the stage, touching the chairlike prop. He sat on it, over the black cover draping it. Now he leaned back. He extended his hand, like a king in command.

"Will my half-brother be here?" he asked her.

"Of course not," she said. Their eyes locked.

Mark asked her, "How old is Gable?"

"Eighteen," Tarah said.

"The same age as the twins," Mark said. The words were like the swift lunge of a sure knife, withdrawn quickly: "Do you really hate my father?"

"With a hatred like love. It has to be replenished," Tarah said.

"You hate him because of the two men?"

"How the hell do you know?" (*Richard opened the door; and the two stood there already naked; she walked toward them, to her prolonged sexual execution, she knew. The closed door stopped the shaft of light that had pointed her way like a sword into the womb of the darkness.*)

Suddenly, looking at Mark, Tarah did not see a child at all. She saw: Richard. Richard as he had looked that savage night that confounded reality. Beautiful. Cold. . . . Anger, murderous fury, clenched her fists as it had that night: *She walked in, she turned, once, to look at Richard, hoping he would relent.*

To contain the spilling anger, Tarah closed her eyes. Gable. The anger ebbed. He had Escaped Richard and this terrible island.

Mark jumped off the chair, the platform. He stretched his lithe body.

Tarah watched him move away from her. What did she feel toward him? An extension of Richard; did she hate him too?

Mark had left the room.

Again he stood at the top of the stairs. Again he looked down at the others in the domed hall. Then he walked quickly along the golden corridors. At the end of the wing, he opened a door, not knocking, knowing it would be open.

Her body covered only by the purple robe, Joja lay in bed. Her red hair fanned on the pillow. She heard the door close. Eyes shut, she said: "Richard?"

There was no answer.

"Mark," she said. This time it was not a question.

Mark advanced toward the bed, over the woman.

Through the window the sun was yellow, soon to turn orange in the late afternoon.

"Why did you ask your father to invite me?" Joja's lips asked.

The boy lay on the enormous bed.

"I slept with you and my father once," he said. "I was naked. And so were you and he."

Joja's eyes opened into the exposed round mirror over the bed, as if she dare not face the boy directly.

"Like this," Mark said. He removed the trunks.

She saw the reflection of his exorbitant body—the white patch at the middle, sheltered from the sun; the dark triangle of hair between his legs enclosing the powerful groin. Her throat choked with longing.

"And you were naked too," he said.

As if her mind had separated itself from her body, one reacting independently of the other, Joja's hands opened the purple robe. Yet her mind cried: *Don't!* It was an alert—a warning which had nothing to do with the fact that Mark was a boy. No, because suddenly for her he was not. Rather, it was a warning that announced a fear of exposing herself to him—as if it were *she* who were capable of being corrupted by him.

"And you held me," Mark said. "I lay between you and my father. You both held me." His voice was soft and hypnotic, mesmerizing—like the beating of the water earlier, the flapping of wings: soft and subdued: rhythmic: yet it commanded.

Then she felt Mark's lips barely touching her neck. To Joja it was suddenly as if he had bent to kiss the imprint of his father's bite.

Malissa lay on her bed, fully clothed as if prepared to rise quickly in any eventuality. Her hands guarded her. "That pitiful Albert—to challenge me," she said to la Duquesa; la Duquesa had just finished arranging Malissa's clothes. The words were clearly an implied warning to the queen in black mourning.

Malissa's eyes closed. But the blue bubbled glasses on the ageless face seemed to remain watching, alert.

Leaving the room quietly, la Duquesa crossed the hallway, knocked softly but urgently at Albert's door—and entered the open room hurriedly before there was an answer.

"Your grace!"

She cautioned him with a black-nailed finger. She closed the door. "She's asleep," she said. Then quickly, as if to verbalize an unspoken alliance: "Why do you put up with her?"

"Because— . . ." He closed his mouth tightly: He would clearly not answer, not now.

"Which one do you want?" la Duquesa asked him hurriedly.

"I don't understand, your grace."

"Tor—Topaze—Rev— . . ."

"You can arrange it?"

"Of course. I'm a superb, convincing actress." Then: less sure: "I can *try*. . . . I think I can get Tor for you. I don't trust the others— . . ." She was already at the door.

"Your grace, why are you exposing yourself to Malissa's anger for me?" Albert asked.

"Because the Duke despised cruelty," la Duquesa said. "He would want me to do this. . . . Often—on rainy afternoons when we made love all day—often he would say that there is nothing sadder than love and desire which pine without fulfillment."

Suddenly there was the loud, unmistakable whirring of the helicopter, descending outside.

"It'll wake her!" Albert said frantically. His hands clutched in terror at his fleshy throat.

The loud whirring of the helicopter continued. It had begun slowly in the distance like the flapping of wings.

Mark heard it instantly. He stood up from the bed in Joja's room. "My father is here!" He put on his trunks.

At the door, he looked back at her. A hint of a promise, long extended, still to be kept?

The recurring rage flowed suddenly into anticipation within Joja. *Richard is here!*

She dressed hurriedly and left the room quickly.

Mark moved along the mirrored halls. He met Malissa coming out of her room.

Richard is here!

The entourage rushed with her, followed by Albert and la Duquesa.

Richard is here!

Downstairs, the others were aware of the loud whirring of the helicopter, and of the excitement seizing the house totally.

Tarah knew: *Richard is here!* Deliberately she gathered all the anger within her, to conquer a vague, sensual, disturbing anticipation.

The fiery water surrounding the island pulled the sun's reflection into its depths.

Now they were all in the enormous hall.

Richard is here!

The glass eye of the arched dome, freezing the sky, glared down at them. From above, the vitreous black and white floor seemed to contain them all within a vortex.

Mark stood on the stairs, Malissa beside him. They all stared toward the white rotunda of columns through which Richard would enter. Mark's clear eyes were red in the fierce light of the late afternoon.

"My father is here," he said.

Part II

9

A black man and a black woman preceded Richard into the house.

"The papaloi and the mamaloi." Mark recognized the voodoo highpriests from the mainland.

Breasts bared dark as grapes, bracelets, earrings, necklaces, amulets, rings thrusting angry stabs of twisted, mottled light about her, the black woman was lithe, her eyes hard blue diamonds locked in coal. Beside her, the man was tall. His shirtless muscular body shone like glossy iron. Crystalline blue, his eyes, like hers, seemed to open into a deep vacuity. Their torsos were painted in shrieking swirls of color.

Behind the blue shield of her glasses, Malissa's eyes smiled.

And then Richard was there.

In a white suit and a deep, deep-blue shirt, he stood under the orange light of the fallen sun which still grasped at the island through the arched dome. Tall, slender, spectacularly handsome, clear irises dark rimmed, set in a deeply tanned angular face—eyes which were like the depths of clearest water, at the bottom of which is a film of black—a face as composed as black crystal—he glanced at each of his guests, recognizing each quickly, even those he had not met before. But his eyes moved swiftly from face to face, searching out one. The arc of his sight paused on Valerie. Then it extended to include Paul.

Malissa captured each swift reaction.

Still holding the branch of wild rose which the priest had given her, Valerie looked away immediately, from Richard to her brother. Her fierce eyes called urgently to the face which gazed fascinated at Richard. Paul felt his sister's hand on his arm, a warm current rushed at him. He looked quizzically at his sister, and touched his lips in a vague gesture.

Malissa shattered the stunned silence. "A splendid, dazzling entrance, Richard!" she congratulated. The rubied fingers were extended toward him, but clearly neither she nor Richard would touch.

"Malissa," Richard acknowledged.

"And the entourage!" Malissa indicated with a dazzling sweep of her hand. "Topaze! La Duquesa! Tor! Rev!" She flung the names swiftly to clear away the irrelevance of superficial identity.

Topaze removed his cavalier's hat and sliced the air elegantly in a deep bow before Richard.

"I'm sorry I've kept you waiting," Richard said to his guests. His voice was like black velvet. Mark descended the stairs and stood beside his father.

"Karen . . . Joja . . . Tarah . . . you look lovelier than ever." Richard began acknowledging his guests. "Karen." His lips hardly brushed her cheek.

The shimmering blackness Richard exuded: It enveloped Karen like a black cowl. She felt a resurgence of life, a tide. "Richard!" Even her voice had a new strength.

Bravo's eyes focused on Richard like the telescope of a deadly gun. As if she would extend her hand to him in greeting, she held out, instead, abruptly, the butt of her whip.

His smile accepted her silent challenge. He glanced at Karen—naming the stakes in the conflict? Bravo's firm grasp on her shoulders claimed Karen.

Staring vacantly like zombies, the mamaloi and the papaloi flanked the sweep of stairs, like guards. To Tor, their objectless gaze reflected his. (He saw: *Eyes on oiled bodies.*)

"Joja." Again, Richard's lips barely touched the actress's cheek.

The intervening years since she had seen him, suddenly they rushed together, fused, evaporated: The only reality remained the brief past with him, the immediate present now: only Richard. "Richard," she said. And she thought feverishly: He's the only one who can resurrect me from the feeling of being dead. But her eyes shifted toward Mark, to include him too. Then back to Richard. Father. Son. Together? Apart? She touched the scar on her neck, kissed by Mark moments earlier, made by Richard years ago. Her soul whispered: Richard. (An impression: *Darkness, darkness!*)

Abruptly Tarah withdrew as Richard approached her, to touch her cheek too with his lips. Even so, she felt herself drawn into his eyes: the black depths beneath the mirror clarity. Even as she felt hatred scorch her flesh with a paradoxical coldness—and her mind was thrust violently into the past: against the memory of sexual slaughter—she had the sensation that her body had opened to welcome him. No. "Richard." She pronounced his name like a sentence of doom.

That handsome, yes, that beautiful. La Duquesa remembered the Duke. Yes, like that, like Richard.

"Your grace," he acknowledged her.

She touched her veil as if to assert its reality.

To gather support from her allegiance, Albert stood near the queen; he stared in awe at Richard, who spoke his name in greeting. Malissa's equal, the only equal she acknowledged, Albert knew. And feared? No, Malissa feared no one.

Richard, Malissa. Rev was aware of two powerful currents of stunning power: Poised. He lifted his knife in introduction to Richard. It could have been an offering.

"Savannah."

The mere utterance of her name by Richard seemed to contain the hint of the revelation of a secret. A mirror! Savannah searched for her own reflection—as if for something to hold onto within a spiraling sea. A mirror! Her eyes riveted toward the base of a giant lamp. Its mirrored surface, a series of concave hollows, distorted her beauty grotesquely. It pulled it apart.

"Blue, you came," said Richard, seeing the youngman for the first time.

Blue nodded. Had he seen Richard before? In a drugged hallucinated haze? A face, beautiful and powerful, not to be forgotten: appearing within hungry orange flames which did not touch it. . . . Blue's flung glance directed Richard's eyes toward his ankle. Richard acknowledged it.

Now his eyes locked with the priest's. "And the archbishop?" Richard inquired.

"He sends his bless— . . . his greetings," Jeremy said.

Then Richard's look returned to Valerie. It penetrated the beautiful façade, it studied it relentlessly. Then he smiled down at the branch of wild rose. "Valerie," he said softly. He embraced her. She accepted his arms passively. When he withdrew, she stared down at the wild rose: crushed by Richard's tight embrace. The petals clung to her breast like caked blood. She clenched them within a fist.

Now Richard embraced Paul. "Richard," Paul breathed.

When she saw Richard and Paul touch, Tarah turned away. *To save Paul—to strike before— . . . !* About to fuse into one, her thoughts dissolved before they formed.

Malissa clutched at the air as if to bring down the silence. The rubies blazed insanely on her fingers. "Enough of greetings and introductions!" she said peremptorily. "If we become bored— . . . !" she uttered the words of disaster. She demanded bluntly: "Richard, what will the entertainment be? We haven't come for miles merely to see your fascinating island!"

"What do you suggest, Malissa?" Richard asked her calmly.

Of course she knew—and he knew—that the entertainment had been determined: There was the waiting stage. He was suggesting to her, then, merely a preliminary sortie. *To keep time moving!* To thwart the fatal boredom she had already warned of! "We could perform tableaux from the Tarot cards," she announced cunningly.

Eager to please, Topaze looked up at her. "Yes, yes, Miss Malissa!" he applauded.

"Her occult bullshit!" Bravo dismissed with bored contempt.

But Malissa's black-ringed finger had become a weapon for slaughter in her momentary entertainment. It was already aimed at the priest: "Of course! The Father could be the Pope!" she named the fifth card of the major arcanum of the Tarot, the ancient cards of divination. "Possessed of the key of heaven!" she described the figure depicted in the card. Her voice changed sharply: "And the key to hell!" Her laughter was like ice thawing, freezing quickly again. "Or would that symbol be too obvious for the good Father?" she consulted Richard.

"Perhaps the Hermit," Richard offered the figure in the ninth card. It was as if he in turn were consulting the priest for his own choice.

"Yes!" Malissa agreed.

"The priest will represent the Hermit's card in tableaux of the Tarot!" Topaze announced solemnly.

(*A confessional booth.*) The priest understood the implied accusation. Had his world indeed narrowed through dual tunnels into a muted corner which allowed life in only through a tiny window—and even that window was screened? The Hermit—...

"Perhaps he should be represented by the Falling Tower," Mark casually named the sixteenth card of the Tarot. His eyes assumed the color of the changing sky cut into a circle by the dome; they deepened into purple. "The powerful tower ripped by lightning." He smiled at his solemn words—yet his eyes, on the priest, conveyed a serious message.

"The crumbling tower!" Malissa described the sixteenth card. "The headlong plummeting of the two figures: Two figures rent apart. Or is it one? A split man. The shattering of a false philosophy! Excellent, Mark!" she congratulated the boy. Yet: The nails of her hands turned inward into claws.

A crumbling tower. Two figures. A split man. The woman was merely attempting in her flippant game— and the strange child in joining it—to utter a wild, baseless prophecy, the priest told himself to keep from responding in anger: perhaps the very reaction the woman wanted to prod.

Malissa went on, as if on a verbal rampage, issuing hints of destruction: "Bravo—the eleventh card! Force!" she deliberately misnamed the card of Strength: referring now to the occult cards not so much for their mystic meanings as for the impact of the readily evoked images within them.

"Force!" Bravo's voice was menacing. (*A man on a woman.* "*Now!*" *The man's body pulled away savagely: And the whip about his neck.*) She recovered immediately: "Come off that mystic crap, man!" she tossed.

But it was obvious that Malissa's black-pearled weapon had found its object there, if fleetingly. It moved swiftly from Bravo in search of other possible victims: "The Fool!" she sentenced Albert with contempt. "On the edge of a precipice, blindly! And the Queen of Swords beside him: the suit of desolation!"

"But *I* have known love!" la Duquesa declared.

"Savannah!" Malissa accosted the stunning woman. "Savannah can be the Moon, dripping blood!"

Blood! Savannah looked quickly into her hand.

Malissa seized the reaction: "Ah, yes; the Moon! The eighteenth card in the major arcanum—eighteen reduced to nine, the number of initiation, Savannah! The torn hymen!"

(*Blood!* "*Cut it!*") Savannah's eyes blackened.

"Dogs baying at the unsullied, but bloody, moon!" Malissa ground on viciously with her description of the card.

"Baying like you!" Savannah aimed coldly at Malissa.

But Malissa was not fazed. Her words propelled her kinetically into further assaults: "Tarah!"

"My card will be The Day of Judgment," Tarah said quietly. Her eyes scorched their message of vengeance on Richard. Her purpose had been announced.

Richard said: "A card of resurrection. Or death."

"Death," Tarah chose.

Malissa allowed the black word to float on the silence. Then: "Or shall you be represented by the Hanged

Man? The hanged?—or the hanger, Tarah?" Not wanting an answer now, she said quickly: "Richard, should you be the Magician—the most powerful figure in the Tarot? Or . . . shall it be I . . . Richard?" And there it was: Her own challenge had been issued, easily. Yes! It would be this season. Tonight!

"Or Mark." Joja's own words astonished her.

The boy glanced abruptly away from his father. As if a secret had been announced prematurely.

Joja felt trapped within two tides. Opposing tides? Or finally conjoined.

Malissa's words had stopped abruptly. Mark. . . . In invading her entertainment so expertly, aiming with such uncanny cunning at the priest, had indeed the boy enunciated *his* bid for power? But he was just a child. Yet perhaps if not now, later. Or *was* it now? Would she then have to confront Richard *and* Mark?

"Is there a snake in the Tarot, Lady Cobra?—for you to play?" Bravo demanded.

Rejecting the insult, Malissa's hands wove an intricate symbol before her, it arched, it swirled, it swept about itself: as if something beyond her were directing its shape and her words: Now the black-ringed finger pointing like a sword lunged at Blue. "The card of Death!" she said. Her hand collapsed, the finger aimed at the tattooed star.

"No," Blue rejected. "It's— . . . over, man," he said vaguely.

Now abruptly Malissa's hands came to life again, floating. "And the Lovers!" she named the sixth card. But this time the accusatory finger found no definite object—it glided from Karen to Bravo, to Blue, la Duquesa, the priest, Joja. . . . Paul, Valerie: It waited momentarily like a spider on an invisible cobweb.

Then the finger retreated. The stabbing hand died. Malissa sighed, suddenly bored: "A game much too complicated," she deliberately rejected her own seriousness. "We must choose another," she said in a dull tone.

Malissa and Richard—weaving the usual trance: advancing, retreating, Tarah knew, almost in admiration.

"Shall we choose sides between God and Satan?" Malissa offered, casually, a substitute preliminary entertainment. The blue glasses faced the priest.

"Yes, yes!" Topaze encouraged gleefully "We'll choose between Satan and God now!"

"Though often the distinction blurs," Richard said.

"Like lovers they begin to look alike," Malissa offered easily. Whatever war would develop ultimately between her and Richard, now their words were in perfect harmony.

"How can *you* speak of God, Malissa?" Tarah questioned bluntly.

"Why, I have dedicated my life to the discovery of Him, dear Tarah," Malissa said seriously. "To ferreting Him out for scrutiny."

The woman's smile, cold as it was, certainly it belied any seriousness to her brutal words, the priest told himself. The words merely sought a reaction: how far, how outrageous they could become. Yet he felt personally assaulted. He must challenge the mockery. By leaving? Flee. . . . The recurrent word. Richard's eyes were on him as if he had spoken it aloud. "Choose by drawing lots?" Jeremy asked lightly, refusing to acknowledge even a sacrilegious seriousness.

"No, not arbitrarily," Richard said. "In such a game we would acknowledge freedom of choice." His smile, like Malissa's, obviated the seriousness of his words.

"I believe it's called free will," said Malissa.

The mamaloi and the papaloi trembled slightly, like figures only momentarily released from a powerful force.

Tor flexed his body, touching it.

Richard turned swiftly to the priest: "Which side would you choose in such a game, Father?"

"The obvious choice." Jeremy still controlled his anger.

"He chooses Satan," Malissa said, her words like acid. "Topaze!" Her hands were live entities again. "Which side would you choose? God or Satan?" she asked the midget.

"You!" Topaze said hurriedly.

Rev pointed his knife at the midget.

"And I," la Duquesa's voice quivered at the edge of tears, "I would choose . . . love." (*"I love you, I'll love you forever, only you." And she extended the flowers to him.*)

"I choose whatever side you're not on!" Bravo flung at Richard.

"They're not serious," Valerie protested. But she moved urgently toward the priest.

"Of course not," he said.

But Malissa had already whirled about to face Blue. "Which side would you choose?"

He frowned at her. (He remembered: *"Lord Susej, I have received a command!" The words had melted on his mind, like a wax rainbow.*) "What?" He searched the tattooed pentagram on his ankle. (*Mouths! Kissing it! Mouths moving up to the blue rubber! The star there, too—stretched!*) But the ram's head, he told himself urgently, the ram's head within the pentagram is missing. "Oh, uh— . . ." he started hazily.

"Between God and Satan—which side!" Malissa demanded.

"It's what— . . ." Blue started seriously. His eyes sought the priest's, as if for help.

The priest made a move toward him. He felt Richard's relentless stare. He stopped.

Blue touched his own forehead—a half gesture—as if to clear it. "See, man, I had to get it together. Diggit, it's what I— . . . See, when Mr Stuart— . . ."

"Decide! Decide!" Malissa's words hammered remorselessly.

"Stop torturing him, Malissa!" Tarah thrust herself between Malissa and Blue. "Can't you see he's taking you seriously?"

Malissa's laughter broke the strange moments. "Why, so he was." She turned toward Richard. "Richard, he was really taking us seriously," she said.

The closed chambers of her mind springing open suddenly—eyes pieces of desperate blue glass—the mamaloi flung herself under the glass dome within the indigo light of heavy dusk.

Malissa motioned for silence. Now the others watched the black woman in fascination.

Contracting her body, she seemed about to crumple onto the floor. Instead, in one stunning eruption of energy, her body became free, her arms were thrust at the dome of sky. Her mouth opened, and it hurled one single word into the waiting canyons of the mansion:

"*Murder!*"

The word released memories like sprung echoes in those who stood about her in a circle: *Blood! Bodies! Clawing hands! Screams! Lights bursting! A gasping child! A black throne! A grave! A shattered body floating in a pool of red! A coffin! Fists crushing staring eyes! A face veiled with blood!*

10

Malissa moved swiftly before the black woman, her rubied hands before her as if to sustain the trance within which the black woman was wrapped.

"What do you see?" came Malissa's words.

"Murder. . . ." the black woman whispered. Her eyes were locked.

"When?" Malissa coaxed.

"Yesterday. . . . And tonight," the black voice spoke.

"A murder committed," Karen interpreted.

"And one to be committed," Tarah pronounced.

"Tonight! Who?" Malissa demanded.

But the trance faded. The blue-glass eyes in the black face opened. Next to the black man again, the black woman's body was rigid and dead.

"What a terrifying prediction!" Valerie's mind had burst with distorted images.

"The beginning of the game," Malissa announced.

But Richard laughed. "No cause for alarm," he directed himself to Valerie. "The mamaloi knows only a few words of English. She witnessed a murder once on the mainland—they practice voodoo."

"Shit, she just wants to make herself seem important with all her heavy predictions, man," Bravo said, directing her words at Malissa.

"Of course," Malissa said. "And that's why Richard brought her here—for our amusement, to keep us from boredom!"

"I'm afraid," Valerie whispered to her brother.

"There's nothing to be afraid of," the priest said to the girl. "Our host—and some of his guests—have an uncanny sense of effective drama." He rejected the scene they had just witnessed.

A grasping, then a sudden release, to produce the ultimate control: It was Richard's tactic, Tarah knew.

"Predictions of doom are the safest to make," Joja too dismissed the scene, haughtily. "She could mean a symbolic murder, and who in his life has not wanted—... ?" (She heard: *A child gasping for breath!* Saw: *A terrifyingly white pillow!*)

As if—correctly—he had expected her to turn toward him at that moment, Mark looked at the actress, and then quickly at his father.

"When the Duke— ..." la Duquesa began.

The whirring of the helicopter—they all heard it.

Blue thought: Cam! The name spun out of his clouded mind, like something always waiting. And then: No, there was no way Cam could be here. He was—... He blocked the rest.

Daniel! Valerie thought. He'll insist we leave.

Anger strangled Tarah with iron fingers. No! her heart shrieked. It couldn't be— ...

Lianne! Joja knew. She felt an unwelcome, jealous rivalry toward Mark's mother.

The whirring ground like gravel into Savannah's ears. A montage of gray rejected memories: *A room, her body.* She heard: *The terrible whirring as if it were drawing the blood.*

La Duquesa *felt* the Duke's presence at that moment. "The Duke and I outlawed unkindness within our world," she reminded them.

Albert sighed for her.

"The games, Richard!" Malissa insisted.

"Tonight," Richard said.

Clearly about to dismiss his guests for now, Tarah knew. He was moving away from them, perhaps to meet whoever had arrived in the helicopter.

Mark made a move to follow him. Then he stopped.

Now the others drifted away from the staring dome, which was like the eye of a glowering heaven.

In the enormous banquet hall, food and wine still waited, intact, like glazed statuary. There had been little of eating throughout the day, little of drinking.

As if, thought Tarah, they were fasting for communion.

She walked upstairs. *Now Richard will come to me,* she knew, *and then he will go to Karen and Joja.* The familiar panels along the walls in the corridors intrigued her anew: the gold silhouetted figures on the brink of self-discovery; or, perhaps, frozen at the point just immediately beyond it. In her room, she looked about tensely. (Remembering: *Two men in the darkness.*) Now she would wait for Richard. Whomever he had gone to meet—if indeed he had—Richard would be here. Soon. And she knew: Joja, Karen—in their rooms they too waited for Richard. But he would come to her first.

Now she looked out the window. The sky was a darkening cave of bitter stars. From this level the gardens formed a symmetrical pattern, like a mirror-image. The alcoves were lighted by soft, subdued lights, hidden among the statuary. From this distance the illumined grottos were like fireflies floating in the night. She saw: A shadowy figure waiting downstairs in the purple pool of night. Who? It looked up. At that moment she heard the door to her room open, close. She turned to face Richard.

"And Gable?" he asked immediately.

"He's well, he's very handsome. We travel together—. . ." she rushed words to cancel other questions, "when he's not in school."

"And except for the interludes."

Her eyes flashed angrily at the words she had sought to avert. "You bastard! You pushed me to it— . . ." (*Naked writhing shadows.*)

"Gable doesn't know." A question? A statement.

"No!" she said. "And if anyone should ever— . . ."

"What would you do, Tarah?"

She looked out at the maze of gardens. There was no moon. Yet the stones on the paths gleamed like the eyes of cats. The shadow waiting there still—it looked up again. In search of one particular window?"

"But what could ever happen to allow Gable to discover?" Richard asked.

Even without facing him, she was aware of his commanding presence. Her love—long shattered into hatred—was like fragments suspended in the present. She attempted to conquer his power with words about their son: "He reminds me— . . ." she started to say "of you," floundered, almost formed "of Mark"; instead she said: "Why did you bring Paul here? And his sister. They're so wrong among the others. They're— . . ." She couldn't use the word. Pure, she wanted to say; pure like Gable.

"I wanted, finally, to meet them," he told her.

"Do they know about their mother's murder?" Tarah heard herself ask.

"Murder?"

"You know damn well— . . ."

"There was an acquittal, Tarah," he reminded her firmly. Then, as if what he would say was of profound insignificance—so that it was the reverberation of his words, the lingering, insistent echo, that would accost Tarah—he said: "Daniel gave Paul and Valerie to me."

It was moments before she could react. "Gave— . . . You bought— . . . !"

"He needed money."

"And you need lives to feed on!" she said with stunned outrage.

"I wanted to help him, and them."

"You gave him all the drugs he needed, you supported him—and them— . . ." She looked at the man she had married, lived with. A man capable of anything in his— . . . What? The exploration of the human soul, he had once named it wryly. "And now —somehow—you're collecting the monstrous debt."

"I wanted to meet them," he repeated.

"What if Daniel hedges on it?" Tarah hissed at Richard. "What if he comes here to kill you, Richard? He's a violent man, capable of anything." She stopped. Would she be satisfied for someone else to slaughter Richard?

Richard's depthless eyes pulled her to him. "Rest now, Tarah, for tonight's entertainment—a play for our amusement," he said. We won't be bored, I promise. It's about a blind queen, Tarah—and the man—the only man—who can restore her sight: with his body."

Quickly, he kissed her on the shoulder—as if branding her with his mouth.

When he had left (Now he will go to Karen, and then to Joja, she knew), she remained by the window. The shadow outside moved; it seemed about to raise its hand.

A signal for whom? Jeremy wondered seeing it from his room. He retreated from the window.

Why was I invited here?

It had been a night like this, so still and ominous. A night which had exploded into a night of howling and death. Death had been a shrieking presence between him and the figure whose paleness was suddenly violated by blood. *The pale, dying hand!* You ran away from the mortally wounded, he thought, but they pursue you in accusation.

Accusation.

Impulsively he returned to the window. The shadow waited. A knock on the door. Even though he saw the shadow outside, he thought: It's him!

It was Tarah.

"I need your help," she said quickly, as if belatedly choosing sides in the earlier game downstairs. Instantly she was caught in the sensuality emanating from the young priest. "You've seen the youngman— . . ." she went on hurriedly.

Blue.

". . . —and his sister," Tarah finished. "They're in danger!"

I gave her the branch of wild rose, the priest thought illogically.

"Why are they in danger?" he asked.

"I don't know," Tarah said in abrupt bewilderment. "This island—it always disorients one; it's difficult to separate the real from the imagined." Then her eyes were on him, boldly; drawn powerfully to the hair over his white collar. So dark. So thick. At his groin it would— . . . She lifted her hand, held his, and brought it to her breast.

He allowed it to remain on the bare, beautiful flesh. He felt aroused. Suddenly he withdrew his hand, looking outside toward the waiting shadow.

Tarah left quickly.

In the hall she saw Malissa talking hurriedly to Richard. Tarah moved away from them.

"That creature—Bravo—she wants Karen," Malissa told Richard. "Show her, Richard!"

"Will that be enough for whatever you want to pay her for?"

"No," said the woman. "That's only a part of it."

Their eyes released each other. Wordlessly, the man and the woman parted.

Karen faced Bravo.

Bravo's whip flailed at her side like the tail of an impatient cat on the edge of anger. "You wanted to see the son of a bitch again, and you have!" There was a stark transformation in Karen, as if she had received a powerful transfusion. "Is it over, then?" Bravo barked.

"Of course," Karen said softly.

"Would you leave now?" But before Karen could answer, Bravo said: "No! Now I have to confront the bastard." She felt an almost delicious wrath toward Richard. With the butt of her whip, she erased from the table the petals from the delicate white flowers which had disintegrated earlier. Before she could have Karen, she must destroy whatever existed between her and Richard, every vestige.

A knock. "It's Richard, I know!" Karen said eagerly.

Bravo faced Richard at the door. "I was just leaving," she said. She would not confront him yet.

Richard's eyes were on her until the door closed.

"Do you like her?" Karen asked.

"She's beautiful," Richard said. "I like beauty. And she's one of us."

"Am I?" she asked.

He did not answer. He kissed her shoulder, a kiss so light it could have been the brushing of a moth's wings. She arched her neck. His lips moved along it. She felt a burning which eased into a feeling of remembered pleasure and longing.

Then he broke the contact, as if he had asserted all

he needed for now. Instantly Karen's body became cold. She looked at him in bewilderment.

"I think your companion is waiting outside," he said.

He opened the door, and Bravo still stood there.

He walked past her. She entered Karen's room. Now Richard paused outside of Joja's door.

Inside: Flowers. Flowers streaked vermilion. Like blood. They were shaped like mouths about to close. Joja looked away from the hungry plant: Richard was in the room.

"You haven't changed . . . in so many years," she told him. Yet she had wanted to hurl accusations at him: Why didn't you meet me last night at the airport? Why did you allow the blond youngman to sleep with me? Why did you send for me? Why did you wait so many years? But all the recriminations melted at the reality of his powerful presence.

"And you're more beautiful," he told her. He kissed her on the forehead, a kiss like dust. "Your play closed?" he asked.

"Yes."

"I know all about it, Joja."

"I had to kill her!" she said.

"Have you been with Mark?" He was touching her neck sensually.

She frowned at the question. "I . . . spoke to him," she said. Her body was warm only where his hand touched her shoulder.

He kissed her on the scar he had made years ago. A kiss like ashes.

Slowly, in order not to break the contact, Joja moved back on the bed. She drew the flimsy dress from her shoulders. Her exposed breasts strained, full. His body pressed over her; she felt his hard, powerful muscles.

"I . . . need . . . you . . . Richard," she recognized her own voice. She yearned to be penetrated by him into her soul.

Suddenly she was aware—though reality rejected it—that in the slash of light which cut the semidarkness of the room from the hall, Mark stood in silhouette.

Then Richard was gone. Only Mark remained looking down at Joja's body, as if it had been prepared for or surrendered to him by his father.

Valerie looked into her palm. She held the rose, crushed, that the priest had given her. The island was grotesque to her suddenly, despite its beauty; like the setting for a terrifying nightmare, in which figures will twist and knot.

This room, suffused in strange blue evening light: In it, the woman who stood suddenly before her—there had been a knock, and her voice had summoned her in—was like an apparition. But she recognized her quickly: Tarah.

"Leave now!" Tarah blurted her warning. "Take your brother with you!" If the girl asked why, what would she answer? Because you're the same age as Gable? Because of the games? The play! Tell her about their mother? About Daniel and Richard? Sexual roulette!

"Paul says we can't do that to Richard." Valerie accepted the woman's warning easily.

"Do what to Richard!" Tarah laughed bitterly. "No one does anything to Richard! No, not yet."

"Will *you* stay?" the girl asked, as if for proof of imminent danger.

"I have to," Tarah said. Through the window she saw:

The lone figure outside within the night's enclosing

blackness, a blackness which transformed the trees into sinister invaders.

A night almost palpable. Shadows hovered about the island like low dark clouds.

Blue stared up at the priest's window.

Jeremy looked down.

Blue: He raised his hand just slightly.

He could have been about to touch his face.

The priest: He disappeared from the window.

Blue: He walked into the blue mist. The path was cool under his bare feet. As if all that had been required to release them was motion, memories swooped on him with the fury of vultures: A house bathed in gray mist, Cam, Mr Stuart, the Blue Woman, the kneeling disciples. He remembered how slowly blood comes at first —reluctantly—so that it seems that placing a hand on the wound will block its flow. Then it gushes. (*Through the fingers: Perspiration stinging his eyes, the bloody hand raised to wipe it: his face a gory mask reflected in the crystal vase on a table. The candle waned. . . . "Susej! Prince Susej!" . . . "You're not hard!" . . . Blood.*)

He shook his head, to withstand the raid of memories. His life was suddenly a pantomime of pursuing shadows. He felt isolated: With all his secrets.

Again within the same statue-guarded grotto formed by hovering vines, Blue waited for Jeremy. Then he saw the shadow like a dark ghost advancing toward him. He stood up. He smiled almost shyly at the priest.

In the filtered, hidden amber lights turned on within the grotto, the cold eyeless statues, warmed, seemed alive; listening attentively.

Blue reached for Jeremy's hand—as if to bring it again to his mouth. But halfway up, the motion stopped. For moments there was no movement. Now slowly the priest's fingers tightened about Blue's hand, which abandoned its grip, the two hands changing roles: Now the priest's hand held the other's, raising it slowly. Whatever the contact would have been, the priest released the other's hand suddenly.

Blue smiled, as if in the unfinished gesture he had extracted a silent promise.

11

Joja had a vision of how she must appear to Mark: her face clouded with rage, eyes like knives. An objectless anger which anticipated its reason: anticipated, because Mark smiled down at her, the incredible smile which was the stamp of Richard's. Joja acknowledged: She desired him as intensely as she desired Richard: As if by possessing the son she would possess the father.

Leaning over her, Mark placed one hand on each of her bare shoulders. She shuddered with sudden warmth, although his hands were cold, although she felt herself veering toward a dark whirling pool. His bare chest touched hers, the vague smile lingered on his face: Joja was swallowed by a wave of yearning: Still, there was the warning of blackness at the other side of desire. She felt his strong commanding thighs against her; and then: the growing desire between his legs—straining against his trunks—already as powerful as his father's. And she felt renewed miraculously: Suddenly she was the child and Mark the initiator! In the mirror overhead, she saw her hands encircle his body.

And then he kissed her on the lips.

The insane wail of a woman rent the house as if sundered from her soul.

Mark stood up immediately. He listened raptly. His face was demonic and beautiful. Then he said quickly to Joja: "Later—we've just been rehearsing for my father's play."

Joja saw his shadow at the open door. Again she was being left empty. A recurrent rehearsal. A rehearsal for what? Richard! Her mind a clash of memories, she reached frantically for the pillow on the bed, hugging it furiously: the new rejection flinging her against another memory of fear: "I had to kill you," she whispered uncontrollably, as if the pillow were both child and the instrument of its murder, "or you would have killed me."

Mark did not hear her. He stood in the hall, the door closed behind him. He waited for the scream to recur, to identify it unequivocally. His face glowed with anticipation.

Recurring, the wail hurled Savannah into a quagmire of memories. (*A man's face! Hatred! Blood! A voice: "Cut it!"*)

"Pure!" she said aloud in her mirrored room. She embraced the word. Purity was an object with dimensions. It was shaped like a hard diamond: clear, unrelenting. Purity—not innocence. Innocence was blind to the world and therefore vulnerable to assault, whereas purity saw it all yet remained unblemished—a radiant part of the horror.

"Pure!" she repeated to her mirrored image.

"Why have you been following me?" Jeremy whispered the words, as if the statues might convey them to hidden ears. Indeed, the statues seemed to listen intently. The night pulled stark green shadows from the grotto.

"*You* followed me." The smile on his lips belonging to another time, Blue looked into his hand.

To remind him that moments earlier their hands had touched? Or to search the outline of the inverted star? "You've been standing outside my window, you wanted me to follow," Jeremy said.

"And you did, man." Blue looked up suddenly. The smile fled.

Jeremy walked back to the house. Its dome blazed above the darkness, lit by the brilliant myriad lights inside.

Before the house, he looked up quickly into the window where earlier the painted face behind the black veil had stared down at him. Yes, it was there again. Looking at him?

La Duquesa moved away from the window, from the spectacle of dark night and shadows. She faced Malissa sitting on the tall chair like an empress.

Tonight, Malissa was thinking. Yes, this would be the fateful—fatal?—season. The confrontation between her and Richard! She felt surrounded by power.

At that moment Tor opened the door of a closet. Arranged in a row on a shelf, an array of masks leered at him. Lifeless faces from some past masquerade. He frowned. (*Eyes on his naked oiled body. Eyes. Other oiled bodies. Eyes. Hoarse commanding voices: "Fuck her!" "Suck him!" "Fuck him!" "Hit her!" And then: His fists! And: Eyes!*)

Topaze sat cross-legged on the floor beside Malissa, the plumed hat on his lap. He was in love with the plush life she made possible. Although he did not believe Albert's mad hints of what became of them, the midget did know that the entourage changed seasonally. And so he was determined to align himself so inextricably with Malissa that he would become permanent. Like Albert. Albert? No! Malissa loathed the pudgy man. Yet there was something which bound the two. What was it? Topaze wished he knew; it would arm him with power. Impulsively, he placed his small head on Malissa's lap, expecting to be stroked like a child.

Malissa recoiled with a gasp. *"Don't ever touch me!"* she shouted.

Panic gripped Topaze.

Rev smiled triumphantly.

The unwelcome contact released a dam of fury in Malissa: a dam which shifted automatically to drown Albert. She stood, rubies screaming. "Albert!" she shouted. "You will wear a dress tonight!" It was a sudden substitute punishment for something evoked.

La Duquesa winced as if a dart had been flung at her. (She saw: *A face: a pale, thin face, sandy hair. Freddy!* She hadn't thought of him in— . . . She heard the echo of a harsh voice: *"Freddy, come here!"*)

Albert stood erect.

"This dress I'm wearing, it was one of the Duke's favorites," la Duquesa said hastily—she indicated the elegant long-sleeved black dress—to shift the vicious attention from Albert, again. "When he was murdered, I had it dyed black. To match my heart."

"Did he give you money?" Rev eyed the mourning queen.

"Everything I wanted," she answered the strange question proudly. "Other women would have squandered fortunes to have him for a single night."

"Albert! Didn't you hear Miss Malissa say you would wear a dress tonight? Answer!" Topaze attempted to make up for his huge blunder. He searched Malissa's face urgently, to see whether he had been forgiven.

"I don't want to wear a dress." Albert tried to make his voice firm.

"The Duke despised cruelty!" la Duquesa's voice choked. (*"Freddy, Freddy—look! Is this what you want?"*)

"Why not go all the way, Albert?" Malissa's fingers dug into the air, as if she were preparing his grave.

"Because I'm not a woman!" Albert found the vestige of lurking courage. "Because, Malissa, if you hadn't— . . ."

Her hands defied him to continue.

Suddenly, again, there was the wail which had earlier gathered all sounds within the waiting mansion: It lunged into the shocked silence it produced; then it drowned in emptiness.

Before dying like a muted siren, it almost shattered the intense blue mood within which Valerie felt caught. Tarah was gone.

Leave. Escape. Valerie's mind crystallized the mesmerizing words. Leave. Escape. Escape. She felt disoriented, as if she had fallen beneath the surface of a blue mirror. Escape. She made the barest motion to rise from her bed. But she felt a heaviness, as if the intense blueness had a physical weight. She closed her eyes. Escape. A strong perfume permeated the room. The odor of lush flowers. She swam on the surface of sleep, rocked by blue waves against a restless shore. Escape. The rush of waves carried the word away, erasing it like a mark on sand. Then again: Escape.

It was then that she saw the figure, an outline cut into the icy blue light.

"Paul," she said.

"Yes, Valerie?"

"We have to leave this island," she said. Her voice seemed to come without her opening her lips.

"Why?"

"It's—..."

"Daniel might be here."

She felt the pressure of his body on the bed. Again she tried to shed the heaviness in order to say that she felt they were becoming objects like the black props on the stage downstairs—that *this* was Richard's play.

She saw her brother's eyes very close to her face; she heard his voice, which was foreign, like another's voice: "Why are you still clinging to that crushed rose?"

She opened her hand, releasing the petals. "Have you talked to Richard . . . alone?" She wasn't certain she had asked the question until she heard his words in ambiguous answer:

"He's an extraordinary man, Valerie."

Tossing in the blue currents of the room, Valerie was aware that her brother was leaning over her. Yes, and his mouth opened—she saw his teeth. He's going to kiss me, to reassure me, like always, even when we were children, she thought. She closed her eyes, shutting out the blue mist. She felt the touch of his lips on the side of her face; they moved down to her neck, so lightly that she was not sure of the contact until it had been severed. It had been like the wings of a frantic butterfly.

Suddenly Paul was gone. Only the strange blueness remained like a presence.

Had she fallen asleep? How long had Paul been gone? There was a definite lapse of time—the room was darker now: The sky was a black mirror. Her body ached as if she had been in a struggle. No, it wasn't her body which ached. It was—...

Suddenly she grasped at her neck, her fingernails

tearing at the flesh to rip away the place which burned there with a steady cold ferocity.

Karen's cool exterior contradicted an inner bewilderment. And so Richard had led her to the point of resurrection—the fleeting contact earlier, that is how she thought of it—only to leave her in a state of suspension. Or had the contact been a promise made? A further test— . . . Tests within which Richard sought —. . . What!

Bravo studied her. First there had been that surge of life at Richard's presence; now a draining. . . . He would be a formidable opponent, Bravo acknowledged. He and Malissa. "What is between Richard and Malissa?" she asked Karen.

"A strange, close friendship," Karen said. "For as long as I can remember. She comes here every season, with a new entourage of youngmen—and Albert."

"Like two challengers, she and Richard," Bravo said. And this thought formed: Pit one against the other and then move in! Her whip seemed ready to thrash.

"Bravo," Karen said suddenly, "let's leave!" She knew: I would have given myself to him again. I can still Escape! she thought.

"No," Bravo said firmly. "Not yet. We'll stay and play his goddamn games. Before the night is over, you'll hate him as much as I do. I promise." Then she was swept by the foreign tenderness toward this woman, a new experience in her savage life.

The wail again. It penetrated the island which now seemed to await it. A long insane wail which broke into racked sobbing.

This time it pulled the others from their rooms. There was the sound of opening doors, of motion, of rushing into the corridors. Tarah, Rev, Karen, Tor, Joja, Albert, la Duquesa—they faced each other along the intersecting halls like live representations of the golden panels. They moved downstairs, no longer so much in search of the origin of the hideous scream as much as if they were being called together by it.

Malissa—Topaze beside her—and Bravo, the two women waited until the others had descended the stairs into the great domed hall. Alone within the golden corridor, the two acknowledged a deadly—close—hostility: sealed by the glaring mirrors.

The wail recurred. Now it shattered the blue mood within Valerie's room. She shed the heaviness quickly, and she stood up.

Fire!

She had the sudden impression of flames lapping furiously about her! A consuming roar! But she did not see flames, and the room was silent.

She ran into the empty hallway. The mirrors clutched at her image, thrusting it violently back into the panels of shadowy figures. She ran faster along the corridor. The sensation of fire increased—although the house was intact.

"Fire!" she screamed. Her voice shattered like glass as she rushed downstairs. *"Fire!"*

Suddenly she stood under the glass dome. Strange faces surrounded her. As powerfully as she had sensed fire earlier, she had the impression of blood on the staring faces!

Their lips were dripping with blood!

"Valerie, Valerie!"

The sensation of fire, the impression of blood—both withdrew at the sound of her brother's voice.

"Valerie, did you have a nightmare?" Paul was asking her.

Suddenly her brother's words freed her from the hideous hallucination of fire and blood. "Yes," she said, looking at Richard's guests. "Yes, I must have been dreaming awake."

And they were all here now: as if finally released from their isolation: Karen, Joja, Tarah—yet Tarah stood apart: Her own planned assault on Richard must be an individual act, merely supported by the others. Tor searched the room, as if for something lost. In a transparent livid-blue dress, Savannah seemed encased in fragile crystal. Saved by the commanding scream from Malissa's insistence that he wear a dress, Albert still hovered near la Duquesa. Rev glanced periodically at Malissa for a signal. Like passive duelists, the priest and Blue faced each other across the great hall. Valerie's eyes on her brother were like embers reflecting the memory of the fire that had scorched her consciousness.

The mamaloi and the papaloi stood like guards flanking the landing of the sweeping stairs. They held wooden rattles: brilliant stones embedded within them like demented eyes.

Richard descended the steps. Mark followed. Now the boy wore black pants, a red open shirt.

Immediately, "The games, Richard!" came Malissa's imperious voice. "If we don't start quickly, we'll become bored!" she warned obsessively. Her hands attempted to enclose all the others in a circle.

"Yes, let's play your games, Richard!" Tarah confronted him. "But there may be surprises this season. Tell us: What tests have you devised?"

"I don't test people, you know that, Tarah," Richard said softly. "They test themselves. No one is here who didn't want to come, no invitation was rejected."

"The two men—you forced— . . ." Tarah accused.

"Perhaps tonight we can face that," he said.

"The game, Richard! What will it be?" came Malissa's impatient words.

"Confessions," Richard announced.

Part III

12

A sudden wind swept through the open windows of the house as if unleashed by an abrupt command. Drapes swirled like lost souls caught in the punishment of judgment. Through the glass dome—as the guests shifted in the sudden wind, their clothes whorls of colors, lights melting like painted honey on the walls—from that height and through the dome that gazed down blackly at them like the eye of heaven, they appeared like frantic dancers performing on a marble grave, the black and white gleaming floor. The thrashing wind withdrew as quickly as it had attacked the great house.

"Confessions!" Malissa accepted. "Oh, superb!" In the changing light, the blue-smoked glasses were purple.

They aren't serious, the priest told himself quickly. Merely jaded, bored people playing jaded, bored games.

Tarah's look shattered on Richard. "Yes!—we'll confess the greatest evil performed on us— . . ."

"Or the greatest evil we've performed," said Blue.

"It may be the same," Richard said slowly.

"And then judge it," Tarah attempted to turn the proposed game quickly to an advantage.

"No judgment— . . ." Richard began.

Mark frowned.

". . . —except our own," Richard finished.

"We should let that occur as it may," Malissa insisted.

Mark nodded.

Richard's silence deferred.

"If not judge it, then avenge it!" Tarah's words fell.

"How the hell do you propose making us play your weird game, man?" Bravo demanded.

Malissa's smile on Richard ricocheted as a stare of hatred at Bravo.

"We may play willingly, Bravo," Karen said, "in order finally to understand— . . ." (*The light! Her hands on the woman's throat.*)

Jeremy looked at Richard standing on the stairs with his son, surveying his guests. So certain that they would all play in his orgy of confessions. "How can you force anyone to confess?" the priest echoed Bravo.

"*La malaspina,*" Tarah warned wryly. "The leaf which produces a sweet narcotic, the blacks say it releases inhibitions, induces confessions."

Did she really believe that? Or was she merely attempting to strengthen their resistance, and therefore hers, against Richard?—their defiance? "Superstitions," the priest rejected.

"No one will be forced," Richard said firmly.

"No?" Tarah questioned. Then to the others: "And there are the drugs always available at Richard's games," she said bitterly. "Just ask the servants for whatever you want."

Servants passing soundlessly among the guests wandered about the great-domed hall like souls in limbo.

"And even if you don't ask— . . . The food, the drinks— . . ." Tarah chose deliberately not to define her warning. Paul's reaction, she grabbed for it. If she could force him to leave with his sister! "But sometimes Richard doesn't need anything like that," she acknowledged. "Sometimes he merely challenges." She said swiftly: "All he had to tell me was that in a room upstairs, in this house, two men waited to tear me sexually apart— . . ." She shot her words directly at Paul: an overt warning of outrage.

"You went," Richard said.

The priest glanced at Mark, apprehensive of the boy's reaction to the woman's words. But the boy's face was impassive, as if he had heard nothing to startle him.

"Confessions!" said Malissa. "We've begun the game!" She propelled it: "And within the confessions we'll find— . . ." Deliberately she did not finish.

"The victimizer in our lives," Tarah asserted. "And the roles may change suddenly," she threatened.

"Indeed, indeed! Excellent!" Malissa approved the shaping game.

"The symbolic blood spilled— . . ." Karen said slowly.

Blue said: "Maybe we'll find the shape of— . . . Uh—whatever—man, you know. Like what we're into— . . . What's going to happen, from what already happened— . . ."

"The victim or the victimizer in our lives," Joja offered.

"Confess?" la Duquesa questioned. "To ecstasy and love? A perfect union? Confess love?" (*"Freddy! Come here, Freddy!" And the narrowing circle of legs. . . . "I'll always love you, just you." And: Shots!*)

"And if there's nothing to confess?" Valerie stood before Richard.

Mark anticipated his father's answer.

Richard waited. His look was gentle on Valerie. "Then we'll confess to purity," he said finally.

Savannah laughed loudly. "Confess purity! What the hell do you mean? Innocence—yes; maybe that has much to confess. But purity— . . . Purity carries its own immunity."

"Your virginity," Bravo spat, "is bought by the highest bidder, like the expensive cunt of a whore! You call *that* purity?"

"Yes!" Savannah did not even wince. "Nobody's had me, Bravo!" She stood before the woman dressed in striped pants and black blouse. "Your tongue's like your whip, Bravo, lashing indiscriminately."

"And always on target!" Bravo reminded her.

Out of a private revery induced by the spectacle of erupting hatred—the memory of a white dying hand jolting the words from him—Jeremy whispered aloud: "To forgive is the greatest . . . accomplishment." He had been about to say "love."

"To forgive God?" Malissa spat. "We'll redefine sin, then!"

"There's no substitute for salvation," the priest said firmly.

"Perhaps there is," said Richard. "To go to the limit of human experience—an affirmation of life."

Tarah's laughter crashed. "You son of a bitch, you can even justify your evil that way."

Suddenly Richard advanced toward his first wife. She waited defiantly for him. His strong arms embraced her.

Joja saw: Mark's lips opened.

Richard's mouth crushed Tarah's lips. Then her body flung itself against his—her hands—fists—encircled his shoulders: The closeness of a lover, the closeness of an intimate executioner—which had it been? As if they had moved too quickly into what hinted of a penultimate climax, Richard withdrew. Tarah dropped her hands to her side.

Escape from Richard! From his son! But the next moment Joja's mind screamed: Make me alive again! And she was not certain whether the exhortation had been directed at Richard or at Mark.

"This whole day—this proposed game of confessions —as you call it," said the priest, "it's a deliberate affront to God."

"Have you found Him clearly enough to know?" Mark's head was tilted in the clear, quizzical expression of a child.

"*Which God?*" Malissa had demanded simultaneously.

"I won't be part of your games!" the priest said. He addressed the words to Malissa, but he faced Blue's fathomless, darkening eyes.

"Because the weight of confessions is too heavy?" Richard asked him.

"And they might topple the Tower," Malissa reminded them of the Tarot card Mark had suggested earlier for the priest.

(*A night. A knock. "Urgent!" The car ripping the veil of rain. "We need you!" An infant dressed in gaudy yellow, pink, blue— . . .*) Without realizing it until the stark-white fingers of la Duquesa rose to touch the mourning veil, the priest faced the queen. "No," he answered Richard; insisting aloud: "Only because this is a mockery."

"Is anything in life a mockery, Mark?" Richard addressed his son rapidly—as if, thought Jeremy, through swift movement he would trap them within the momentum of the game.

Mark shook his head: No. He asked the priest, "Will you flee, then, Father?"

"We'll leave with him!" Valerie said to her brother.

Richard's eyes studied her carefully.

"No, Valerie," Paul said.

Richard turned away.

The priest looked at Mark. Flee. ("*Let me go!*" And: *Fleeing!* And: *A corridor. Thighs hugged by black leather. Breasts leering like eyes. Laughter! . . . Fleeing!*)

"Isn't that your role, Father?" Malissa asked frostily. "To hear the worst?"

"Isn't it?" Blue said.

A feeling of revulsion. Then again Jeremy remembered: The tarantulas floating in a black cloud across the desert highway. The hideous creatures so isolated in their dark evil. Facing Blue now as automatically as he had faced la Duquesa—and Blue was looking deeply into his own hand: a reminder of the still, amber moments in the grotto when their hands had shifted roles? —the priest knew that he would stay. Unequivocally now. To protest the outrages, yes—and to find, finally— to try to find—the shape of his world: accepting, on this island, an important challenge.

"The game is confessions! We'll become bored unless we play quickly!" Malissa reminded.

"Who will begin?" Richard asked.

Valerie breathed deeply: A strong, sweet scent had seized the house, like incense, as if exhaled by the walls themselves. Merely the island's lush, flowered evening odors, commingling, stirred earlier by the invading wind. . . .

Richard moved toward Karen. Bravo blocked his path, the whip before her, booted feet braced. "If you touch her, I'll kill you," she threatened him.

Richard passed her, ignoring the threat.

Now he approached Paul. Valerie moved closer to her brother, to protect or be protected. Richard passed Blue; he seemed trapped in a crystal world. Savannah, in hers. The priest—like a general ready to plunge into battle after painful indecision. Tor, a statue waiting for life. Rev, an executioner seeking the executed. Careful not to brush against her, Topaze moved quickly toward Malissa. La Duquesa touched her veil as if for protection.

Abruptly Richard addressed Malissa: "Perhaps you'd

like to start, Malissa. What would you confess?"

The moment was wrong. And Richard must know it: This was, then, merely another reminder of the confrontation between them: It *would* be this season, she knew with excitement. But the first phases of the game, they would play those together, like other times: allies—until the perfect moment. Malissa raised the hand with the black ring, just raised it: Yes, Richard, you and I will play too. But not yet.

Bravo laughed a raw, derisive roar: "Confess what turned you into a bitch, Malissa! A sexless bitch! A sexless bitch in heat!"

Albert's mouth opened automatically. Bravo saved the reaction.

"*You* begin, Bravo!" Malissa chose her words like weapons in a duel to be fought later. "Tell us what it feels like to be so inadequate that you had a man prepare— . . ."

(*The whip a noose about two necks!*) Bravo cut the rest of Malissa's sentence with a thrash of her whip.

"What could you find out about me in your game?" Savannah offered herself. Suddenly she felt inviolable. She would face them, willingly, in this test, a test she must pass, finally, for the total vindication of her life.

"Scrutiny might sully your precious purity," tossed Bravo.

"Nothing sullies purity," Savannah insisted. "It exists or it doesn't—that's all."

"Important only to you," sneered Bravo.

"No," Richard contradicted. "Without it her beauty would be like all other beauty: and therefore nothing."

Rev raped Savannah in his mind. The magnificent virgin slaughtered publicly. His body, hers. The violation of her purity would arm him with power.

"Purity. Inviolable by its very definition," Richard

said, as if presenting the premise for evidence to be weighed. "It exists or it doesn't—is that what you said, Savannah?"

The others looked at the woman of the legendary beauty.

Savannah nodded. "Yes!"

"It's too soon for Savannah," Malissa whispered hurriedly to Richard. "We should save her for later." Richard's silence indicated agreement. "Tor!" Malissa offered the bodybuilder instead.

Muscles like carved ice, the muscleman flexed at Malissa's bark, the only clear response he was capable of.

And Savannah knew: The attention would return to her—the examination was essential, to her, to them. But her challenge—her blunt assertion—had been formidable: She had armed herself with announced confidence, and that had been her intention: a thrust made in order to gain strategic strength, to achieve a favorable position, before the inevitable attack.

Tor. Obviously chosen as a mere exercise; a preparatory ceremony would ensue, Tarah evaluated the strategy of the shaping game. Certainly the enormous muscleman meant nothing to them. Presenting no challenge, he would provide them with a maneuver which would speak to the others by implication: a hint of their power, paving the way for other confessions.

"What can you confess?" Richard asked Tor. There was an ambiguous note in his voice. Something tinged with— ...

Certainly not pity, Tarah rejected; he was incapable of that. It was amusement, she told herself; disguised, cruel amusement. And so he and Malissa were proceeding.

"Confess, Tor!" Malissa commanded in mock seriousness. But she spread her rubied hands like rigid stars before him. When they had captured his eyes, she closed them quickly, as if to clutch him within her fists. Only the forefinger choked by the black-pearled snake remained extended like a threat.

"Certainly there's something never spoken, to be spoken now," came Richard's soft voice. "A weight to be removed, finally," it seemed to offer compensation.

The cruel imitation of compassion to coax others to his will, Karen thought: the expert erection of an arena within which to attack.

Now Malissa's hands flashed open again.

In Tor's mind, her rings became: *Eyes!*

Malissa made a swift sign before him—it could have been a parody of the sign of the cross, inverted. "Speak!" she commanded, and this time there was no mockery in her voice, only an unequivocal demand.

Straining flesh, Tor's muscles seemed about to explode.

At Richard's glance, which merely glided, the mamaloi and the papaloi sprang to sudden life. Instantly they flanked Tor. Then they shook the beaded rattles before him. A sweet scent stirred.

"Tor . . . Tor . . . Tor . . . Tor . . ." Malissa's pronouncement of the name was rhythmic, like the evening ocean's advancing tide. Her fingers flashed open, closed, open.

Tor's face struggled for an expression. His muscles expanded, attempting to release emotions crushed within the overly developed, massive body. "Once— . . ." he said.

Yes, so quickly he was in their control, la Duquesa knew. But why? Did they indeed have black powers?

"Once," Malissa echoed Tor. The word purled, like

reverberating circles of water moving outward, fading, embracing their own ghosts. "Once— . . ."

Marginal players now, the others watched: A sacrificial confessor had been chosen. For now it was not them.

"Our bodies were painted gold!" Tor shouted suddenly, in abrupt wonderment at the recollection.

"You performed in an exhibition," Malissa knew.

"A sex exhibition. Naked!" said Albert excitedly. He stood before the muscleman, like a comical ringmaster before a mighty lion.

Malissa allowed the pudgy man to advance: As long as it served her purpose, she would permit Albert this; and she would not herself have to draw out from Tor details which would disgust her: Though she loathed sex—as if it were a stalked enemy—she accepted its use as an instrument for the acquisition of control.

"Yeah, naked—painted gold," Tor's mesmerized voice said. "A guy hired us off the beach."

"Many of you—all with beautiful bodies," Albert offered.

"Four studs, three chicks," said Tor. "There was an audience."

"Hundreds!" said Albert.

"About twenty," said Tor. "Men, women—they just sat and watched."

Richard retreated from the immediate arena. He watched the others from a distance, occasionally glancing at Mark.

As if instructing him, the thought occurred to Tarah. . . And: Yes, clearly, Tor was no challenge; only a part of the spell to be woven like an iron web about the others. Richard and Malissa. They had merely set the confession into motion. Now it spun kinetically—and Albert was their unwitting surrogate interrogator.

"You were on a stage?" came Albert's exacerbated voice.

"Yeah," Tor said. "On a stage—the seven of us naked, our bodies painted gold: like we were . . . moving statues. The people sitting before us called requests."

"And they resembled undertakers," la Duquesa said abruptly from her own resounding memories.

"Like at a mass funeral," Blue said from his.

"Yeah, like that," Tor said.

"But then I met the Duke— . . ." la Duquesa's voice broke.

"The requests, Tor!" Albert pled. Afraid Malissa would break that much of proximity, he dare not move closer. But the bodybuilder's perspiring body enflamed him.

And Tor's body expanded, as if words, thoughts, must rebel against resisting muscles in order to form. He blurted: "The people in the audience, they'd yell: 'You, the blond one, fuck the dark-haired woman!' 'Fuck her, fuck him, suck him, hit her!' Like we were gold puppets! Large, gold toy bodies!" (*Eyes, eyes, eyes, eyes, eyes, eyes, eyes eyes eyes eyes eyes eyeseyeseyeseyeseyes. . . . Fists! Screams!*)

Expertly, Malissa filtered the sound of Tor's words— extracting the sound of anguish—from their sexual meanings. The preliminary entertainment was better than she had anticipated.

"The man who hired us—he squatted very close, watching," Tor said.

"He had eyes like pits," Blue said.

"A creep, a weirdo," Tor said.

"The Duke despised those words," la Duquesa protested. "He said nothing in life is weird—except cruelty: and the horror of unfulfilled love— . . ."

"And a man was taking movies," Tor went on in a

daze. "Like to pull our bodies into a tiny, black trap."

Savannah saw: *The flash of light, flooding, steady, hot —like white lights over an operating table which may soon stare at a bloody corpse.* She knew: Her own interrogation must come swiftly, the test passed conclusively.

Valerie was not listening to the brutal recitation of words. But she saw their reflections in a vicissitude of expressions on Paul's face. . . . The moments in the blue haze of her room earlier, they seemed covered over by fragile glass now; splinters of remembrance—at moments tinged with fear—progressively more tenuous, like a fading dream.

"And then— . . ." Albert coaxed Tor feverishly, rushing before Malissa might chop off his words.

"Then— . . . *Then!*" Tor shouted.

The tone of his voice! Malissa knew. The moment! The fatal self-knowledge! Instantly she was standing before Tor.

The rattles hissed a deadly whispered demand.

"And then— . . ." Tor repeated.

"What, damnit!" Bravo joined the interrogators.

"Confess!" Topaze insisted gleefully, flexing his biceps in a parody of Tor.

"Tell them whatever the hell they want to hear so they'll fucking stop picking your head, man!" Blue shouted at the muscleman—but it was as if he were shouting to himself about other interrogators. ("*He told us it was you!*"—words battered his mind.)

"Say it, man!" Rev commanded. He knew: The confession would finish Tor in the entourage, and his own position would be strengthened.

"What, what, what, what!" Malissa pulled at Tor's mind.

Again the rattles hissed their deadly warning: like the fatal spitting of an angered snake.

The sweet scent rushed Valerie. Did it accost Tor too? He seemed to inhale deeply. Did the scent emanate from the shaken rattles? The island's flowers— ...

13

"And then for the first time I saw myself," Tor spoke.

Blue saw: *His own distorted face of long ago, revealed in a leering mirror.*

"Like I jumped out of myself," Tor's words were tortured. "And I saw: Just a body. And eyes staring at it."

Blue remembered: *Twenty-four accusing eyes. His life on exhibit.*

Tor continued dazedly: "I was a painted body performing for blank eyes, and what they were watching was two of us fucking the same chick. I was entering her— ..."

"From the back, the other from the front," Tarah said suddenly. "And the woman howled with something that was neither pain nor pleasure but the surrender that precedes dying, and no one heard."

"She was trying to prove she was still alive," said Joja, understanding.

"But she merely emphasized her long, long death in life," Tarah said.

"You didn't have to go up those stairs," Richard said to his first wife.

"You let me go!" she said.

"You went, Tarah."

Jeremy accosted Richard: "How can you allow these horrors to be spoken before your own son, a child— ...?"

Mark looked at the priest. At that moment, in the youthful face of the boy there was an ancient knowledge.

"Horrors?" Richard questioned the priest. "The capabilities of the body? So limited by its own orifices, the position of its limbs. Horrors? The limited entrances. What is all that? . . . Yet the infinite capabilities of the mind. Its dark caverns— . . ."

"Which you have explored so intimately!" Tarah fired at him.

"Of which I've seen so much," Richard said.

Valerie saw in Paul's eyes a glow like that in Mark's.

And Mark's eyes shone as if at some premature victory. He was saying to the priest: "Is it really *me* you want to protect from these words?"

Jeremy moved back, away from Mark.

"The woman felt rent apart, but not by the physical act," Tarah pulled the attention swiftly from the priest; returning it to Tor—attempting to use his words as a weapon in her shaping war against Richard.

"She felt empty," Joja said angrily. Her eyes sliced at Richard, Mark.

Joja's vacillation. Tarah evaluated the actress as a potential ally. One moment Joja seemed to be outlining her own attack; another, drawn powerfully to Richard, to Mark. . . . She could join either camp.

"And then, Tor?" Albert questioned, but now the exacerbated voice was mildened by a note of pity.

"I saw myself," Tor went on. "Like when suddenly you run into a mirror you didn't know was there. Flesh. Just flesh. . . . Then I jumped off the pile of bodies. I rushed with my fists at the staring eyes. To close them! . . . There were screams. But then— . . . Then I just . . . returned . . . to the pile of gold-painted bodies. . . ."

Albert closed his eyes. Tightly.

The mamaloi and the papaloi shook the rattles ferociously before Tor. Then the hissing beads expired, dead.

"You were a piece of meat, that's all," Malissa hurled triumphantly. "And you finally realized it." There would be no further use for Tor. She turned away in boredom.

Tor wiped his perspiring face. An expression had finally formed on it: an expression of years-long, never-understanding, never-faced torture, till now. For moments that performing statue of himself had been imbued with a terrible vision: the glimpse of his throttled soul: the snuffed spark of identity. Now his body set again rigidly in resignation. Like chilled wax.

The mamaloi and the papaloi retreated as if from a fresh grave.

And Tor flexed.

"This is cruelty!" Jeremy shot at Richard and Malissa. "There are things which shouldn't be examined!"

Richard seized this weapon: "Even in confession?"

"In the quiet of the confessional— . . ." Jeremy said haltingly.

"Life isn't lived in silence, Father!" said Richard. "You can't subdue the shouts of living to the whimpers of dying."

"Confession leaves a vacuum, which can be filled only with absolution." The priest determined that his words would not sound rehearsed. "If confession doesn't lead to communion— . . . What have you offered this youngman?" He pointed to Tor, who stared blankly as if unaware he was being spoken about.

"The revelation of his emptiness!" Malissa spat. "Of his inflated weakness—like his inflated muscles. Only that!"

Tor was through, Topaze knew triumphantly.

"He wasn't aware of it until you ripped him apart!" said Karen.

"Who now?" Malissa again propelled the game.

"The virgin whore," Bravo chose Savannah. "She wants to be questioned."

"The unapproachable Savannah, the unassailable Savannah," Richard gave the signal, "whose beauty is matched by her purity—what could she possibly confess to?"

Savannah eyed them imperturbably. The test! And she would win! Must win! Finally!

The midget stared up at her with a sensual leer.

The mamaloi and the papaloi stood suddenly before Savannah, their rattles ready to hiss before a new, possible victim.

Savannah did not retreat, did not wince, did not lean back. With the command that grew from the knowledge of her superb beauty, and its power, she raised her hand imperiously, freezing the hissing of the vicious rattles.

"Tell us of the inviolability of purity—and the origin of such purity," said Richard.

Purity, thought Tarah. A word he used often. In contempt. As if it affronted him.

(*"There is your purity!"*) Karen glanced quickly away from Savannah: A surrogate part of herself would be attacked.

Richard's relentless pursuit, Joja thought. But of what?

"A purity more expensive than an experienced-whore's cunt," Bravo repeated her assault on Savannah.

Savannah laughed gloriously; her laughter was amber, like champagne. "Your words can't touch me, Bravo," she said. "Not the first time, not this time." She would willingly allow the intense scrutiny. The style of her life, strengthened each day of her existence, inevitably it must be proved: all a rehearsal for now!

"Of course her words can't touch you," Richard said. "Because there's no flaw in Savannah's beauty." He spoke with grave seriousness. "It's that which has made her a legend."

Was Richard, then, an ally? Savannah wondered. Or merely an enemy of Bravo. Did he want her to emerge triumphant? And she would!

"She exists only because there's no flaw to her beauty," Richard went on. "A perfect gem: Find the slightest flaw—and it's destroyed. Totally."

The priest said: "The greatest flaw could be invisible."

Blue stared at the empty tattooed star.

"You mean the soul," Richard said flatly.

"That isn't for discussion at this moment," said Malissa.

"It's the subject of it all," said Richard.

"Find the flaw!" Mark's words were sudden.

(*Black blood!*) Through the sheer pale-blue material which adorned her body, Savannah touched her glorious breasts. Richard understood—yes, he was her ally, she thought.

"Is there a flaw, Savannah?" Richard asked her casually.

"No—because she needs no one!" Joja's husky voice defended. Shifting again—first allied with Richard, then opposing him—she might extract a vicarious victory in Savannah's unswerving stance. "Because she never needed another in order to be complete. *That* is her flawless purity. And she may teach *us* now." Her eyes sought to include Karen, Tarah—but Mark captured her look, holding it firmly on him: on the clear, beautiful, dark-lashed eyes.

"I became the Duke, and he became me," said la Duquesa; "yet we were ourselves."

"How long did you live with him?" Rev asked her lazily.

Avoiding facing him, la Duquesa said: "As long with him as without him: an eternity."

"Where?"

"Wherever he was—that was the universe."

"Confessions!" Malissa exhorted.

"The flaw— . . ." Mark repeated. There was no discernible emotion in his voice.

"A flaw in Savannah would be fatal," Richard said.

"Ask whatever you want!" said Savannah. She would answer all their questions. Years of her life had provided a rehearsal for these moments. Now!

But instead of questioning her, Richard touched a panel of buttons on the wall: smothering the lights in the giant hall. The chandeliers sighed softly into blackness. In the darkness, the dome which had revealed the night's intensity relented, lightened. From its height the guests were anonymous black shadows.

"A mute confession," Richard announced.

Now a white panel intruded on the blackness: a screen; and then a projector slid from the wall, responding to the touch of another button. Quickly there was a shaft of cold-white glaring light, a tunnel through the darkness.

Rubies gleaming like red eyes amid the black gouged eye of the pearl on her forefinger, Malissa thrust her hand insanely into the shaft of light: a giant silhouetted spider on the screen, asserting its power. "What are you going to show us, Richard?"

"A film which captures the origin of purity," came Richard's voice.

No! screamed Savannah's heart. She had rehearsed for

an interrogation which would not come. The question would not be allowed—only its answer. Already she saw, on the screen, the remembered, despised room:

In a mansion. A giant soft red bed like a dyed marshmallow. On either side of the canopied structure: bronze statues of a man, a woman: naked. And the parted red drapes revealed: a girl, shatteringly beautiful, young, in flimsy nightclothes. The body stretched languorously, the lacy material slid off. Embracing the gloriously naked flesh, the leering eye of the camera glided up her thighs, to the light brush of amber hair, delicate like a powderpuff. Then quickly: a closeup of the perfect, stunning face.

"It's Savannah!" said Bravo.

"A mute confession indeed," said Malissa.

Joja felt a sense of vicarious defeat.

Tarah's body was flooded with rage. Yet her eyes stared fascinated at the screen. It was not *her* life recorded.

Flashing into the tunnel of light like a huge firefly, Topaze somersaulted before the screen. Suggestively he thrust his hips in a lewd sexual gyration, and his small hands grasped at the nude image on the screen.

The façade—the carefully erected, sustained mask of years—it remained intact on Savannah's face as she confronted the image on the screen, trapped in silvery hues—the shade of purity, she thought. And her mind opened to the memory of that fatal day: the whirring of the camera, the sound itself capturing her body; the flood of lights drenching the room in icy white, like an operation room. The fatal day. The point from which she had cunningly reconstructed her life. Toward this moment, then?

Her long hair loose, the girl on the screen cupped her breasts softly. Now her hands caressed the tanned flesh: Between her legs, her fingers parted the opening, delicately, as if to expose a precious jewel.

The flickering on the screen was reflected in Paul's eyes: Valerie looked there, to filter reality; but the reflected reality attacked as powerfully.

Now there was a man on the screen. Also naked.

Savannah's face turned quickly away.

On the screen the man's lips were pulling at the girl's nipples. Now his mouth was on her stomach, hungrily.

Bravo hit the back of a chair with the butt of her whip, an ambiguous punctuation mark.

Immediately, Malissa turned from the screen. She knew what the film would reveal now.

The man's tongue brushed the body, which was like light honey. Now his head burrowed into the brush of the girl's pubic hair. The camera angled: The man's tongue dug into the spread lips between her thighs. As if to connect the two orifices, the man kissed her on the mouth. His cock the arrow ready to pierce, his body arched like a bow. Then the hard swollen organ lunged into the girl. Suddenly her body jerked.

Savannah's nails dug into her palms.

The camera shifted quickly to the rough grinding of the man's buttocks—to avoid, but it had caught clearly, the racked reaction of the girl's intense pain: the traumatized horror on her face.

(*"Cut it!"* Savannah heard the hated voice from the past. The whirring of the camera had stopped momentarily, again to avoid capturing the gory slaughter of her body.) Even now, Savannah reacted to the fierce, remembered pain. She stifled a moan—remembering: Her hand blocking the blood flowing from her ripped thighs, her head flailing against the pillow. Layers of pained remembrances had colored the red blood black, black in her mind.

Suddenly Savannah stood up, intercepting the shaft of white light, the outline of her body flung onto the steely screen, the flickering of the sexual movie projected on her own body now as if to claim it from the past. "I bled!" she shouted. Two other silhouettes joined her stark outline against the screen: the black man and the black woman. Enlarged by the light, their rattles were raised like axes. "He hurt me! He tore me up! I hated all sex!" The rattles hissed.

Mark saw: For one instant Malissa had brought her hand to her face. Then the look that hungered for violence returned.

"The torn hymen of the Tarot!" Malissa gloated savagely.

Bravo's laughter growled: "A botched sex performance for a blue flick!"

Malissa announced triumphantly: "And so the unapproachable Savannah, who wore her 'purity' like a badge— . . . It never existed."

"Pain, not purity—*that* kept you from becoming a common whore," Bravo said vindictively. "But you did anyway—a whore with a unique gimmick!"

The lights came on, the screen rose, the camera disappeared. The chandeliers blazed.

"Savannah confesses before overwhelming evidence! Superb, Richard!" Malissa congratulated.

But Richard's dark face did not register victory.

What the hell more does he want from her? "Are you proud of this!" Tarah stood furiously before him.

"What existed was revealed, that's all."

Tarah was startled: Richard's lips had not moved to form the words. His face was as inscrutable as black ice. Then she realized: It was Mark, not Richard, who had just spoken.

"Is he here?" Savannah yelled.

"Who?" asked Joja. Her breathing came unevenly: Each slaughter bringing her nearer to the decision she herself must make.

"The bastard who tore me apart—so I can kill him!" Savannah shouted into the house.

"How could he be here?" Malissa asked, but with interest, eyeing Richard; remembering the surprises at other seasonal games. "An anonymous man, no doubt; how could he— . . .?"

"There is your purity," Karen sighed, as if to herself, remembering those words, spoken long ago to her.

Like a panther finally approaching a long-stalked prey, Bravo advanced toward Savannah. Now she placed her hands firmly on Savannah's bare shoulders. Then she drew her to her.

Needing suddenly what she had never needed before—to feel protected—Savannah did not draw away.

Roughly, Bravo pushed her back. "I don't want you, you sullied bitch!" she struck.

14

Savannah retreated. She had needed a test of her iron stance: to perfect it. Passed, it would have ultimately choked the brutal scene of painful initiation rendering the imitation purity "real." But she had not prepared for a confrontation with the recorded reality of the slaughter. Now, in sudden recognition, she stared at Tor: They were shells, magnificent, empty bodies.

"You can have her for yourself, pimp!" Bravo turned on Malissa.

"I never wanted her," Malissa said quickly. Now

Savannah would be spoken of as if she had once existed in sharp focus—but no more. "Nor anyone else!"

Bravo's husky voice became a deliberate, mocking simper aimed at Malissa: "Someone to love, Malissa! Why not? It's obvious she needs someone—finally; and you need someone too, Malissa."

"No one," Malissa rejected in a controlled voice. "No one. Ever." The long fingers were like jeweled daggers.

"Everyone needs love," la Duquesa asserted.

Bravo moved in on Malissa. "Everyone *loves* you, Malissa! Nobody hates you!" she roared. "Love, love, love, *love!*" she spewed the repeated word like poison in the woman's ear, to kill.

Malissa pushed the word away. The purple-shaded eyes murdered Bravo.

Now Bravo's voice broke into a roar of contempt. Again to feel out the potential for insurrection, she spun about toward Albert: "Why do you stay with her?"

"Because— . . ." he began with difficulty.

"Because he's a fat little man!" said Topaze peremptorily, stretching his own small body as if his assertive words would enlarge it. "Without Miss Malissa there would be no entourage, and *that's* why he stays!" It was his overt bid for a permanent place in the retinue.

Bravo ignored the midget. "Tell us, Albert! Why?"

"He has nothing to tell," Malissa declared.

"Why don't you want him to speak, Lady Cobra?" Bravo questioned.

"Why don't we hear from *you,* Bravo?" Malissa spat. "Tell us about the man you had prepare your women for you."

"Only at first—and then they wanted only me."

"But there was the exception, wasn't there, Bravo?" Malissa shifted the tide of battle.

Bravo winced, barely but perceptibly.

"A *man,* Bravo!" Malissa used the word "man" as Bravo had used the word "love" against her.

"I coiled my whip about their fucking necks, and I made them kneel before me—the man *and* the bitch," said Bravo. "Okay. That was the one exception. *I've* confessed. Now you tell us, Malissa: Why don't you let Albert speak? Are you afraid he'll tell us what becomes of the people you collect? Is it true, Malissa, that you're hundreds of years old and need regular transfusions of fresh young blood!" Then, aiming indiscriminately, striking in every direction: "Was Albert your lover once? Were you *always* sexless?"

"Speak, Albert," came Mark's voice, unexpectedly.

Malissa's face expressed rage. Her eyes shifted quickly from Mark to Richard, exhorting him to chastise his son.

But Richard said nothing.

Topaze mirrored Malissa's expression of rage.

"Yes, speak, Albert!" la Duquesa proclaimed her own rebellion against Malissa. "If you do, you may be free of her!"

Malissa's purple-glassed eyes swallowed the queen.

"Tell about the pain of the humiliations, the taunts— . . ." the voice behind the black veils exhorted.

"How do you know?" Rev said.

Topaze was nervous, Rev was joining the interrogators, a rival Topaze must destroy.

Behind the dark veils, the voice said: "Because my life with the Duke was so perfect that I ache for those who haven't known love." Tears darkened the veil. "Candles never lit, giving no light."

The unlived life, thought Jeremy.

"Who are you, Albert?" Bravo rode on relentlessly.

"I'm Albert!" he shouted.

"We'll question Rev!" Malissa said, to indicate that she would ignore Bravo.

Rev frowned. "My tattoos!" he blurted, anxious to please Malissa, yet equally anxious to thwart the slaughtering attention. "Each stands for a perfect hustle! Diggit!" He opened the leather vest, exposing the jungle of tattoos. "Now question the midget!" he offered frantically.

"What could he possibly confess?" said la Duquesa. "To confess you have to feel agony, and he has no feelings."

"Why *should* I have feelings?" the midget questioned. "I'm perfectly formed!" He exhibited himself proudly. "And my cock is the largest— . . ."

"*Tell us about Malissa, Albert!*" Bravo would not be thwarted.

Resuscitated, the mamaloi and the papaloi flanked Albert, rattles ready.

The pudgy little man covered his ears to block the hiss.

"Get away from him!" Malissa shouted commandingly at the black man and woman. She glared at Richard for allowing this charade. They must still be allies for the purpose of moving the others into the dark caverns of the game.

But the black man and woman stood steadfast beside Albert when there was no reaction from Richard.

And Rev made his formal bid for power: "You want me to kill them?" he asked Malissa suddenly.

Malissa glanced at Bravo. "Not *them*." She made a motion of slicing—perhaps the inverted sign of the cross.

Understanding—but his eyes questioning Malissa carefully for unequivocal approbation—Rev stood before Bravo. His knife opened before her with a deadly *switch!*

Bravo looked with a slashed smile at the tattooed man.

Malissa sent silent commands. No, she would not allow Rev to use the knife now: It was merely a further maneuver to steer Bravo from Albert—the game required improvised rules—and it was also a statement of warning, of the ultimate thrust against her.

Rev pointed the knife at Bravo's throat.

The priest protested: "I won't allow— . . ."

"Are we playing destiny now?" Mark asked.

So fast it appeared to be one movement, Bravo brought the coiled whip up in both hands, knocking Rev's knife to the floor. Disarmed, Rev cowered before the raised whip. "You petty fucking little coward!" Bravo said.

"Don't— . . ." Rev started.

Malissa did not even glance at Rev, and Topaze sensed a victory for himself.

Bravo's boot pushed the knife away. It slid on the spiraling floor to the tip of Blue's bare feet. It pointed to the tattooed star. With a cry, he kicked it away. Gleaming, the knife glided across the swirls of the floor. Now it pointed at the priest.

"Father Jeremy," came Mark's words quickly, "to whom does a priest confess?"

Live entities within the dead bodies, the blue-crystal eyes of the mamaloi and the papaloi shifted to the priest.

Jeremy picked up the knife.

"Father, let's leave this terrible house!" Valerie's voice broke. Her eyes moved past the archway of this hall into the room where the stage waited. "Something terrible will happen!"

Yes, leave it! Tarah's mind screamed at the girl. But it was Paul her eyes—and Valerie's—implored.

"Will you leave?" Blue asked the priest; there was a mournful tone in his voice, but the lips smiled.

The priest did not answer, but he did not move away.

Valerie backed away slowly from the priest. *Is he one of them?*

The priest dropped the knife.

Rev rushed for the weapon. Armed again, he stood staring about him in search of a victim, any victim another might choose for him.

"Your pose is over, you posturing petty hood." Bravo turned her back on him.

"Put that knife away, you fool!" Malissa lacerated.

Bewildered, Rev obeyed.

"*That* is Rev's confession," Malissa announced contemptuously.

"Now can I have him, Malissa?" Albert whispered.

Hatred draped Malissa's face, like the queen's black veil. Albert retreated meekly, knowing: No, he would have no one as long as Malissa held the awesome power over him.

Not joining Savannah and Tor among the slaughtered, Rev touched the knife now in his pocket, asserting its dormant presence.

Her blazing triumph over Rev had only whetted her desire to confront Malissa: Bravo attacked: "*That's* how much you *love* Albert, Malissa! You'd have someone kill for him!" she taunted.

"Love!" Malissa formed the word with abysmal disgust. And she turned defeat into victory: "Love is as foreign to me as it *was* to you, Bravo, until— . . ." And her eyes, her jeweled fingers named Karen as the subject of the unfinished words. Now the words shaped like bullets: "We'll!—question!—Karen!" She had aimed expertly:

The threatening whip fell lifeless at Bravo's side.

And so she had forced Bravo, finally, to withdraw—for now, Malissa knew. And she knew too: Through Karen, yes—it would be through her that she would pay Bravo back for all this. But it was not yet time for Karen.

Richard nodded: The mamaloi and the papaloi retreated like shadows from Albert.

"How can anyone despise love so much?" the priest said. (*"I love you! Don't let me die— . . . !"*)

"Because to love is to become a victim," Karen answered.

"The perfect love I had with the Duke— . . ." began la Duquesa.

"A dark guy?" asked Rev abruptly.

"Tanned from season to season." La Duquesa drew the veil more securely over her face. "A bronze pearl — . . ."

Joja, Karen—they flowed toward Richard. Like a jury about to pass judgment—or defendants announcing their confessions, their own sentences. Tarah watched, studied.

Richard looked slowly at the three women.

Joja stopped. Her heart screamed: *I need you, Richard!*

"You make love sound terrifying," Valerie seemed to accuse them all. What terrible games are they really playing? she wondered. A trap to catch me and Paul!

"It is," said Tarah. "It's merely a word, misused for 'hate.'"

The mamaloi and the papaloi followed Richard's gaze on Tarah. Their rattles rose.

Defiantly, "I don't need them to elicit my . . . confession!" Tarah said. "I'll shout it only too gladly." She addressed the others: "Listen! When he was through with me, he told me two men waited for me in a room upstairs. A challenge. I knew he'd withdraw. I walked up those lighted stairs, he followed me to the door. Two men, already naked, waited. I entered. Richard didn't relent. The bastard just walked away—entombing the darkness which contained me and the two men."

"You didn't turn back," Richard said.

"What do you want to find, Richard? Finally, what?", Karen asked him.

"I merely opened the door for you, Tarah," Richard said, as if, mysteriously, that were Karen's answer.

Karen saw: *A door opening into another dark room. Legs, flesh— . . . And crushed roses.*

"And turned me into a hunter!" Tarah accused Richard. "I even worked in a whorehouse after that!" she announced to the others. "I didn't need the money, of course not—Richard is most generous with that: I needed the hungry youngmen to fill— . . ."

"The pit," said Joja.

"Is that really your confession, Tarah?" Richard asked almost gently. "Is there nothing about Gable?"

This time the beaded rattles shook before Tarah's face. She saw: Dazzling pinpoints of color. She breathed deeply, deeply. "Gable? My son? We were confessing to the worst in our lives. And I've confessed it: I've confessed *you*, Richard!"

Malissa's smile congratulated her, an unsuspected challenger.

"There are no restrictions," Richard said. "We'll allow each confessor to tell the good in his life."

"Good requires no confession," Jeremy said.

"Things are not always as they seem," said Richard.

"Not here, not in your inverted world," said Tarah. Then swiftly: "You want me to tell about Gable? All right then: He was born into his father's strange world, where love revealed itself as hatred."

"When examined closely," Richard said.

"And so I fled with Gable," Tarah said. The black man and woman faced her like guards. "Yet despite my son's purity, Richard had stirred a hunger in me which is his mark."

"And before me, Tarah?" Richard interrupted her.

She answered automatically: "It had been the same as after." Swiftly she tried to counter herself: "But you gave it pause. . . . And then it was over, and it was the same. But worse," she added quickly, like a witness underscoring her allegiance or hostility at a trial. "Shadows—shadows, that's all they were; bodies which I needed, attempting to satisfy with numbers— . . . But always away from Gable—to protect the only purity that had emerged from the corruption of his father."

"The investigation of Savannah's purity revealed— . . ." Malissa reminded, without finishing.

"Gable's is *real* purity," Tarah said firmly, her eyes on Paul and Valerie. "He didn't suspect where I went—he never does, because the pure conceive only of purity."

Mark listened as if at an important initiation.

"Now I've confessed the worst and the best!" said Tarah.

"But have you?" Richard still challenged.

"Why should we justify our lives to you?" the priest interrupted.

"Only if you feel compelled to," Mark said as if the question had been asked of him.

"What gives you the right to play— . . ." the priest addressed Richard; he paused, he had been about to say "God." He finished: ". . . —to play Satanic inquisitor?" His look included Mark.

"Satanic inquisitor!" Malissa clutched the words in

her eager fingers, destroying the words, re-creating them: "Do you suppose Satan too hears confessions? As selective as God, does he too investigate profoundly to choose those worthy of damnation and hell? Would one, then, confess the evil? Or the *good?*" Her laughter was seized by Topaze's.

"A judgment in hell," Blue spoke aloud.

A perverted "purification" was occurring. Valerie's thoughts were like deep knives. A "purification" for a terrible communion!

"But you, Father Jeremy," Richard said. "What gives *you* the right to— . . . grant absolution for living?"

"For *sin,* not living," the priest corrected. Then: "I was ordained," he said—and stopped. His words instantly boomeranged. He was being baited into reciting his qualifications to play— . . . Richard's deliberate pause had been unequivocal. . . . —to play God.

Richard turned quickly back to Tarah.

Malissa knew: An important one, his investigation of the priest would come in phases throughout the evening.

"Is there nothing else to confess, Tarah?" Richard asked his first wife.

"I hate you, Richard." Swiftly Tarah attempted to block any further interrogation.

15

Now Richard's words cracked with the fury of a snapped whip: "What if I told you that Gable is here, Tarah; that he heard everything?"

"Is my half brother here?" Mark asked eagerly.

Tarah had taken a step toward Richard. She stopped.

There was no way Gable could be here. The words had been calculated to disorient her. She would resist his move. Suddenly she felt very strong. The moment to attack! Enlist Karen and Joja! "What would *you* confess?" she questioned Richard abruptly.

Instantly Mark looked at his father.

"Tell us, Richard: Why did you invade our lives?" Tarah included Joja and Karen—she must count on them. "What did you want to find?" she pursued.

Mark still watched his father.

"Tell us why you prepare people," Tarah flailed. She waited, for a signal from Karen, Joja that they would join the attack. "You make actions inevitable, you choke alternatives," she continued to accuse Richard. Still no reaction of support from either of the women she needed as witnesses. "You leave only one avenue open— . . ."

"And then even that avenue closes," Karen finally joined the assault, an ally Tarah could count on.

Malissa knew: Sudden alliances would be formed tonight, and allies might turn into enemies. "Why, they might be talking about your God," she tossed flippantly at the priest.

"I identify the avenues," Richard said to Tarah, to Karen.

"You use lives for your amusement," Tarah continued, determined to enlist Joja: "Like props on a stage — . . ."

The actress's magnificently sculpted face looked up at Richard—at the beautiful, inscrutable man who had dominated her life from the moment he entered it, so totally that it seemed to her he had ruled even the earlier parts of it—her life before then a preparation to receive him completely. Suddenly she could not join Tarah and Karen against him. Not now. "The roles I played— . . . constantly trying on new masks, to find the one I could live with— . . . Richard drew the masks, and I came to life."

"So briefly!" Karen reminded her, and herself.

"Yes—until he discovered whatever the hell he wanted to discover!" Tarah felt threatened by Joja's assertion.

Blue was aware of the sweet scent wafting through the hall in recurrent waves. Outside, lush flowers breathed within the dark night. Suddenly, like velvet, a calmness contained his turbulence: Within it, the priest shone in luminous clarity. So young—almost too young to be a priest. Cam. Cam's face constantly on his mind like something drowned in the memory of spilled blood, rising recurrently to its surface.

"A confession! We must have a confession quickly!" Malissa's fingers ripped the silence to shreds.

Mark nodded at Joja. He bit his finger, lightly, between the rows of perfect teeth. He nodded again.

Vaguely Joja began to understand the abortive encounters with the boy throughout the day. She stood suddenly before Tarah.

The actress would be a witness now, Tarah knew. For whom?

Malissa's purple-shaded gaze moved like a scythe from Richard to Mark to Joja.

"When I was a child, I placed a doll against my heart because that's where I felt empty," Joja said.

Tarah frowned. Joja was a witness in Richard's support.

Mark had already said: "You felt empty then."

And Joja understood unequivocally the meaning of the broken encounters with the boy. Emotional extortion. The harsh words flowed darkly into her mind. Her allegiance with his father, and therefore him—against Tarah—that was what Mark had been extracting, cunningly, throughout the day. In exchange for— . . . the sexual promise first issued when he stood naked outside her window. And Richard—had he allowed it all?

A doll. A womb. Jeremy wrenched away from memories: *Lips, an orange heart. The enormous stomach about to open to give hideous birth. Bandages.*

"You wanted a child, that's all," Tarah tried to dismiss Joja's ambiguous but powerfully disturbing testimony.

Mark's crystalline-marble eyes were on the actress, capturing hers. Slowly, he touched his neck.

"No," Joja said. "I was empty before Richard. A body forming inside me would have drained life from me." (*The child smothered with a pillow. "Die! Die!"*)

Still determined to turn the tide of this interrogation, "It was Richard who rendered you empty!" Tarah prematurely asserted the verdict she must prove.

Joja offered the words to Mark: "Richard resurrected me."

"Only for moments!" Karen said.

"And then he turned you into a live corpse without him!" Tarah thrust. "When he was through—brutally! —like a vampire who's drained all the blood!"

Valerie stared at Paul's lips. As if a fist had pulled out the memory, she remembered: Her brother on the bed with her, his face— . . . She touched her neck. There was the wound. "Paul," she whispered quickly, "when you were in the room before I came down— . . ." She deliberately suspended the words—a question or a statement.

"I haven't been in your room, Valerie," Paul said.

You're lying! Why? Lodging in her mind, the unspoken words disoriented her: The giant hall waltzed slowly before her. It stretched on waves of colors, the unformed words floating sinuously within them, becoming the colors themselves: then only one:

Red!

She touched her neck again.

"Yes, and then I felt dead again," Joja acknowledged. She turned her head violently from Mark, severing the control of his intense eyes, rejecting, for that moment at least, the terms of extortion.

Tarah breathed in momentary triumph. "And so it was Richard who made you aware of living within death!" she tried to force the necessary accusation from Joja.

Mark glanced at Richard, as if expecting him to speak. When he didn't, "The word she used was resurrection," the boy offered. His eyes, the beautiful sensual eyes; his lips, the promise of them; his body: The radiance of his supreme sexuality enveloped Joja. "The doll—your empty heart—long ago," he insisted.

Tarah stood deliberately before the boy, blocking him from Joja's sight. "She merely wanted a child!"

"No—I killed her!" Joja said. "I smothered her!"

"Confession!" Malissa accepted. "And is it addressed to God or Satan?" she demanded. One hand grasped for the night cut in a circle by the dome, the other for the spiraling black and white funnel of gleaming floor. "*Which* one?!"

"Maybe when you confess, that's when you *know*," Blue said aloud.

The beaded rattles trembled before Joja, pinpoints of colored, shattered fire assaulting her eyes.

"You killed the child— . . ." Malissa coaxed.

Joja heard words—her words: "It was during a play —the last play I was in— . . . The role of a woman who hides her child to conceal her age." Suddenly she was transported to that tense stage. "But at the end of the play she resigns her youth to her daughter, an acceptance of life drained from her, of death in life."

"How old was the child?" Malissa's question came like the calculated interruption of a prosecutor.

"Twelve. No—fourteen," Joja changed the age quickly.

"Mark's age!" Malissa understood the quickly revised testimony. Against whom? She would determine that later.

The rattles continued to tremble, as if to force more words from the actress: "I played the role night after terrible night," she said. "And it was all wrong! I was fading, emptier each night. So I changed the ending. I made up new words—whispers at first coming from my own—my real—soul, for once." The emotional words—directed at Richard, and Mark, at Tarah—formed with the paradoxical calm of someone pronouncing rehearsed testimony, knowing on whose behalf, yet allowing the possibility of reinterpretation.

The rattles renewed their insistence. Joja continued: "The audience began to whisper, the whispers grew, became angry shouts: 'Louder, louder!'—like a judgment on my muted, masked life. It was then: Instead of surrendering my life, this time to that despised daughter —... *I smothered her for stealing my life!* The curtain fell—and I was still holding the pillow over the gasping child." And so her own cunning strategy had shaped: The words had allied her to Richard against Tarah, therefore also to Mark—yes; but she had at the same time issued a warning to Mark which Malissa had seized intuitively: The announced symbolic murder of a child his age. A possible rehearsal?

"You killed her?" Mark asked, smiling.

"I would have," Joja answered coldly; "they pulled

me away. I only killed the child she represented. So you see, Tarah," she fulfilled her part of what she viewed now as an unspoken contract between herself and Mark; and was Richard also party to it? "So you see, no, I didn't want a child."

"Richard had already rendered you empty, you merely recognized it on that stage!" Tarah still struggled to enlist Joja.

"And then Richard's invitation came," Joja said.

"And you accepted," said Richard.

"And I accepted," said Joja with finality.

She had moved too rashly, too early, propelled by the first hint of the actress's wavering toward Richard, Tarah evaluated her blocked attack. She would not withdraw, no; but she would not advance further for now. Not yet. She had announced the war—her demand that Richard would play in his own game of confessions.

Mark's black smile. It received Joja's allegiance. She had thwarted Tarah's initial thrust.

Joja touched her face, her beautiful mask. Her purple eyes on Mark enforced her counter-threat of extortion: Her allegiance was not absolute. She would hold him to the day-long promise. She remembered: When she held him. Years ago.

Like a vulture in search of prey, Malissa circled the giant room. From person to person. There would be more—much more, and exciting—from Tarah. But for now the attention must shift. Otherwise, a premature climax might ruin the rest of the game. She would lead them to the next encounter.

She passed Savannah, a rejected mask of beauty. And Tor, another mask. Through! So easily, so expertly revealed. Would Joja join Savannah and Tor, now? No. She seemed strengthened by her confession—there would be more from her. Topaze—he would be easy; he was trying desperately to please her, and he might therefore be formidable against Rev. It amounted to this: How much more could the midget provide in the pursuit of others? She would extend his period of trial. Blue.

Blue.

Malissa's purple stare. Her hands: Extended.

Blue's eyes: On the vortex of black and white spiraling at his feet.

The priest: He moved toward Blue.

Malissa's hands: They withdrew.

Blue's ankle: The inverted pentagram.

Was Richard saving the blond youngman for the handsome priest to draw out in confession? Malissa savored the revelation. Paul and Valerie, then! Oh, something exquisitely special. Richard had given only the most vagrant of hints. . . . Question Bravo now? How to move? To move yet? Bravo was strong. The game had developed several clear leaders. But one must always watch for the silent observer studying the active players. She glanced at Mark.

Mark.

Richard's brooding strange child.

Would Mark plunge overtly into the current of power? Indeed, had he already done so? Richard pitted against Mark! The sudden thought seized Malissa with its startling possibilities. There had been the boy's look on Richard when Tarah challenged his father. She would study the boy carefully.

"Your grace!" Malissa chose finally.

Instantly the hollow eyes of the mamaloi and the papaloi riveted on la Duquesa.

The queen touched her black veil; it would be her shield from Malissa.

"Don't look into her eyes!" Albert whispered urgently to the queen.

"We've heard so much of hatred," Malissa said. "And we've agreed that we may confess to the . . . good . . . in our lives. We will, however, be allowed our own definitions! . . . Perhaps, then, your grace, you'll allow us to hear something about— . . ." She could not pronounce the word now. In that context, it belonged to a foreign language she did not understand.

"Love?" la Duquesa finished for her. "Even the word frightens you, Malissa. Why? I'm not afraid of it. Love, love, love, love, love. See, it's easy. I'll gladly tell you about love."

"Why should *you* want to hear anything of good, Malissa?" Karen asked.

"Because the darkness, which I adore, is brightest immediately after the dark blaze of light, which I abhor!" Malissa said.

"The moment I met the Duke, my life became a rhapsody," la Duquesa told them.

"Don't look directly at Malissa, your grace!" Albert insisted. "Her eyes, her hands—that black ring—they can force you to say things you don't want to say."

"I'm not afraid!" la Duquesa said. "Even death, ugly, black death—like that horrible black pearl on your finger, Malissa—even death came eventually to contain the beauty of our love, like the perfect frame about a perfect painting. Otherwise, the beauty might spill over."

"Confess, then, to perfection," came Richard's voice.

"You pervert words with new meanings," said the priest to Richard. (*"Don't let me die! I love you!" The pulled hand!*) "You despise even the concept of love." He did not look at the queen.

"Some might contend that it's an unnatural condition," said Richard, "that it invaded man's pristine savagery like a disease."

He was being taunted into a reaction to be examined; Jeremy allowed the dialogue to stand for now.

Topaze asked la Duquesa: "Where did the Duke have his kingdom?" His face was set in a serious expression. His hand floated idly over his groin.

"Oh, dukes don't have kingdoms, dear," la Duquesa said gently, "they have duchies. . . . But the Duke abandoned his lands, his holdings—all his aristocratic rights —when he married me."

"You're preparing to try to mock her love, aren't you?" Suddenly Valerie defended the black-mourning figure.

"Merely to inquire into purity," said Richard, as if presenting evidence of a recurrent crime.

"Like Savannah's purity!" Bravo laughed with contempt.

Hearing her name, Savannah looked about the room as if in search of something irretrievably lost. Tor stared at her as if at a ghost. The shadowy servants looked at the two, for the first time, in abstract recognition.

"Savannah's purity never existed," Richard said firmly. "But does that mean— . . . ?" He stopped. His eyes sought Valerie, as if demanding that she supply the unfinished words.

16

Suddenly Valerie seemed frightened, so vulnerable, so pretty to la Duquesa. The queen felt a growing compassion toward her—moments earlier the girl had defended her. To thwart the annihilating attention that Richard's look conveyed—and now Mark's, then Malissa's; and the black man and black woman advanced toward the girl—to thwart that, the voice behind the black veils said: "I'll confess about my life before I met the Duke! *That* should satisfy your longing for the worst." And she recited quickly a sad litany to her past: "Old houses among crouching sinister palm trees, the stink of weeds. Bodies sprawled nightly like mangled shadows; a crushed daisy chain. A funereal orgy. Women as receptacles—nothing else—for sailors, marines, thieves, the cruel vagrants. A sexual wake." The queen issued words calculated to force their interest away from the girl. She had succeeded:

Richard's eyes released Valerie. Malissa's followed. But Mark's did not yet relent.

Blue remembered: *The procession of blood. "Susej!"*

"Dark rooms, bodies, men and women," la Duquesa continued her black litany.

"Only men," Rev interrupted. "I know that scene. Dark pads, grass, pills, queens— . . ."

"*Women*," insisted la Duquesa.

"Studs like me and queens like you," Rev said emphatically. He looked at Malissa: Her eyes acquiesced; she was granting him a reprieve from his humiliation by Bravo. He moved toward the queen.

Topaze's eyes narrowed on Rev like the sight of a gun. Rev was attempting to reassert himself within the charged field of shifting power, and Malissa was allowing it. Lewdly, the midget cupped his groin in his hand and thrust his hips toward la Duquesa, to steer the attention away from Rev.

Coolly la Duquesa avoided looking at the midget.

Rev pulled the attention from the midget: "Yeah, I know that scene," he tossed at la Duquesa. "Diggit—I'd wake up in the morning in someone's pad, and this painted man's face would say, 'Fuck me'; and of course I wouldn't be interested. So if she'd lay some bread on me, I'd let her blow me while I slept—of course I didn't need the bread; I was in the big time, man." His voice gained authority. He would restore the image Bravo had bludgeoned. Then he would go after Topaze. And the dike, he would take her on too! "Queens tripped out over my tattoos," he said toughly. "They'd redraw them with their tongues."

Albert's tongue protruded hungrily.

Desperate for attention, Topaze pointed: "Albert's *tongue,* Miss Malissa!"

Allying himself doubly with Malissa, Rev deliberately tortured Albert: "Diggit, I even got a tattoo on my dick!" he announced.

"But you've mentioned the perfection of your love, your grace," Richard reminded the queen.

"Love came when I met the Duke," la Duquesa said.

"In spring?" sneered Rev.

"In spring," said la Duquesa.

"And he died— . . . ?" Rev went on.

"In winter," said the queen.

"Did *you* kill him?" Tarah shot unexpectedly, attempting to trace within another's life the path from love to hate to murder.

"No!" la Duquesa said quickly. "Why should I destroy our perfect love?" Now she knelt as if before a grave. Her hands slowly mimed the placing of a wreath on the stone of death. She leaned forward to kiss it. Behind the veil, tears glistened like black beads.

Rev studied the face behind it.

"I met the Duke— . . ." la Duquesa started.

"At one of those weird parties?" Rev asked. Recurrently glancing at Malissa for approval—given—Rev felt his power being restored, even if on probation; he would pass that test.

"Of course not," said la Duquesa, turning away from Rev's intense stare. "He wouldn't have been caught dead among such trash! I met him . . . oh, in a shimmering mansion, with many, many floors—eight, to be exact. We went— . . . to the penthouse! In elevators! You could see the dazzling city!"

"Was it a glasshouse?" said Rev quickly.

"As a matter of fact, it was. Yes—it had so many windows! You could call it an elaborate glass house! With windows like diamonds!" la Duquesa said. "And in the glass house, the servants were— . . ."

"In uniform?" said Rev.

"Oh, yes, full uniform—of course."

"Black?" Rev questioned.

"No—blue," la Duquesa corrected.

"Oh, it was summer," Rev understood.

"Late spring," said la Duquesa. "And the other guests at the fabulous gathering—all selected quite carefully— . . ."

"Wanted?" Rev interjected.

"Yes—desired; sought after— . . ."

"An assorted group?" Rev asked.

"There were many titles," la Duquesa explained. "We were announced— . . ."

"By the servants in black," Rev finished.

"In *blue*," la Duquesa corrected, "it was late spring. . . . They escorted us in by the hand. . . . And even among all those beautiful guests, even then, the Duke was dazzling beyond dreaming!" Still kneeling, she addressed an invisible grave.

"The Duke," said Rev, moving in viciously, "did he have a tattoo which said, 'Born to Lose'?"

La Duquesa frowned. "Why— . . . As a matter

of— ... How did you— ... ?" Quickly: "Of course he did not have a tattoo!"

"Yeah!" Rev insisted, his eyes only inches from her face, as if to penetrate the black veil. "And he had two others—two birds on his chest flying down toward his nipples!"

"No!" la Duquesa regained control more quickly this time.

Alerted, Malissa moved in on the veiled figure. The hint, the clue! The game! The confession!

"Don't look into her eyes—look away from her rings!" Albert warned the queen again.

"He was gentle, he purified me of my lurid past," la Duquesa said. Eyes closed, she leaned forward again to mime the kissing of the grave.

Swiftly Rev stood before the kneeling figure, his crotch thrust toward her.

La Duquesa's eyes opened on it. She recoiled quickly.

"You met the Duke in the glasshouse," Rev hurled viciously at the kneeling queen in mourning. "You saw him for the first time in jail."

Blue remembered: *The ugly, gray, monster building where you were booked after being arrested: heavily glassed, barred: the "glasshouse."* Remembered: *A fat, ugly detective: "He told us!"* Now Blue shook the words. But remembered: *A courtroom the color of dirty sheets. The blue rubber with the star. "Isn't this your trademark, boy?"*

"The Duke! In jail?" la Duquesa tried to recover. "How dare you!"

"Yeah!" said Rev, encouraged by Malissa's smile. "He was busted—one of many times. Your duke was just Duke, that's what they called him—and, baby, like he was just a petty hustler. You saw him in jail: He'd been busted for armed robbery—and you for masquerading in drag!"

"I was never in jail," la Duquesa protested.

Staring sadly at her, Albert stood closer to her.

"Yeah, you were, baby," said Rev. "And so was Duke."

"Superb!" Malissa's hands swirled excitedly, as if to frame a perfect confrontation.

Topaze looked at her desperately. He would have to move soon—somehow!—to topple Rev!

Dazed, as if reality were pulling at her too strongly—and the beaded rattles of the black man and black woman needled her painted eyes even behind the veil—la Duquesa said: "He loved me!"

"Shit," Rev sneered. "I knew Duke. He dug getting queens hot over him. He took them for whatever they had, he even made them hock their goddam drag clothes!"

"Your dark prince!" Malissa mocked.

"I remember you, baby," Rev told the queen. "I tried to recognize you from the first—only you kept covering your face with that crazy black drag. But with all that shit you just laid on us—man, I connected! The glass mansion—that's the joint, man! And the men who announced you were cop-pigs who brought you in handcuffed. Baby, I remember you now—you're the hung-up queen who bailed Duke out of jail— . . ."

Gathering her dignity and her black veils, la Duquesa rose. "He loved me," she said softly.

"He never even let you get near him!" Rev ground on. "Man, he laughed about this queen who kept giving him bread and he never even let her touch him!"

La Duquesa's eyes overflowed with black, painted tears. She turned to the priest, as if he could stop the cruel violation of her dreams.

The priest wrenched his eyes away from her. (*Another painted face!*)

"Yes," la Duquesa's sad voice asserted now. "Yes, I did see him the first time in jail—and my heart embraced him, instantly! It's true I bailed him out. I borrowed money, I sold and hocked things. Then I arranged to meet him in a park after I got him out. I even gathered some flowers for him." (*"I love you, Duke," she remembered her words to him; "I'll always love you—just you, Duke!" He took the flowers and started plucking the petals, smiling his half smile.*) "And he loved me," she asserted.

"You never even made it with him!" Rev fired.

"Yes! Once— . . ." la Duquesa blurted.

"Oh, yeah!—yeah, that's right, I remember," Rev said. "And, man, how he laughed about it. One night, when he was stoned— . . ."

La Duquesa remembered: *Yes, stoned, drunk. I had dressed especially for him. My favorite gown. Green velvet. It had sequins.*

". . . — he let you blow him," Rev finished. "Then he tore your drag dress!"

(*The scattered sequins, like gleaming tears on the floor.*) "He loved me!" la Duquesa's words erupted passionately.

"He didn't even let you finish him off," Rev laughed savagely. "He jerked off on your false tits and face, man! He used to describe your face smeared with makeup and cum!—he said he thought he was coming in colors!"

"I would have conquered the cruelty!" la Duquesa asserted. "My love would have made him gentle—if the cops hadn't killed him!" She turned to the others: "They shot him down on the dirty street, like an animal —the filthy cops! If not," she said slowly, her voice breaking, "if not, my dreams— . . . Yes!" she insisted.

"Yes, he would have come to love me—I know it; I just know it! And he *did,* before he died!"

"The pigs got him when he was running away. He left this other dude behind," Rev laughed. "They shot the Duke."

"I heard the shots, I rushed to him, I knelt over him, I held his head," la Duquesa went on. "The cops tried to pull me away. 'I'm his wife!' I cried. The Duke opened his eyes. Just once. And his lips parted, about to form a kiss."

"About to say, 'Shit,' " Rev said contemptuously.

"No! At that moment he loved me, truly, at last!" la Duquesa knew. She moved stonily like someone accompanying a corpse to burial. "If he had lived, it would have all, all, all, all been true," she insisted. "And his love would have destroyed Freddy forever."

"Freddy?" Rev questioned. Secure in what he saw as his regained stature, he drew out his knife—to him, the symbol of his regained courage—and he began in rehearsed toughness to file his fingernails.

"Yes—Freddy," sighed the queen. "That was— . . . That used to be my name— . . ."

"Yeah!" Rev trampled on the memories erected from her longing dreams. "Duke used to call you Miss Freddy; he even did an imitation of you."

The queen's face tore with pain, the veil was glued with tears to her cheeks.

Angrily, "*There* is your purity, Richard!" Karen said abruptly.

As if in reaction, Richard's face whirled toward Valerie.

Valerie said to him: "You wanted to corrupt her memory of love!" But she was facing Paul.

"It wasn't real."

Valerie heard the words; but—her eyes closed suddenly because what was revealing itself as reality was glaring too harshly at her—she was not sure whether they had been uttered by Richard. Or Paul.

Suddenly, knowing the seizure of power could not wait, Topaze lunged at Rev, grabbed the knife. The midget stood before him, the sharp weapon inches from Rev's crotch.

Rev looked down in terror at Topaze. "What the hell— . . . ?" he started.

Topaze laughed. The point of the knife touched Rev's cock.

"Don't!" Albert shouted.

"Please—take him away!" Rev pled in a shaken voice.

The priest moved toward the two. How far would such scenes actually be allowed to proceed by those in control? The mere outline of violence?

"Cut his yellow balls off!" Bravo shouted. "*Cut!*" She made a savage motion with her whip.

Topaze drew the knife back as if to slice.

The priest advanced.

"Please— . . ." Rev begged. Perspiration draped his face, his body.

Her words forming like icicles, Malissa said slowly: "Why don't you grab Topaze quickly, Rev? Just one swift move, that's all it requires. Certainly you can overcome him."

Topaze understood Malissa's words as a taunt at Rev. The midget held his position, secure in Malissa's approval.

"But . . . if I . . . don't— . . ." Rev looked at the knife, ready.

"Try," said Malissa; her voice was hard ice now. "You have nothing to lose."

"Except his balls!" Bravo flung.

The midget's hand jerked back.

"Enough!" Malissa crowned the midget the obvious victor. "Enough, Topaze. We have all heard—and seen—Rev's confession. Twice."

His momentary restoration of power squashed by the midget—the probation withdrawn, and so it had all been for nothing!—Rev stared at Malissa in open hatred.

Imitating Rev, Topaze strutted away, dropping the knife.

His eyes still buried deep into Malissa, Rev retrieved it.

They had allowed Rev to proceed in the terrible exposure of the queen. Then they had permitted the midget his horrible charade. Slowly, they were discarding those whom they trapped. Yet might they still avenge themselves? Jeremy braced. This was just the beginning of the fierce war.

Like a black shadowy statue, la Duquesa stood between Savannah and Tor: also shadows.

The mamaloi and the papaloi: Their rattles: They waited: Sinister dormant weapons.

"I want to confess!" It was Blue.

"Confessions belong in the confessional," Jeremy said instantly.

"No. Confessions long to be screamed out—not to fade into meaningless whispers," Richard contradicted.

"Yeah," Blue agreed vaguely. The fixed smile, the intense serious eyes. "A righteous confession, man," he said. This public confession would be his way of *forcing* the priest, finally, to listen. And why? It was that answer which Blue would attempt to extract.

"Confession—without absolution— . . ." the priest said again.

"If Satan does extract confessions as the price for entering hell," Mark said with a smile, "what kind of absolution would there be, then, Malissa?"

The priest looked at the boy. "How can you allow your son to listen to this— . . . ?" he repeated to Richard. "To expose him to all this blackness! You deprive him of the right to make the correct choice."

"To the contrary, he can choose more clearly—whatever the correct choice may be," Richard said. "But the only proof would be if he confronted another raised in an atmosphere more to your approval, Father. Then who would— . . . ?" He paused. "Who will survive?"

Like a sudden antagonist, Mark faced the twins.

Lashing out in fury, Tarah said: "What makes people mere objects in your experiments, Richard? We're not blind to your power to manipulate."

"A knowledge of corruption—is that power?" Richard said. He turned to Blue. "You wanted to confess."

"And willingly choose *whom* to confess to!" said Malissa excitedly. "Perhaps you should begin, 'Satan, forgive me for I have done good!' " she parodied the rite of confession.

"Don't allow this," Jeremy said to Blue. It was suddenly as if Blue's confession, withheld, would seal his own. "It's a mockery."

"A mockery?" sliced Malissa. "A mockery to confine life to whispers in a darkened booth—that, yes, is a mockery! He should confess to *us*, Father, who have knowledge of what you call evil. *We* can measure it. Whereas you, how can *you* measure evil? How can you absolve what you don't understand? Or do you understand? Do you, Father Jeremy!"

Embarrassed immediately after he had done it—but having responded to a powerful compulsion—Jeremy made the sign of the cross, swiftly: "In the name of the Father, the Son, and the Holy Ghost!"

Malissa hissed: "In the name of Satan, His son, and the Black Angel! ... *Now* the scales are balanced, Father! Your side and ours! *Now* the sides are poised evenly! *Now* the confession can be heard and weighed—by *both* sides."

"Maybe, finally, there will be only one side," Mark smiled.

"How dare you use those words of sacrilege before me!" the priest accosted Malissa; he could not face the boy.

"How dare *you* use those other words before *me?*" Malissa flung back ferociously. "Does it occur to you that *they* affront me as powerfully as mine do you?"

17

The priest turned from the woman.

"Run away!" Mark hurled at him.

"Not ever again," the priest said firmly. "I'll face all of you." Now he looked directly at Mark.

"Confess!" rasped Malissa to the priest.

"Not to you!" said the priest.

"We'll see," said Malissa.

Blue said quickly: "Father, forgive me, for I have sinned."

"Satan, forgive him, for he may have done good!" Malissa intoned.

"Don't tell them anything!" the priest yelled at Blue.

"I want you to fucking listen, goddamnit!" Blue shouted back. In the grotto the priest would have walked away from the worst. Here, caught in the microscopic scrutiny of the others, it would be much more difficult.

Yet the priest had turned away angrily.

Mark reminded him: "You were never going to run away again; you were going to face us now."

The priest did, his eyes black like coals about to burn.

Blue had gambled correctly. "Now both sides, like they're listening, man; and finally I'll know where I'm at," he said, almost imploring.

"Help him to find which side!" Malissa said to the priest.

Again Richard was withdrawing from the tight cluster. He would listen from a distance, separated. He knew—and Malissa knew now: Whatever Blue would confess would be determined paradoxically by the priest —even by his resistance to it.

Now from the symbolic glass chamber which contained his life, visible but separated from all but himself, Blue's words would come, willingly: without preparation, at times forming out of sequence on the acid-coated fringes of his mind, which would open expelling the dam of memories: images trapped in a dark, shattered kaleidoscope: "I had never seen Mr Stuart, though he must have seen me, somewhere," he began. "The Blue Woman, she'd heard of me. Like Mr Stuart, uh diggit—he was only a telephone voice that called to refer me to clients: I was so popular people made appointments way in advance: Sometimes they just grooved seeing me naked. Man, I began tripping: like looking *past* a mirror, swimming in it very still while you're standing before it and it's really glass. But all that love— people digging me, my bod, righteous paying for it, but it wasn't enough, I didn't really fucking want any of them—and after the sex, man, I rushed to myself in the mirror."

Savannah glanced at her reflection in a large mirror among the panels of gold, waiting silhouettes on the wall; between her and it: an empty corridor of space. Within it stood the fading outline of her former image: the mirror now linking the row of panels with her own reflected gold silhouette.

"And that is your confession," said the priest hurriedly to Blue.

The mamaloi and the papaloi faced Blue, but their rattles did not hiss.

"No, man," Blue said inevitably. "It's about Cam."

Cam. The priest's body tensed, as if before an enemy. "What did Cam look like?" he heard himself ask. The echoing irrelevance of his question struck him. He had asked it only to withhold the parody of confession, and not because the answer was important to him, he explained to himself.

Blue glanced at the priest. Like you, he thought. But he said: "He was . . . very handsome." And then he was lulled backwards, across time past, and his voice snagged on a memory: "Cam, I didn't— . . ." he started. "I met the Blue Woman— . . . I rode in her silver Packard— . . . Cam." His mind tumbled over the gravestones of buried memories: "The Blue Woman had this crazy pad in the hills, we *drank* acid, man. The whole day was a trip; and the night—the night, diggit, man, it was like *riding* on a black bird flying against the sun!" His words —conveying his mind's images—swirled like a multicolored ribbon in a reckless wind.

"You already carried the inverted star of Satan?" Malissa attempted to shape the confession.

"Uh—what? The star— . . . Satan's sign has the ram's

head inside the pentagram, man. . . . Diggit, I wanted the star on my cock first. Oh, yeah, sure, I already carried it," Blue said. "I even had it put on the blue condoms."

"You warned your victims with it," came Richard's controlled voice.

It seemed important to Tarah that she protest at that moment. Yet she was fascinated into attention by the spectacle of this beautiful blond youngman—so young, so corrupt. In sudden reaction, she grasped for the image of Gable.

Blue's voice rose: "Then Mr Stuart kept calling to tell me my clients had canceled my assignments; he kept saying they preferred Cam!" Calmly, the torrent of his memories ebbing: "The Blue Woman," his words went on like a tape spliced out of sequence, "she drove around looking for me in her silver ride. Diggit, it had black curtains. Her chauffeur wore chains, man; he was like one of her slaves. She was beautiful—young, with blue makeup, man. At night she painted her body blue and pasted white feathers on it. She was searching for me because—uh—she had—diggit—uh, what? Oh, yeah, you know, uh, man, oh, what? Oh, she heard I carried the sign. But not the ram's head inside the star." Now he frowned and smiled at the same time—the heavy black eyebrows glowering over the curled lips: as if dual memories, one terrible, the other amusing, were vying for this mind. "Then the murder happened," he said.

Looking at Blue, Jeremy thought in resignation: I will confess. He corrected his thoughts quickly: *He* will confess.

"There was a trial," Blue stumbled. "They had the blue rubber there. Twenty-four eyes in that jury box. On me, man."

Something buried—overheard—surfacing. *A trial! Murder! Daniel! Their mother!* Valerie felt trapped in an avalanche of fire.

"The card of Death!" Malissa reminded them at Blue's words.

Blue retreated now within the mist of his ravished mind: "A huge pad in the hills. The Blue Woman's. There was a pool surrounded by inverted crosses. And people, men and women—their faces painted in many colors; their bodies almost naked. Painted all red, once —a procession of blood, they said. . . . Cam! . . . At the trial— . . ."

The word badgered Valerie's awareness: *A trial, a trial, a trial!*

Again to move beyond the act burning in his mind: "Once, diggit, one of my clients burned a nude picture of me; and he put up a holy palm cross on his door on the day I saw him regularly—just to see if I could cross it, man!" Blue thrust the words at the priest.

"And did you cross?" the priest asked tensely.

"No," Blue smiled. "The cross freaked me out."

"Shit, he thought you were a vampire," Bravo derided.

Blue said: "The Blue Woman, diggit, she called me Prince Susej—that's Jesus spelled backwards. I was the Lord Satan's prince. But only like on probation, like till there was a heavy test."

The rattles still did not hiss before him. They had not even been raised.

"The imitation of evil, the ritual of evil, nothing more," the priest attempted to dismiss it all. "Insignificant cults."

"Yeah," Blue's mind converted the priest's words into others. "Yeah, like that: And the Blue Woman was naked on the black throne. She was painted blue. And I wore only the blue rubber, man. The disciples, men and women, they performed before us: Weird things, man. And they'd kiss the inverted star on my foot while I fucked the Blue Woman. And then I'd stand and they'd lick the rubber and the woman's cunt. And once with a long black rosary, they tied a boy and a girl— ..."

The priest interrupted in outrage: "Did you actually invoke Satan?"

"Yes!" Blue said.

"And did he answer?" asked Malissa.

Suddenly Blue looked at Richard, then Mark, now at the priest: as if his mind were seizing a composite of the three faces. "When I was tripping, I saw a beautiful dark face once," he mumbled. *"Was it him?"* he shouted.

A heavy silence throttled the words.

Then: "The murder!" Malissa demanded.

"The Blue Woman told me the Lord Satan wanted another sacrifice," Blue muttered. "I thought that would be the test."

"*Another* sacrifice?" Malissa's gleaming hands attempted to pull out words.

"Yeah, there had been, you know, birds, animals," Blue said. "Now the Lord Satan required a human sacrifice."

"Cam," the priest whispered aloud.

Blue's voice was clear now: "He was one of Mr Stuart's boys—he was eighteen."

Eighteen. The same age as Gable. The unremarkable coincidence penetrated Tarah's mind sharply.

"He was a Satanist?" the priest asked.

"Who? Mr Stuart? He was like thirty-five," Blue said. "I didn't know it then, man, but he was like a high priest at the Blue Woman's rites. Diggit: He'd sit behind a black scrim, and just watch. He'd told the Blue Woman about me, and the inverted star. That's when she went out looking for me. He wouldn't tell her where. And finally he brought me and Cam together, at that weird pad in the hills. He just said it was a heavy assignment, man. This time there were only the four of us—Cam, myself, the Blue Woman, and Mr Stuart—it was, uh, you know, the first time I actually saw him—or knew it was him behind the black scrim. We were naked—except Mr Stuart; this time the scrim was drawn, he sat on a tall draped chair and watched: like at a real heavy play. And then— . . . And then— . . .!"

"Then!" the priest yelled.

Blue's hands covered his face. He blurted: "I drew Cam to me! It was the first time I had ever touched anyone that way!" Now he stood close to the priest. Without touching him, he mimed the movements he was describing.

"The beautiful closeness that exists only in dreams," la Duquesa said.

"And then— . . ." Blue stuttered. "Then— . . . the greatest horror in my life!"

"The murder," the priest said, accepting it.

"No." Blue frowned. "You don't understand. The murder wasn't the most horrible. The greatest horror was— . . ."

"What!" the priest shouted. Suddenly he wanted to hear the confession he had been eluding throughout the day—the confession Blue had been determined to force on him.

"The greatest horror was that— . . ." Blue went on, ". . . —that Cam didn't— . . . That Cam wasn't aroused by me! *He wasn't even hard!*" The dark blue of his eyes seemed to funnel swiftly into an open wound. "See, always before it was other people desiring *me*—*their* desire of me, just that, turned me on, like they were mirrors. But with Cam— . . ." His mind jumped: "I moved away from him, understanding—trying to reject him, to save my own world. But it was too late. Mr Stuart was laughing. And the Blue Woman stood on the stairs, her hands like wings, and she kept yelling: 'A new dark prince for Satan! A new Lord Susej!—I'll carve the ram's head on his ankle with my tongue!' "

Now the rattles hissed before Blue. The sparkling beads stabbed his eyes.

Bravo roared with derisive laughter.

"The one person you desired— . . ." Joja began. "The only one who might have filled you. And you haven't been able to become aroused since then," she understood the morning's angry incident between them.

"And that was the most terrible moment of your life," Karen said incredulously.

"That you lost in some ugly game. But how?" Tarah asked.

"How? Well—uh— . . ." Blue began vaguely. "In wanting someone finally, I had failed the most important test: That's why Mr Stuart had brought me and Cam together, that's why he'd told us both that our clients had canceled assignments for the other—yeah, he set us up as rivals—to see who would never *need* anyone else: And *he* would be the Lord Satan's righteous prince."

"Not to need anyone—is that to win?" Karen asked.

"Yes!" Joja announced, the toughness that had propelled her through life asserting itself. She had aimed the word at Mark, verbalizing to the boy the possible withdrawal of her earlier implied allegiance to Richard; her reassertion of counter-extortion.

Alerted, Mark touched his bare flesh at the low opening of his shirt.

"And so you killed Cam!" Malissa said excitedly to Blue.

Blue looked at her in bewilderment. "Kill Cam? No, I didn't kill . . . Cam."

"But the murder!" Malissa said, as if a prize were being withheld from her.

Memories on the surface of Valerie's mind, like flotsam: *A murder, a trial, suicide, murder!* Her brother's face, fascinated, gave her no hint that the words were stirring memories within him too.

"Confess the rest in private!" the priest made one more attempt to thwart Blue's words.

Malissa said: "Oh, the holy father is indeed determined to be the only one to enjoy the youngman's confession!" Cunningly, "But what guarantee do you have that he *will* listen then?" she asked Blue.

"I don't enjoy torture!" the priest said.

"Do you come alive only then, only through listening, alone, to others tell you what you call their . . . 'sins'—which is really the shape of their lives?" Malissa asked. "Without sin, where would you—*and your God*—be?"

His right hand raised by his left, Topaze stood before Blue. "Cam was the winner!"

"But later— . . ." The words came from Blue's bowed head.

"Later did *you* reject him?" Bravo asked eagerly.

Blue raised his head. The sinister smile had conquered his face totally. "After the murder, *then* Cam was aroused by me. I was determined! All I had to do was just stand before him! And then it happened. Then *he* advanced. And then we made love, Cam and I. On the blood!"

"Whose blood?" Malissa demanded.

"Mr Stuart's," Blue ansewered. "I thought I told you. Cam killed him." He stared down as if at a dead victim at his feet. "Diggit, man, Cam hit him with a heavy lamp, he smashed his skull. Then we made love on his blood. The Blue Woman was chanting over us, and Cam and I made love over and over. There was blood on our bodies, our hands, faces. We rolled in Mr Stuart's blood!"

A burst of red shattered on the priest's mind.

Valerie thought easily: Murder. Until she heard him call her name in alarm, she did not realize that she had flung herself against her brother.

"Why did Cam kill Mr Stuart?" It was Tarah who asked the question, as if from another's motivation she would strengthen her own resolve. "Because he was outraged by his manipulation of others' actions? Because he wanted to close the staring, accusing eyes?" With surprise, she heard the echo of the meaning of her own last words.

"What? I told you, man," Blue uttered. "What? Oh, yeah. Like Cam knew Mr Stuart always carried a lot of bread, and wore all kinds of jewelry—but he wouldn't give it to Cam. Cam tried to get me to help him rip off Mr Stuart. But I wouldn't do it—I even split from the room. When I came back, that's when I saw Cam— . . ."

"After you made love, you didn't want to go with him?" Bravo asked. *"You* no longer wanted *him?"*

Blue said: "Yeah—I didn't want him any more. . . They caught him at the border, with all the bread and jewelry he'd ripped off Mr Stuart. I was busted too. So was the Blue Woman. There was a trial. The pigs told me Cam said I'd done it. But I confessed."

"You *had* to tell the truth—that it was Cam who murdered the man," the priest said.

"Oh, yeah, sure, man; and the Blue Woman, she testified to that too. And Cam stole— . . . I was acquitted," Blue said flatly.

The priest sighed, as if the word—acquitted—were an omen.

"You drew his confession admirably," Malissa's words attempted to jar the priest into the ironic recognition of his part in the anxious confession.

"And Cam— . . ." The etched smile on Blue's face was fierce. "Cam was given life."

"You were smart, man!" Rev congratulated him. "You didn't split, Cam did."

"I was innocent," said Blue.

"Innocent," the priest echoed.

"Innocent," Richard revived the fading word. "Murder as communion over a slaughtered corpse. An act of love. But imperfect because the object murdered was not the object loved," he seemed to evaluate Blue's confession.

"What terrible perversion, to believe that—even for you," the priest said.

"An act of love, perversion?" Richard said.

"To call murder an act of love— . . ."

"The ultimate purification of another, perhaps," said Richard.

"We're balancing the scales, Father!" Malissa said. "An *accurate* evaluation!"

"Don't listen to them!" Valerie yelled at the priest as if she were afraid they might win him over.

"I can't conceive of an instance where that could be true," Jeremy answered Richard. "Love unites, murder alienates. It's the difference between communion and sin: Irreconcilable absolutes."

"Murder performed to purify," said Richard.

Valerie's hand clutched her brother's arm.

"When the Duke— . . ." began la Duquesa. But the rest of the words were impossible to form now. The myth of her love lay shattered.

Richard asked the priest swiftly: "To whom do you confess, Father?"—echoing his son's earlier unanswered question.

"To another priest," said Jeremy.

"But what can a priest—a pure, young priest—confess to?" Malissa asked.

Richard's eyes pulled Blue's onto the priest.

The smile on Blue's face drowned in a sea of dark expressions. "Now you," he said to the priest.

18

"I have nothing to confess to you," said the priest in a firm voice. (*A hand, blood.*)

"There is always something to confess," said Malissa. She aimed recklessly: "Someone you killed!" Her hands, cupped, offered the last word to the priest like a present. Quickly, she withdrew them—tearing jeweled claws again—and she laughed.

"Or someone you wanted—want—*have* to kill!" came Tarah's sudden words, but they were directed threateningly at Richard. She understood Malissa had offered the act of murder as confession only as the worst for the priest to refute.

"Or someone you couldn't live without—and so perhaps you hastened the absence," said Karen.

"Confessions deal with a powerful figure in one's life! An act!" Malissa coaxed the priest.

"Who was it in your life, Father?" Mark looked down at his own body, stretched lazily. Quickly he intercepted Joja's eyes on him.

Then Richard moved in on the priest like a deadly animal about to attack.

The marble-blue stare of the mamaloi and the papaloi burrowed into the priest. The red beads on the rattles shone like drops of liquid fire, burning blood.

"Was it a woman?" Richard thrust suddenly at the priest.

"Or a man!" Malissa followed swiftly.

"A woman!"

"A man!"

"A woman!"

"A man!"

"A woman!"

The priest stared expressionless at them.

Then Richard broke the mesmerizing rhythm, leaving a funneling vacuum of silence. He shattered it abruptly, his words tossed violently like stones into a lake, trembling currents swallowing others: "Since we can't arrive at the gender of the person we seek in the Father's life, we'll refer to that person as him-her-it!"

"Don't call my mother that!" the priest fell into the trap.

"Oh, is the game called Catch, Richard?" Malissa asked delightedly.

"And so we've found the powerful figure," said Richard without surprise.

"And so easily," Malissa said with an edge of disappointment.

The priest forced his composure. He would not allow them a shade of victory. "Why should you want to hear about that? It couldn't interest your jaded curiosity for horror—because I loathed my mother purely— . . ." *Loathed!* The accidental word reverberated in the priest's mind like the pealing of an infernal bell sounding doom. "I meant that I *loved* her purely," he corrected himself hastily.

"Pure loathing," Richard said.

Mark said: "A confession can be one word."

"Indeed!" Malissa approved.

The rattles hissed before the priest. He was aware of a lovely scent. As if the rattles were emitting it, it surrounded him like mist. Instinctively he turned his head, avoiding breathing it. "I clearly meant I *loved* her," he repeated. "It was a logical, perhaps inevitable, slip in view of the constant recitation of hatred in this house."

Richard's unyielding stare, Mark's lips parted as if to form a question, Malissa's savage, wounding smile, Blue's accusatory eyes, almost black: They attacked the priest silently.

He knew: They had seized the slip as the key to the confession they wanted to extract from him. Because of that, his love was on trial. He would defend it, easily: "If I hadn't loved her, with all my heart, how else could I have stood the recurrent illnesses which ruled her life and therefore mine?" That memory freed another: "The odor of death," he remembered aloud, "hung about us constantly." He added quickly: "And it was made tolerable only by the very love you question."

"Death smells like sex," said Blue.

"Rancid," said Karen.

Albert touched his hand to his lips, as if to block the words forming.

"If I hadn't loved her," the priest continued his defense, "would I have allowed her life to absorb my own?"

"And she loved you, very much," Mark drawled.

Looking at the boy, hearing the soft words, Joja thought of Mark's mother.

"So much," Jeremy said, "that she couldn't bear to die without me." (*Death. The body, still fighting, surrendered—the soul shrieked into eternity, howling its loss. Rage, pity, love—a war of emotions.*)

"And you couldn't bear to see her die, without you," Richard said.

"Yes," Jeremy said. "I couldn't." Don't breathe deeply! he thought as the rattles hissed again. The drug which forces confessions, *la malaspina,* he reminded himself, dismissing the thought quickly; he would not allow himself to be trapped by their calculated props. "And so there is nothing here for your scrutiny," he finished.

"Of course not," Richard said. "You've convinced us that the slip was indeed accidental. Clearly you meant 'loved.' Not 'loathed.' An accident—and not the representation of the dichotomy in your life: not a confusion between love and hate."

"Confuse the two?" Malissa pretended outraged incredulity. "Why, it would be as difficult—or as easy!—to confuse good and evil, reality and dreams, God and Satan!"

"I don't share that confusion," the priest understood her taunt. "Love frees, and hatred ties— . . ."

"You were close to her, to your mother," Richard said.

The priest's hands locked tightly: a chain: "Bound together like— . . ." he began, and stopped, knowing again he had sprung a waiting trap.

"But love frees," Richard seized his words expertly, "and hatred binds—you said 'ties.' "

"Words change their meaning," the priest said. Now he inhaled, deeply.

"And yet you've upheld—your phrase—the existence of 'irreconcilable absolutes' throughout the evening," Richard countered. "Does 'loathe' then change into 'love'?"

"Of course not; you don't— . . ."

"Love unites, murder alienates—you said that

earlier," Richard's rapid verbal assault continued. "You could not conceive of murder as an act of love. But now you say love frees, and hatred ties. Which is it? Which, Father!" And now he struck: "You hated her."

"Shut up!" Jeremy's fists hardened. The eyes darkened in his blood-drained face.

"And you wished her dead," Richard pronounced.

"No!" Jeremy protested. But suddenly a note of pleading entered his firm voice.

"The lifting of a heavy weight, Father," Paul's voice offered. "If you verbalize it— . . ."

Had her brother joined the interrogators? Valerie saw the intimate stranger.

The priest heard his voice protest: "I even stood and watched her as she died as if that way— . . ." *As if that way I could die with her.* Those words, formed in his mind, were blocked as the rattles trembled in a frenzy before him: glittering beads like tiny, coaxing demon-eyes.

The priest heard his voice finish: " . . . —as if that way I would force her finally to leave me!" Had he truly uttered those words—not the words he had intended? The part of him that resisted this confession listened in astonishment, in shock, to the echo of the words wrenched from him by a force too powerful to overcome. Something *made* me speak those words! he told himself in disbelief. The drug— . . . *La malaspina!* Is it real then?

The demonic rattles! Again they trembled, seemed to exhale.

Now the priest breathed deeply again, defiantly. Suddenly he was two people—one listening, the other speaking; one resisting, the other anxious to surrender; confessor and confessee: one ripped apart from the other by the sundering confusion of accidental words. Then the resisting part of him whispered calmly to Richard, and to the part of himself that had spoken the unwelcome words: "You've tricked me into pronouncing those words—but that's all."

"Tell us!" Blue shouted at the priest. "Get out of your fucking dark confessional, man! Become human!"

Become human.

Become human!

Become human!

Human— . . . That?—Blue's exhortation; an accusation?—a judgment? The incongruous, suddenly assaulting memory of their hands touching briefly in the grotto? Or was it the overwhelming, suddenly lovely scent, lulling him?—just that? Or would he offer the words to them willingly only so they would not pry them even more threateningly from him? Or to prove his mangled humanity? What made Jeremy at last form words long entombed in icy darkness?: "She clung to my hand, my mother," the words had already Escaped, "and she cried, 'Don't let me die!—I love you!'—her bloodless, dying hand still clutched mine!" He touched his own hand, withdrawing one from the other swiftly; remembering: "I pushed it away—finally! I yelled, 'Let me go!' I remember: Blood! And then I flung her hand away! And I ran out!" The words hurtled against the blackness of the calm, apathetic glass dome. He waited as if the silence would pronounce an inevitable judgment. Then: "Is that what you wanted to hear?" he flung at Richard and Malissa. "Does *that* make me human?" he asked Blue.

Blue frowned, as if the question merited long, careful deliberation. Slowly, he shook his head: slowly: No.

"Then you meant what you said," Karen sighed wearily at the priest. "You loathed her." (*"I hate you!" "No, no, baby, no!"*)

"My love for her was real," the priest still defended, "and it was love—crushed, mangled by her brutal demands for my life. She drained—like a vampire ... But even then there were times when love shattered the hatred; times when hatred shattered the love. Love— ..."

Stop there! Tarah's mind exhorted him. She knew: Yes, she yearned for him. And it was his purity she desired. Is that what they sought to destroy with his confession? *Stop there!*

"The tumbling tower," Malissa named the card of the Tarot that Mark had chosen for the priest earlier.

"Or is it still to crumble?" Mark asked casually.

"You have to pick up memories from the grave," la Duquesa said sorrowfully. "Perhaps something miraculous will make them grow."

The priest exhaled the perfumed air.

"And then?" Mark asked.

"Then I became a priest," Jeremy said.

"The pure—grasping—love of a mother," Malissa spat her evaluation of the priest's confession. "The equally pure love of her son! Like a fake jewel!" she buried the words. "Like la Duquesa's imaginary love—Rev's courage! Tor's inflated body! And Savannah's purity!"

"Purity," Richard echoed. A clue to a profound mystery, the word hovered over them. Silence gathered as if by a conspiracy of sound and motion: a waiting, stark, demanding presence.

Then sound and motion resumed as if on direct order of Malissa's commanding hands: as if a movie reel, merely stopped to capture a single frame—order within the tumbling anarchy—had begun again. "The game! Confessions!" Malissa said hungrily.

"Miss Malissa requests that the game continue!" Topaze announced like a page.

"And so you fled!" Malissa assaulted the priest.

"To insulate yourself against the roar of life," Richard said.

Tarah stood near the priest, to convey her strength to him, to allow him to withstand them. *He* must resist them. An alliance with him? she wondered. Or did she merely feel drawn magnetically to his fierce, inviolate sensuality? (his naked body—the image lodged in her mind)—was she determined to keep the appearance of purity, even if it was not real?

"He sheltered himself within the confessional," Mark said as if reciting an anecdote. "Easy to listen to life, there. His world was peopled by cold statues in a church. Statues without eyes."

Jeremy remembered: The statues in the dark alcove. Among the lush embracing trees, the glorious star-shattered flowers, they had seemed to listen, to watch raptly.

"All filtered by stained-glass windows!" Malissa stood near the priest, separating him and Tarah, to sever the current of strength she detected between them.

"He didn't give a damn about anyone or anything except his own beautiful salvation," Bravo joined the interrogators.

"He was afraid of the world." Valerie heard Paul's words without shock this time.

Now Blue's eyes were like dark fire on the priest: "You ran away," he said in judgment. "You lived only with shadows and whispers, and those belonged to others. Man, you tried to Escape all righteous human contact."

Raided furiously by their words, "It's not true!" the priest said finally.

"Then tell us," said Blue. The smile lingered incongruously on his lips. "You said you wouldn't run away again—not ever—and that means from your head too, man. Face your memories! Become human!" he repeated the powerful, accusatory words.

Jeremy knew: Now he would allow himself, and them, to listen to other voices long stifled in the past. "It's not possible to Escape," he said. "Life attacks. It comes roaring at you."

"The game is confession," Malissa's voice was solemn. The rattles hissed.

And again the priest breathed very deeply. "Even within what you call the shadows of the church— ..." he began: Not a confession, no; he would not confess to them, he insisted to himself: What he had already verbalized—and what he would now say: that was his bid to join the savage humanity he stood accused of fleeing only in self-protection. And perhaps too—suddenly!—was there something of cunning? Had his stance indeed been too rarefied, too distant? In revealing himself as vulnerable, might he then be able to enlist the others to move against the gathering tide of evil in this house? Indeed, he glanced at Tor, Savannah, Rev—still restive—la Duquesa: Was there in them something to be resurrected to avenge the slaughter?—and in those who might follow. The priest said: "There was a youngman—I saw him often, always sitting in the front pew when I said Mass, always watching me— ..."

"And you were aware of him." Blue stared into his hand, directing the priest's eyes there; a reminder of a silent promise witnessed by shadows and blind statues?

"Not until later—in retrospect—when he came to the rectory, one night, late; it was raining," the priest said. " 'I need you!—we need you!' he told me. A woman was dying, his friend, he said."

Tarah felt a sense of premature defeat.

"We sped in his car. To an old house. Up dark steps, along a maze of hallways, yellow lights, yellow shadows—the youngman with me." Specters locked in the prison of the priest's mind sprang forth starkly now: "Doors opened, seminude women—black-strapped leather corsets cutting into the white flesh—they stood in the hall, terrible leering painted faces staring at me— . . ." He thrust the images at Blue as Blue had thrust the images of his private hell at him.

"You were in a brothel," Tarah understood, and her heart felt smothered.

"Yes! And through the open doors," the priest rushed, as if, once spoken, the words and the images would die forever, "I could see: Bodies laid out like aroused corpses." Now he addressed la Duquesa, forcing himself to face her: "We entered a room, semidarkness like gray velvet, some of the women I had seen in the hall crowded in, like a tattered army. A woman was lying on a bed, moaning, in labor."

Tarah said: "She was bearing your child?" She felt afraid of the answer.

"And the youngman?" Blue asked the priest.

"He just stood there and watched me as intently as he did at Mass. His eyes were like scalpels." Jeremy went on: "The face on the bed was soft, childlike, as if a very small girl had painted herself, her hair was bleached, her lips an orange heart. Her painted fingernails clutched at her swollen stomach. I touched her—in fascination. Something was wrapped about her waist! Bandages! I unwound them. And I knew then that the . . . creature . . . in labor was . . . was— . . . !"

"A man!" la Duquesa hurled the word at him.

"Yes!" the priest whispered. "A . . . man! Then I saw a small bundle pressed against his stomach. It was a doll.

A tiny grotesque little carnival celluloid doll; the man had tied it to his stomach. And the doll was painted pink, yellow, blue. It had green-dyed feathers and sequins!" He stopped, to contain the assault of memory. "The women in the room began to laugh, their mouths were red—as if they had been smeared with blood —..."

Valerie closed her eyes.

"Then the man on the bed," the priest continued, "brought the doll to his chest, to feed it from his false breasts! And with a sigh ending the simulated labor, he fainted! ... I turned angrily to question the youngman who had brought me there. He shouted at me, *'This is where life is!'* "

Gathered, the silence now flowed like a river.

"So you see," Jeremy said, "you were wrong. I only tried to Escape."

As terrible as the images evoked had been, nothing the young priest had said had violated his ... purity— his *sexual* purity. And that was important to her: Tarah breathed easily.

Blue stood before the priest. "No, you couldn't run away. Nor ever, man. And now here you are, like the rest of us."

19

Savannah stood up, like a ghost in search of flesh.

"Now who, Richard?" Malissa would not allow a moment's respite. It was all moving too excitingly, too perfectly; a pause would thwart the gathering momentum. She craved more.

As if in answer, Richard, the mamaloi, and the papaloi stood in a triangle, Richard at its head, like an arrow aimed between Valerie and Paul.

Swiftly Mark stood beside the twins—but apart: as if to juxtapose himself with them.

Valerie's heart beat against the wall of her ears. Or was it her brother's heartbeat she heard?

"Leave them alone!" It was Tarah.

The priest had stationed himself beside Valerie. "She has nothing for you to destroy!" He felt even stronger now: The revelation of vulnerability had called up all his power to resist.

Blue stood a distance from the priest, to observe him more totally.

Paul looked at his sister, then at Richard, as if ruled by two powerful currents. Now he met her imploring gaze—and he nodded: as if (or did she merely imagine this? she questioned herself, reality occurring suddenly in shifting waves)—as if exhorting her to look at Richard.

She met Richard's look.

And he was smiling at her. And so was Paul now, a mirror-image of Richard.

She felt a violent implosion within her, a smashing. Behind closed eyes she tried to seal the shattered world. Blackness would restructure it.

Frantically Tarah turned to Karen: "It's your turn, Karen!" she said quickly, to draw the attention from Paul and Valerie. "Your confesssion is next!" She was almost pleading. And her tactic had worked:

Richard faced his third wife.

Almost too willing to release Paul and Valerie from scrutiny, Malissa thought.

"I confess to the violation of purity!" Karen said suddenly.

"And to hatred for Richard!" Tarah tried to draw the essential words from her, her tactic reinforced now, against Richard.

"Yes, to that too!" Bravo spoke for Karen.

"Tell us!" Tarah insisted.

"I was pure when he married me," Karen said.

"And what sullied that . . . purity, Karen?" Richard asked.

"You! When you led me to my mother—naked, in bed, groveling with another woman!" she yelled at him.

"He exposed it," said Mark. He looked at Joja, to extract her allegiance again: a reminder of the extortion?

The actress stared coldly at the boy. She deliberately withheld her needed support against Karen's assertion. Withheld it longer. Still longer. Mark's lips parted; he drew his tongue over them, looking down at his body. And Joja responded: "And Richard's action released you, Karen."

"I loved my mother *because* she was pure," Karen said. "And then Richard opened the door into the room where she and the other woman were, legs tangled, breasts—. . . 'There is your purity!' Richard said to me; and then I hated her, I wanted to kill her, I rushed at her—. . ."

"Your mother had made you frigid," said Joja. Mark's acknowledgment of her renewed allegiance: He touched his body. "And Richard freed you," Joja continued.

Tarah glared fiercely at the actress. Still a witness for the defense of Richard. "And then he didn't want you," Tarah reminded Karen.

"But he had freed you," Joja uttered words; she still faced Mark.

"*Now* she's free of him!" Bravo said.

"Is she, Richard?" Malissa questioned cunningly.

Karen moved slowly toward Richard, as if finally to confront him.

"How dare you bring us to this depraved place?" Valerie was able at last to form the accusation.

"I invited you," Richard said.

"How dare you expose us to all this? Paul isn't aware of what's occurring here," she said, avoiding looking at the stranger her brother was becoming.

"But you, Valerie, are you aware?" said Richard. The question was emphatic—the answer important.

"I do know, Valerie," Paul's voice filled the silence.

Richard turned away.

"This isn't our world!" Valerie shouted.

Now Richard seemed to wait for words which perhaps only she could pronounce.

"Such moving love," Malissa's lips barely touched the last word. "This brother and his sister!"

"It is, yes, it is!" said la Duquesa. "Why don't you leave it alone?"

Valerie said to Malissa: "You don't understand it because it's pure."

"Pure," Richard pronounced.

"If Daniel were here— . . ." Valerie tossed the unfinished threat at Richard.

"Daniel agreed to your coming," he said.

"But he didn't know what you'd expose us to!" Valerie protested.

"He knew," Richard said. "He's known all along."

Tarah realized: He would reveal to Paul and Valerie in brutal moments the horror withheld from them for years. As if to render the inevitable less painful by shortening it—if only that—Tarah rushed words: "Your father made an arrangement with Richard."

"Your father gave you to me," Richard said.

The mamaloi and the papaloi became rigid. Erect, painted, black corpses.

Richard's words released others in Valerie's consciousness: *Suicide! Murder! A trial!*

Paul made no reaction of surprise.

"How can you *give* people?" Jeremy said.

"He *sold* them!" Malissa understood. "And later Daniel murdered Hester!" The wild jeweled gestures of her hands turned inward now, devoured themselves hungrily.

Mark's face registered interest.

Even though her hands blocked her ears, Valerie had heard Malissa's words. "He didn't!" she shouted. And remembered: *Whispered voices quickly silenced by her presence.* All a nightmare in reverse: as if she were wakening *into* it.

"He was tried for her murder!" Tarah once again attempted to rush the climax, to render it less cruel—and perhaps to propel them into leaving before— . . .

"No!" Valerie insisted.

"Your father gave you to me before you were conceived," said Richard.

The words bolted out of Valerie: "If Daniel were here, he'd kill you, Richard!"

"Can this nightmare be possible? What are you trying to discover?" the priest blurted at Richard.

Mark awaited his father's answer.

But there was none.

"No one buys anyone," Valerie seized control.

"Your father had an expensive habit—his money was all gone. In drugs." Richard's calm voice belied the brutal words.

"Lies!" said Valerie.

"He's telling the truth," Paul accepted easily.

Eagerly? Did he already know? Since when? Had

Richard told him only earlier? The blue moments—
... Valerie looked at Richard with a rage which flooded over to her brother.

"I needed a child," said Richard.

"But I was going to have Gable—you knew I carried him," Tarah said.

"I needed another," Richard said. "At the same time."

"What were you plotting even then?" Tarah asked. "What demonic experiment were you already preparing?"

The rarefied years. The beautiful seclusion. It was over. What was important now was to save Paul, Valerie knew.

Still calmly, almost gently, Richard went on pronouncing the terrible words: "Your father didn't want to be sure, ever, that the child which would result from that night was really his. Or mine."

"Oh, God!" the priest understood.

"Both of them took her!" Tarah yelled. "They called it: Sexual roulette!"

Malissa glanced at Paul, then Mark.

"You may be their father, then—and still you allow — . . ." the priest started.

"It's all a lie!" Valerie shouted. "None of this is happening!"

"I fled with Gable, to protect him from this hungry evil," Tarah said. "But that's what you counted on all along. . . . *Is it, Richard!*"

"And because of remorse for the disgusting agreement," the priest said, "their father killed the poor woman."

"Hester agreed to the arrangement," Richard said slowly. Then to Paul and Valerie: "Daniel did not kill Hester."

"I knew it," Valerie said.

"Did *you* kill her, Richard?" Malissa said.

"She committed suicide," Richard said; "she deliberately made it appear like murder so Daniel would be punished." Again the sound of the terrible words was incongruous, the voice almost compassionate.

"What is the purpose of these hideous revelations?" said the priest.

"What is the purpose of confession?" Richard countered.

"How she must have loathed Daniel, to long so powerfully for revenge, even with her life," said Tarah.

"But she didn't have the courage to kill him herself," Richard said to Tarah.

"How do you throttle evil like yours?" the priest pronounced the overt declaration of war on Richard.

"You exorcise it with a stake," Mark said with a smile.

I have to save Paul! The thought draped Valerie's mind like a shroud. Suddenly she embraced her brother. Tightly. Paul's body pressed against his sister's. Richard's gaze did not waver. Then the tight embrace ended. Valerie turned to the priest, feeling an accusation. She had to explain: "I have to save him, Father! From *them!*"

Jeremy turned away from the girl's intensity, which judged him ambiguously. Blue's cold eyes pounced on him.

"Are you one of them too?" Valerie asked the priest. And she moved apart from them all.

"Oh, splendid!" said Malissa. "A beautiful game! Superbly played! The best in a lifetime of seasons!" Fed by the crushed lives, she looked sinisterly beautiful. "But now the most crucial aspect of the game: We must not allow it to lag!" Her hands seemed determined to set the very air into motion. "There is still much more!"

A deliberate postponement: Richard had turned from Valerie and Paul. Tarah, Jeremy flanked the twins like guards.

"Topaze!" Richard's pronouncement of the midget's name announced his willing retreat from the twins.

The crucial test of his permanent position in the entourage? Topaze looked beseechingly at Malissa.

The impervious purple-glassed eyes told him she would leave him to survive the attention on his own: The encounter might provide a few moments of amusement.

"What's it like to be a dwarf?" Rev tossed at Topaze.

Topaze winced at the despised word. "I'm not a *dwarf!* I'm a *midget!*" he protested.

"A freak!" Rev was re-entering the arena of power.

"I'm not a *freak*," Topaze shouted, "I'm perfectly formed, and my cock— . . ." Then desperately he jumped into the air. Challenging space, he somersaulted in a full, perfect, graceful loop. He landed expertly, flawlessly on his feet, his cavalier's hat slicing in a flourish before him. And he smiled anxiously.

Now Malissa released him from the scrutiny: "And *that* is Topaze's confession!" she allowed gaily.

Topaze looked gratefully at her.

Rev felt as if he had been abandoned in a glaring, hostile, savage light.

"Let Albert confess." It was Bravo.

The smile fled Malissa's face.

"I've told you he has nothing to say," said Malissa.

"But you said earlier that there is *always* something to confess, Malissa," Bravo reminded her. "Let's all play the game!" She glanced at Richard, and she nodded. That glance, that nod—they told him that for the purpose of these moments—and only these moments, because she despised him—they might become allies: "Is the game still called Catch, Malissa?" she taunted.

"Catch Malissa?" Richard asked wryly. "No one can . . . catch . . . Malissa."

"Kneel!" Bravo commanded Albert suddenly.

"I forbid it!" Malissa said.

Terrified, Albert looked from one woman to the other.

Bravo's whip cracked over the man's head. "Kneel!"

"He does what *I* say," Malissa said.

"We'll see!" said Bravo. She would take a dangerous risk: She had humiliated Rev, yes—but by that very fact she might restore his posture for her purpose: her early victim, an ally for now. "Rev!" she plunged. Her desperate risk worked:

Rev joined her swiftly. There was power there too, and Malissa was irrevocably through with him.

Malissa understood the alliance: Bravo was moving to trap Albert.

Bravo said: "Open your vest, Rev!"

"Don't, Rev!" Malissa shouted.

Rev opened the black leather vest, exhibiting the tangle of tattoos.

"He *did* it, Miss Malissa!" Topaze gasped incredulously. "He disobeyed you!"

"Look, Albert," Bravo parodied admiration, "aren't Rev's tattoos beautiful on his bare flesh?"

Albert moved toward Rev's torso.

"Albert!" Malissa barked.

Albert froze. He had become a mere object between two storming vortexes of power.

Bravo was already saying to Rev: "Take your vest off!"

Rev removed the leather vest.

Albert swayed in fascination.

"Move back, Albert!" came Malissa's voice. Her rubied hands destroyed the air before her.

Retreating, Albert pulled his eyes from Rev's tight torso.

Malissa smiled.

Bravo commanded with just one word: "Rev!"

Exuding the violent sexuality, Rev stretched his body.

Albert's eyes were riveted to it.

"He's moving closer, Miss Malissa!" Topaze announced.

"Go to your room, Albert!" Malissa demanded.

Albert began to move away.

Bravo intercepted him, forcing him to turn. "Look!"

Rev allowed his hand to dangle lazily over his own groin.

"If you kneel, you can have him!" Bravo struck.

Panting, Albert knelt.

Bravo exhaled in triumph. "You see, Malissa, he *did* kneel!" she said victoriously.

Malissa felt defeat strike like a bullet in her heart. She struggled to regain control. "Get up!" she barked at Albert, her hands like swift swords.

Inches from Rev, the kneeling man did not respond.

"*Get up!*" Malissa commanded.

Albert was like a statue before Rev.

"Miss Malissa *demands* that you get up, Albert!" Topaze growled.

Rev looked boldly at Malissa, then down at Albert. *His* triumph.

Now Bravo circled the kneeling man like a panther. "Albert, tell us— . . ." she began.

"I forbid this!" said Malissa. She faced Richard.

Richard did not intercede.

Mark smiled.

"Tell us about Malissa!" came Bravo's voice.

Hypnotized by the scene, as if they were witnessing the swaying of cobras, the others watched the confrontation.

"Tell them, Albert!" la Duquesa said suddenly. "Finally free yourself from her!"

"What does she do with the entourage once she's through?" When Albert did not speak, Bravo motioned to Rev, who understood:

He spread his thighs, boots planted firmly.

"She— . . . She— . . ." came Albert's tortured voice.

"What!" Bravo demanded.

"Sometimes— . . ." he started.

"Albert!" Malissa's lips thrust the name.

Albert shook his head.

Aware that he was wavering—that she must move swiftly—Bravo signaled Rev again: He reached for Albert's head, as if to pull it against his body. Instead, he held it away.

Paul blocked Valerie's view. She heard only words.

"Tell us, Albert!" Bravo commanded.

"She killed— . . ." he stammered.

Malissa rushed at him. But her words were controlled: "You lying fool," she said. "Shut up, now, or I'll— . . ."

"Miss Malissa is: going: to commit: *you:* Albert!" Topaze warned in a clipped voice.

Bravo blocked Malissa. "She won't do anything to you, Albert. I'll protect you. And you can have Rev!"

"She pushed one . . . out of a window when he— . . . He was a beautiful youngman," Albert said. His gaze was pasted to Rev's thighs.

"Liar," Malissa said calmly.

"And once— . . . she gave heroin to— . . . Then she deprived him—for entertainment."

"Albert's imagination!" came Malissa's steely laughter. Bravo signaled Rev to move back.

Albert shouted: "She uses their blood to stay young!"

"You stupid madman," said Malissa. "I'll commit you for all your lies."

Apart from the others, Valerie saw the strange scene, heard the strange words. Are we in hell or in an insane asylum? she thought. It was as if they were all objects in a terrifying experiment. Suddenly disoriented, she looked at the dome over them. The black sky.

Tor's body tensed, as if to stir the blood within him.

A potential ally? Jeremy wondered.

Albert's imploring look begged to consummate the contact with Rev.

Malissa's jeweled fingers tore the air. Now she moved in with deadly accuracy: "Tell us about Karen, Bravo!"

"Leave her out!" Bravo warned. She glanced quickly at Karen.

"Confessions are sometimes made with a single glance," Malissa interpreted. "You won't get her, Bravo!" She looked at Richard: a reminder: allies against Bravo.

Bravo struck her own thigh with the whip. "We'll see!" she said. Then she knew: She must possess Karen before them all—*that* would be her true victory. She turned savagely to the kneeling man. "I'll let you have Rev if you tell us: What the hell are you to Malissa? Who the hell are you?"

Rev's hand relaxed its grip on Albert's straining head—but only for an instant; it still held it away. Albert's mouth gaped in expectation.

"Tell us!" Bravo shouted.

"I'm— . . ." Albert stuttered.

"Albert!" Malissa flung the name like a sentence of execution.

"Her father," Albert whimpered. "I'm Malissa's father."

20

Malissa towered over Albert. With abysmal disgust she formed one word: "Filthy," she said.

"Confess, Malissa!" Bravo hammered ruthlessly.

Malissa defied the rattles suddenly raised before her by the black man and woman—her hands stopped the terrible hissing. "Confess to what?" her words defied too.

"Perhaps to a father who molested you," Bravo grasped, "and whom you've paid back with interest!"

"Albert is insane," Malissa said evenly. The purple-shielded eyes turned on Bravo. Your time will come, she thought, I'll slaughter you.

Perspiring, flushed, Albert quivered toward Rev's spread thighs—but Rev still awaited the signal from Bravo. Indifferently Bravo motioned him to move away. Instantly he released Albert's head—and he turned from the whimpering man.

Albert closed his eyes.

La Duquesa held out her hand to him, to help him up.

"Thank you, your grace," Albert said.

"The Duke was kind," the words echoed beyond her control as she attempted the painful reconstruction of her dream of love.

"He *is* your father!" Bravo pursued Malissa.

"He's a babbling liar," Malissa said.

The black ring on her finger: Blue saw it. Then he

looked at the night-encased dome over them: like a huge magnification of the pearled ring thrust accusingly at heaven.

"Whoever you are," Jeremy questioned Albert, "whatever you are to her, how did you come to be so utterly in her power?"

Albert released the buried words: "I was afraid."

"No!" Malissa shouted. "It was because I knew the shape of power!" The jeweled hands rose: Slowly. They opened into wide stars—which she crushed suddenly into fists: a hint of the convolution that had brought Albert down.

"Why don't you kill her, Albert?" Bravo said calmly; she nodded to Rev.

With equal, cold amusement—soaring on the crashing waves of power—Rev pushed his knife on the floor toward Albert.

Malissa glanced at it as if it were an insect.

Albert bent, retrieved the knife from the black and white swirl of the floor; he held it in his hand—and he stared at Malissa.

"Think of all the tortures," Bravo said. "If you use it, Albert, you can control the entourage."

"Cut her guts out!" Rev yelled.

"Use it," Bravo said calmly.

Albert dropped the knife. "I can't."

"Why?" Bravo demanded harshly.

How far would they have gone? *Was* it merely the ritual of evil? Jeremy wondered.

Malissa laughed. "Why? Because he's as much of a coward as Rev."

"No, Malissa," came Albert's injured voice. "It's because . . . I . . . still . . . love you."

Malissa was before him. "Don't use that word before

me!" she commanded ferociously. Her hand reached out to strike him. But she withdrew it. Even that amount of contact would contaminate her.

Then she moved away from Albert. No—she discarded him.

"And now you, Richard," Tarah's voice ended the silence. "Let's hear *your* confession. We must all play the game." And so she had renewed the assault which Joja had aborted earlier. It had to be now—the moment when there was an implied split between Richard and Malissa: Would Malissa join the attack? And who else?

"Yes, now you, Richard, you play!" Heady with her success with Albert, Bravo joined Tarah. She must attack now, in front of Karen.

Karen stood erectly as if she realized she would be the prize in this challenge.

Tarah had gambled on Bravo's support. But could she still count on Karen?

Mark glanced immediately at Joja.

The actress withheld any indication of her allegiance: the steady reminder to Mark that it was not absolute.

Mark touched his neck.

Now Joja moved toward Richard.

"You don't need him, Joja!" Tarah asserted. She had deliberately not named the object of that need: Richard? Mark?

Bravo sensed a disturbing reaction in Karen, an uncontrolled, barely perceptible thrust of her body toward Richard. "Nor do you," she addressed Karen firmly. "You don't need Richard."

"None of us needs him!" Tarah said. "He's just managed to make us feel so. Destroy the figment of his power—merely by turning away from it—and you destroy him!" she moved. "Yes, let's play confession, Richard! Perhaps your confession will free us all!" She turned to the black man and black woman. "Now shake your rattles before him!"

The mamaloi and the papaloi did not move.

Tarah's eyes openly enlisted Malissa.

Malissa waited.

"Stand before him!" Bravo shouted forcefully at the black man and black woman.

Mark said quickly: "But there's been so little from you, Bravo."

"And from you!" Bravo turned on the boy.

Tarah allowed the attention to shift. She might be able to use Mark's words in her move against his father.

The boy was being challenged! To be questioned. About Richard? Malissa welcomed the spectacle. In any event. If the boy trapped Bravo— . . .

Bravo commanded the black man and woman: "Stand beside Mark!"

Again they did not move.

Bravo raised her whip in menace.

Still, they did not move.

Mark said easily to them: "Stand beside me." Somberly, they did. Painted, black bodies. "This is what you wanted?" the boy asked Bravo. "And now what?"

Tarah advanced swiftly: "Tell us what it's like to live with Richard!" she said. "To grow up in his rancid evil."

"Living without secrets," Mark answered without hesitation. "Without fear. . . . Do you want to justify the life you've imposed on Gable by questioning mine?" he accused Tarah.

Was it so! Had she come back to confront Richard? Only for that? Or to justify the life she had created for her son? To destroy her doubts, *"Play your own god-*

208 · *The Vampires*

damn game, Richard!" she yelled, turning again to Richard, and away from Mark's accusation.

Rev touched the knife in his pocket. He might *still* become an instrument of power. Tarah's. He took a step to join her.

"Yes, Richard, now you." Even as she heard the echo of her own words, Malissa wondered whether she should pull them back.

"Is it now, Malissa?" Richard asked her.

And was it indeed now? Join Tarah and Bravo, for these moments; an allegiance of enemies? she wondered. It would be a formidable alliance! But no. There was still the play, the waiting dark stage. And, importantly, there was this: Her own confrontation of Richard must be— . . . Her mind, pausing long, chose the word carefully: Pure. . . . Her smile on Richard withdrew the challenge for now.

"Your confession, Richard!" Tarah repeated obsessively.

Mark's face: His eyes: Reflecting the exposed sky, they were black, black.

Joja: Her hand: On the scar Richard had made years ago, the scar Mark had brushed with his lips. Suddenly: She had assumed he was enlisting her against Tarah, on Richard's behalf. But—and this was the sudden thought—would it be, ultimately, against Richard, against his own father, that he would attempt to use her? Swimming precariously within the waves of the boy's sensuality, Joja felt afraid.

"Confess, Richard!" Tarah's words pounded.

"Confess?" Richard said softly, with amusement. And then fiercely: "Why did you come back?" he fired at Joja. Allowing no answer: "And you Karen?" he demanded. "Tarah?"

"To kill you," Tarah said.

Richard's smile received the verbalized challenge with something of admiration.

Again silence was trapped in a violent maelstrom.

Tor stood up, his body flexed, assuring itself recurrently of life. Savannah studied the servants gliding about the house: Live shadows.

Suddenly Paul felt like a stranger in a foreign country who discovers that he knows all its streets and alleys, although he has not been there before. Only the climate of this beautiful island had been required to stir into fruition the emotions burgeoning within him.

Valerie was the first to see the gossamer white figure floating down the stairs—a woman beautiful yet terrifying. In lace, like a violated bride. Her eyes glowed in the pale, demented face.

Now the priest saw the woman approaching like a frantic ghost. The white lace clung to her slender legs.

Paul saw her. Then the others.

A vision of faded purity, the white figure moved ineluctably toward Richard.

Swiftly, Mark advanced to meet her.

As if assaulted by the piercing fragment of a broken memory, the woman in white turned her head away from the boy.

Now Richard moved ahead of Mark.

The boy stood beside him, quickly.

"Mother," Mark said to the woman in white.

The glass dome revealed a silver-black sky.

"We've been waiting for you to join us, Lianne," Richard said to his second wife.

Lianne seemed to attempt to recognize the faces before her, to locate them within the lucid patches of her ravished mind. "Have you already begun the games? One year— . . ." She wiped away the unformed words with a vague motion of rejection. "They said I— . . . Their words were— . . . They said I *rushed* into insanity!—and they were talking about me! . . . What is the game, Richard?"

What horrors has she been exposed to? Jeremy wondered.

Joja's eyes followed Mark, who stared relentlessly at his mother, the spectral smile just barely forming on his face. Jealousy stirring; a violent sense of rivalry within Joja. Without reason, she told herself.

Thoughts swam turbulently in Valerie's mind as she studied the woman in white.

Tarah faced Richard. "I accept all your corruption —but this!—to bring this insane creature here!"

"How dare you call me that!" Lianne turned on Tarah. "I'm blessed with— . . . With Richard!" she finished. "Every day was night, I remember the darkness, laughter trapped in it! Who are you?" she asked la Duquesa. "Death!" Lianne recoiled. "That death exists— . . ." She emitted a terrible scream, a howl— the scream that had rent the house earlier and had seemed to summon them together into this domed hall. "I want to live eternally!" She stretched her lithe body, as if to stretch her life. "I wouldn't even hate hell—if we were alive there."

Richard kissed her, gently, very long.

Her body relaxed.

When he released her slowly, she whirled around toward the others. "To exorcise evil you have to slaughter it!" Facing Mark directly—but not looking at him—she clasped her hands before her; and she raised them, as if clutching a deadly stake. "And the heart is the source of evil!" She plunged down with all her force: miming exorcism: the burying of a deadly stake into an astonished heart. Then she said: "The mamaloi and the papaloi always precede murder. Will you be the murderer or the murdered?" she asked the priest.

"No!" he rejected quickly.

Then she rushed at Valerie: "Is it you!"

Her eyes! Like my eyes! Valerie thought.

"Or you?" Lianne asked Paul sadly. Then she looked at Blue.

"No— . . . Already, it— . . ." Blue stammered. The ram's head, he thought febrilely, the inverted star is incomplete without it!

"Is it you?" Lianne asked Bravo.

Bravo's hand clasped Karen's shoulder. Karen shook her head.

"You, Malissa!" Lianne accused.

Superb! Malissa thought.

Then Lianne stood before Albert, very long. Moving, she avoided the black ominous figure of la Duquesa. She frowned before Rev—then Tor. Savannah. Topaze. "Tarah! Where is your son!" She spun around.

"Away," Tarah said tersely.

Already Lianne was addressing Richard. *"Richard— . . . ?"* But the intense question dissolved only for those moments. Abruptly she faced her son for the first time this day. "You, Mark? . . . Or I?"

Then she rushed howling into the other room, where the draped props waited on the stage like the black memories of an abandoned nightmare.

Part IV

21

Richard touched a button on a wall panel. Light flowed into the room, illuminating the stage. The props on the platform were like gravestones.

As if the light had carried them in on a current, the others followed Lianne and Richard into the hall.

"The play," Tarah said aloud. She felt doom—but lightly, like a black feather.

Torsos aflame with perspiration, the mamaloi and the papaloi stretched braceleted arms as if to tear down the sky. Their rattles fell with one more deadly hiss to the floor.

"But the confessions haven't ended," Malissa protested. "Lianne! There's still Lianne!" Exultant, heady with excitement, she would fence with Richard.

Her face white, her eyes shining as if trapped alive within a corpse, Lianne started: "I confess— . . ."

At her words, Mark mounted the stage quickly, looking down at her as if challenging her to continue. Richard faced his son abruptly, as if Lianne's words had stirred mutual memories.

Like two powerful directors, Mark and Richard, Jeremy thought. Jaded bored people involved in jaded games—*just that!* he insisted again.

"Confess to what!" Malissa demanded of Lianne.

Lianne walked to the edge of the round stage. Her eyes, Mark's—they grappled fiercely. "I confess . . . *to the existence of Mark!*" Then she laughed before her son.

Rage blackened Mark's face. He took a step toward his mother. Richard stood swiftly next to Lianne. She turned her head abruptly from her son as if to free a vulturous memory; her laughter became a growl, dark, sensual, the laughter of rape.

Once again, the unformed smile flickered on Mark's beautiful face.

Lianne retreated suddenly, within a hidden chamber of her mind.

Peremptorily, "What is the play, Richard?" Malissa questioned. She realized the confessions would indeed continue, flowing within the play. They must not be forced now.

"About a queen, a blind queen," Richard announced rapidly, "and the man, the only one, who can restore her sight."

"Fraught with possibilities!" Malissa admired, looking at her rings as if mysteriously they would determine her own role in the proceedings. "But there are only two roles."

"There will be several versions of the same play," Richard clarified.

"And what will the queen be like?" Malissa asked.

"Determined—to the point of murder," Richard described. "And passive. Perhaps empty. Sullied. A fake. Frail. Hollow. Lucid. Strong. Evil." He paused. "Pure."

"But that's what we'll discover," Mark interjected.

"The roles haven't been written," Richard said.

"And the youngman—the man who restores the sight of the sullied queen— . . . ?" Tarah could not control her words.

"Sullied?" Richard intercepted her word. "Have you chosen already, Tarah?" Then he answered: "He'll be whatever the queen needs . . . to restore her sight. And he too may be blind—he'll be choosing his own role."

"He would have experience in everything black, man," Blue heard himself say, "to be righteous purified."

"No," Tarah contradicted. "He'll have a luminous purity. With no knowledge of corruption, to cleanse the woman." Despite her words, a kaleidoscope of sensual images colored her mind.

"A violent prince," Rev asserted.

"A powerful one. Here!" said Topaze, touching his groin. "Not a fake one armed with a knife!"

Joja thought: A new role. Finally the role never to be abandoned? Determined by Richard? Or Mark?

"And the ending?" Malissa's hands demanded a spectacular answer.

"The ending of the play is an open question," Richard said. He went on: "The players may wear masks."

"A symbol of a flaw, the origin of their blindness," said the priest, caught.

"Or perhaps no flaw exists," said Richard.

"Will *he,* the man . . . be freed—from his blindness, too?" Valerie heard herself ask.

"We'll see," Richard said.

"But if the players are masked, how will the choice be made?" Malissa eyed her rings like dormant weapons.

"Through intuition—and the magic of human contact," Richard said wryly.

"Sexual contact," Tarah said aloud.

"Perhaps," said Richard.

The terrible mockery of purgation—after confession. A parody of absolution. Communion. The word flashed into Jeremy's mind. Communion with what? Sullied by confession into purity! Words were assuming inverted meanings. Communion had become excommunion. . . . That they might agree to act within the strange play— at the same time that it seemed impossible, Jeremy watched the fascinated, anxious faces. And so again Richard was creating the disorienting momentum that had catapulted them into confessions. And there were the drugs, he reminded himself. That was important. The heavy scent of *la malaspina* hung over them like a cloud—which must be resisted, the priest knew. . . . He said suddenly to Richard: "You've pulled out what you call our confessions—which are nothing but shadows of our lives— . . ."

"Stark, clear shadows," Mark interrupted.

"But what if we refuse the roles you assign?" the priest continued. His eyes sought Tarah's, which responded. A pact. Allies! Then he felt Blue's electric eyes pulling him away.

"You can reject any role—or alter it," said Richard.

First our pasts, now our futures. The control of our jagged lives—and will we allow it? Karen wondered.

"What qualifies you as director of this play?" the priest asked Richard.

"A knowledge of evil, of course."

It was Mark who had answered. Forming completely, the smile on his face belied the seriousness of his words.

"We'll act willingly in his weird play!" Bravo addressed the priest—and knew: On that stage, before them all, she would possess Karen.

Already he had won over at least one powerful participant, Bravo. The erection of the powerful spell, Jeremy told himself; and he could almost view its intricate structure. Yes, Richard was expert at creating the binding ambience of hallucination. We've got to seize control! Jeremy thought.

"And you too will play." Tarah's words shaped their threat at Richard. Within his own play she would trap him.

As if to enter through the circle of the black dome

they had left behind, the whirring helicopter ground directly over the house. Now the sound, moving away, became a descending murmur. There would be at least another guest on the island.

Cam! thought Blue. The Blue Woman?

Suddenly livid, Tarah looked beyond the windowed wall, into the island. Anticipation, fear convoluted into the other.

"Daniel!" Valerie thought aloud.

Paul felt a fury which waited to find its object. Their father? Here? But *was* he their father? Looking at Richard, Paul felt for a sudden moment as if he were staring at a mirrored reflection of himself—but not of what he was; rather, of what he might be.

Malissa's words snatched the attention from the helicopter. "The first queen!" she demanded the play begin.

Richard faced her from the elevated platform.

Sitting lazily before the stage, Mark studied the two carefully.

"Savannah! Who will be your prince?" Richard's voice questioned. He drew the dark shroud from the large square prop on the stage. With a heavy sigh, the drape fell, a crush of black on the floor; revealing:

A velvet throne. A throne which could be an altar. Three steps led to it. Beside it, two half-masks waited; blind, sealed eyes.

Savannah moved onto the platform, the center of the stage—as if she were mounting a scaffold from which she might yet be saved, and vindicated. "I'll be the queen," she said.

Another willing actor! Swiftly! Caught in the trap being shaped with perfect symmetry and cunning. The hypnotic trance claiming each like poison, Jeremy evaluated.

"The mask," Malissa reminded quickly. She knew the

scenes must move rapidly. It was an axiom of the games that momentum was important; any pause might allow the players to question their participation.

"I won't need the mask," Savannah rejected.

Richard agreed with a nod. "There are varieties of blindness."

Savannah had understood this: She was being allowed a possible resurrection: Through her pulled "confession," they had destroyed the elaborately wrought, sustaining structure of her fantastic life. Now she would be offered a means of restoring what had been crushed, and she might yet regain her shattered image through her choice. "I'll be the queen because I feel empty." Her voice was firm, indicating her resolve. "And I want to regain what was lost."

"A purity you never had," Bravo reminded her cruelly. "Pain, Savannah—not purity!"

"It sustained me, and so it was real while it existed," Savannah said. "And maybe now I can make it exist again. If I can alter the act— . . . Pain into . . . fulfillment."

"Perhaps in your choice of prince— . . ." Richard suggested.

Malissa realized excitedly that the play would have no predetermined shape. Like a new river, it would choose its own course. It would be whatever each wanted it to be, a mirror each might shape. But the mirror, too, might assert itself! An excellent entertainment! she approved Richard's device.

"But who can accomplish that? Pain into fulfillment? Fulfillment into purity?" Savannah glanced from guest to guest.

Tor moved toward the throne, perhaps bidding for the role of prince, perhaps only for an identity, any identity.

Savannah's eyes paused on him—but only to acknowledge a similar loss. How could emptiness fill a vacuum? Now her eyes, on Blue, recognized another loss. Now on Richard, they questioned, demanded. Would she choose him?

Malissa prepared for Richard's reaction. Oh, he was forcing Savannah's gaze away! Away from himself—as if he could not or would not provide the answers to her unformed questions: shifting it almost as if by physical force to— . . . Mark! No— . . . To Paul! And quickly away! Saving him? Shifting it unequivocally to:

The priest!

As if by the black command of Richard's eyes, Savannah descended the steps before the throne. She stood before Jeremy. Slowly, she untied the gold sash about her waist: and she drew the pale-blue dress from her shoulders. It slid easily to her feet without a breath. She stood naked before the priest. In the diamond light, her glorious body seemed translucent, like a delicate, golden shell.

Blue: His hand: It opened quickly like a bursting star: A reminder. And now his look dropped to his ankle, to the uncompleted symbol of his violence: A warning.

Tarah: Her face: It turned abruptly toward the priest, as if he might betray *her*.

Valerie: Her hand, lightly, on her brother demanded that he look at her.

Malissa: Her fingers: They locked: The red rings an uneven row of red drops, like a necklace of blood, broken by the stark black pearl.

"Purify me, Father!" Savannah said to the priest. She held her hands to her breasts, as if in offering.

Blue: His mouth. His hand. He touched one with the other.

"Purify me!" Savannah's touch melted on her body, her hands flowed smoothly along the honey torso, down, toward her thighs, holding her hands before her, open, toward the priest, as if to form an entrance for him: into that violated part of her which might yet be sealed by him: "Fill me with *your* purity!" she said, as if in a trance.

Tarah's eyes burned on the priest: *Don't!*

He turned away from Savannah's naked body. "You've hypnotized this girl; with your terrible revelations of her life, you've made her so vulnerable she's in your control!" Jeremy accused Richard, without looking at him this time.

"You're *afraid!*" Malissa lacerated the priest. "You're still running away!"

Turning to him, the priest seemed to appeal to Blue for contradiction.

But Blue's impassivity acquiesced in Malissa's judgment.

"The priest rejects— . . ." started Richard, and corrected himself: "The *prince* rejects the flawed queen in the play."

Savannah retrieved her dress from the floor. She covered her nudity, veiling the violated body. Acknowledging her loss—forever—she moved toward the shell of Tor, who met her. Beautiful statues, they stood before each other. Trapped.

"But for whom, then, will you be the prince?" Richard asked Jeremy. "Not for Savannah, who chose you, wrongly then, as the instrument for her purification?"

"Why, she wanted to seize *his* precious purity!" Malissa parodied indignation. "And he wants only to save himself! But from what, Father Jeremy? Or should I say: For *whom!*"

Quickly Valerie moved toward the priest, as if they had begun to choose allies in the terrible war they called a game. She waited for Paul to join her, but he remained standing apart. Like sudden antagonists, the twins faced each other across the infinite distance of a few feet.

Allowing the question to remain like a sword poised over the priest, "The play," Malissa said, "the play's moving slowly. Who'll be the next queen?"

"You!" Bravo attacked. "A sexless queen!"

"Or you—the queen-prince!" said Malissa. "Perhaps you'd choose la Duquesa as your prince!" she spewed.

"And you would choose Albert!" Bravo countered. She would assume a role in the play, yes; but the time must be right.

"Your grace— . . ." Richard addressed la Duquesa.

La Duquesa's face glittered with tears like black sequins. "I'll be the queen in search of— . . ." The words waited, still difficult to pronounce: In search of the Duke! Finally she was able to finish: "In search of my prince." Once the words were formed, her voice gained authority. "I'll prove that my memory can sustain the cruel assault. I'll find no prince except the resurrected memory of my Duke. And that memory will sustain me, again." In a stately pavan with an invisible partner, she ascended the throne. Framed by the black veils, she sat there, a shrouded ghost in black.

"You'll attempt to purify the tarnished memory," Richard understood.

Like Savannah, she was being allowed the possibility of resurrecting her trampled dreams. "Yes," la Duquesa said. And those dreams began the process: Duke, Duke! *The* Duke!

"You'll be faithful to his memory?" Richard emphasized.

224 • *The Vampires*

"Yes!"

Rev looked narrowly at the queen, as if to place her on target. He had used her before in his bid for power, he would do so again. Yet twice he had been defeated after brief, flashy victories. This time he must proceed as if through a minefield.

"My eyes are already blind to everyone but the memory of the Duke," la Duquesa rejected the mask Topaze had handed her. "My mourning veils are my mask; they turn all others into: Shadows. Because my beautiful Duke justified my life; he converted me from a receptacle into the object of pure love. Oh, on rainy afternoons he brought me presents, and I would give him one in return: my love. Yes, I'll be faithful." She sat on the throne, allowing the lover, twice slaughtered, of her imagination to seize her again, totally; locking the memories as one might lock a treasure; attempting now to bury it beyond violation by another. "Yes! Definitely!" The outline of the dream began to incarnate: "I remember now clearly: The Duke *did* form a kiss on his lips right after the cops shot him—when he saw me, for the last time— . . ."

Issuing a silent, understood command, Richard's eyes were drawing Tor forward; or so it seemed to the priest.

The muscleman mounted the platform.

"Your grace," said Richard, "is this your prince?"

22

La Duquesa gripped the sides of the throne, as if otherwise she might sink into a dangerous ocean. Yet propelled by a greater demand, her hands rose—though haltingly—toward Tor's massive chest. This was the closest she had allowed herself to come to a man, a sexual object, since she had cradled the dying Duke in her lap. A body, Tor stood very still before her. "My . . . fidelity . . . is on trial," la Duquesa whispered a warning to herself. *"The Duke was true to me!"*

A fluid game, whatever they made it, whatever each saw in the role he chose to play: That's why they would accept it: To search among the shadows of their pasts the shadow of their destinies. Joja looked at the queen in black, so totally seized by the role, the test. And who would be her own prince?—*her* destiny? the actress thought with excitement and fear. And premature defiance.

La Duquesa's hands rested on Tor's shoulders— lightly, not fully committed to the touch. Moving lower, her fingers became heavier. Then quickly her body became rigid, as if flushed by a powerful memory; and her fingers withdrew abruptly. She leaned back on the throne. "No," she said. "This is not my prince. My prince is dead."

Her triumph over Richard, Tarah knew in disturbed, vicarious relief.

But already Richard was directing another phase of this play. His eyes questioned Blue.

But Blue glanced at the priest: A silent message to Richard.

Richard nodded at Topaze.

The midget looked up at Malissa for approval.

She gave it: The black-choked finger pointed to the throne.

With exaggerated quietness, Topaze stationed himself on a stool before la Duquesa; her eyes were still sealed.

"Is this your prince, your grace?" Richard asked.

Leaning over, Topaze whispered into the queen's ear: "When my cock is hard, it's— . . ."

226 · *The Vampires*

La Duquesa's fingers moved forward.

"We could go upstairs, or outside!" Topaze said; he knew that if he trapped the queen, the fact would emphasize Rev's failure—and it would strengthen his own place in the entourage by contrast. "I have the largest—..."

Now the queen's fingers floated over the midget's elevated body—without touching him, merely outlining his form. Rigid again, she withdrew. Again she sighed: "My prince is dead."

Rev laughed at the midget's defeat.

Fighting the rejection, "If you feel it just once, you'll *want* it!" the midget shouted angrily at the queen.

"My prince is dead," la Duquesa said firmly.

She was being tested again—exposed by the confession, tested by the play. Was Richard allowing the restoration of her dream? The priest attempted to find a pattern. Or was it all merely sated anarchy?

Topaze had turned helplessly toward Malissa, trying to read her face.

"And so she's proved her fidelity, the purity of her reconstructed love," Tarah said urgently to end the test with la Duquesa's victory—as if her own fidelity would be vindicated. Fidelity? The word jarred her. Faithful to whom? Through all the encounters, the sexual bouts ... faithful to whom?

"Dead?" Lianne echoed the queen's last word. "I hate death, the soul howls," she said. "Unless it's purified." Looking at the queen on the throne, "Certainly she'll find someone to bring her to life," she formed vague words.

To stop Karen's reaction, a shudder, to Lianne's words, Bravo's fingers tightened on her shoulders.

Rashly assuming command—sinewy tattooed body

arched—Rev stood before la Duquesa. Only a spectacular triumph would restore his squashed power.

Aware of his overwhelming, violent, sensual presence, la Duquesa leaned against the throne.

"Is *this* your prince?" Mark asked.

Within the play, the silent contract between her and Mark would finally demand the fulfillment of its terms, Joja knew. And if she could not possess Richard again, she must possess Mark.

This time the queen's fingers did not even reach out tentatively toward Rev. As if to shackle her hands to it, she gripped the sides of the throne. She had always given herself to those who would hurt her! "The Duke is my prince," she said hurriedly, "and he's dead." Through the black veil, Rev was an ominous outline.

Then Rev growled harshly: "Cummere, Freddy!" And his hand dropped over his groin.

Freddy!

The name exploded in the queen's mind. The despised name of her childhood pulled her into a quagmire of memories, of other times. She reached quickly for the mask she had rejected earlier, and she covered her eyes with it.

"Cummere, Freddy!" Rev commanded coldly: the voice the queen would recognize of all the savagely desirable men who had used her, hurt her cruelly, and used her again.

"I'm not Freddy," she said. But her voice hinted of a nervous boy's.

"Yeah, baby," Rev insisted, "you are Freddy. Diggit—you're the skinny little queer who was afraid of the studs he dug—because they'd laugh at you after they'd used you, even beat you up and rob you. But when they came back, you let them use you again!"

"I'm *la Duquesa*!" the queen strengthened her dignity.

"Freddy!" Rev clutched the name tightly.

Malissa watched him in admiration; he would not accept defeat.

"What . . . do . . . you . . . want . . . from . . . me?" Now completely the queen's voice was that of an effeminate, terrified boy. Still, her body resisted even as it edged on the throne. "I'll be faithful to the Duke!" she whispered urgent words which might save her.

Rev crushed viciously: "You're not faithful to no one, Freddy, because you're no duchess—you're just the skinny little hung-up queer Freddy. And That's All!"

La Duquesa dropped the mask from her face. Her eyes were wide and frightened.

Don't surrender! Tarah's mind demanded.

"Good God, stop this torture!" said Jeremy.

"The memory of the Duke will cleanse me!" The queen covered her eyes with her hands over the veil.

"Freddy!" Rev used the name as the fatal weapon against la Duquesa. They were all watching him. Yes, he was formidable. He could feel power. And now he thought beyond a permanent place in the entourage. Beyond a partnership with Bravo. Or anyone else. He had become one of them! Legs spread, "Blow me, Freddy!" he whispered harshly into the queen's ear.

Near the throne—as if he could support her—Albert clenched his pudgy hands into round fists, but his mouth had opened automatically.

The queen *felt* a silent howl within her that was the total of all the unscreamed screams of her life. With a whimper—the bare manifestation of that buried howl which acknowledged the return of Freddy—he fell on his knees before Rev.

Looking down at him disdainfully, Rev pulled the

mourning black veils savagely from Freddy's head. The frail veils ripped with a cry.

Freddy looked up at Rev with undisguised desire.

"And so both the Duke and la Duquesa are dead," Richard pronounced the requiem.

"And Freddy lives again." Malissa turned away.

Contemptuously Rev withdrew from Freddy as he had from Albert.

Freddy remained kneeling. His mind kaleidoscoped: Yellow shadowless bars! Dim gray streets! Crushed rooms coated with velvet grime! A past now the future. Only the memory of imagined love and fidelity had blocked the terrible dam of the past. Black veils tattered, dark lipstick smearing his lips like black blood, he stood up. And he looked savage. He stared at Rev. His tormentor. No—an instrument of torment. It was Richard who had led them into the deadly games. Richard's stone-bright eyes, like funnels sucking them all into his world. His physical beauty. Richard, as unattainable as Duke.... To avenge the crushed dream!

Apparently shapeless, the play was revealing a stunning inevitability about it. Aware of a growing anticipation within her, another part of Tarah knew she must stop the cascading movement.

"Death!" A white shadow, Lianne rushed toward the erect prop to the left of the throne. Pulling the black drape, which sighed, she exposed the stake within whose hollow the long knife was buried like a final punctuation mark on the stage.

Valerie turned from it, as if from the exposure of hidden violence.

The stake. The knife.

Exorcism! the priest thought suddenly, feverishly. Release the evil!

They all stared at the knife, a symbol of power waiting to be seized. Intense whirling currents seemed to shape about the stake. Radiating into waves of hatred, into a beautifully constructed web.

Mark's look passed from one to the other of his father's guests, a look carefully collecting their reactions.

Swiftly! Lianne pulled the knife from the stake. She moved with it toward the velvet throne. Clenching the knife with both hands, she raised it high, held it poised. Now her eyes flashed about the room as if selecting a victim. With a powerful thrust of her frail body, she buried the knife into the throne.

Paul's hand reached automatically to touch his heart.

"We'll kill death!" Lianne shouted. And she plunged the knife again and again into the throne. "We'll exorcise the greatest evil—death! Kill death!" she chanted.

The mamaloi and the papaloi echoed: "Kill death! Kill! Death! Kill! Death!" And their own hands plunged invisible stakes into the frenzied air.

The priest rushed to Lianne. "Stop it!" he demanded.

Lianne crumpled to the floor. Abandoned there, the knife remained plunged into the throne. Released, Lianne stood up, frowning, as if already the scene she had enacted was lost in her mind.

"Your evil is awesome," the priest said to Richard.

"And is *your* good awesome?" Richard asked the priest. There was a trace of weariness in his tone.

"*Is* it, man? Your good—*is* it righteous?" Blue echoed, facing the priest.

Valerie stared at the knife. It could tear her world.

Jeremy turned away. From Blue. From Richard. From the deadly, hollow stake.

"Who'll be the next queen?" Malissa was unsated. "Perhaps a pure queen!" She walked toward Valerie. "Capable of resisting all impurity. But will she?"

Now Paul joined his sister. She touched his hand. It was cold.

Richard stood between Valerie and Malissa.

"Oh?" Malissa seized his sudden reaction.

And so did Mark.

The most powerful ally against Richard! The thought excited Malissa with its possibilities. Mark turned against his father! But if she moved overtly to bring about the split and she was wrong, she might be crushed between them. A deliberate tactic, rehearsed by father and son, to mislead her? She would wait, and watch more keenly. . . . Her choice of Valerie had been arbitrary. It was Richard's sudden reaction that goaded her on now: "Indeed, whom would Valerie choose?" her words knifed. "Perhaps Tor—his powerful muscles to protect her purity! Or that youngman—Blue—for the veneer of purity, with the profound knowledge of evil! But certainly hers is more than a façade. Perhaps Rev—his colorful tattoos might entertain her sense of beauty," she laughed. Her jeweled hands formed mocking distortions of her words. "Whom would she choose?"

Paul's hand tightened on his sister's. The anger on his face warned Malissa.

But Malissa continued the taunting—and although it was directed at Valerie, it was Richard whose reaction she was determining: "Would she choose Topaze? The test of purity must be powerful!"

Valerie saw: Their eyes: A jury about to pass judgment. On what? A crime not committed.

Albert heard Malissa's pounding voice—no longer words: just hammering sounds, inflections, taunts.

"The priest!" Malissa continued relentlessly. There had been no indication of approval from Richard in her assault. Why? A postponement? Something supremely

232 • *The Vampires*

special, saved? "Who could be purer than the priest? But we've seen his reaction to Savannah. Yet Valerie's purity would match his—they might save each other."

"Leave my sister alone," Paul said.

Looking at him gratefully, Valerie no longer saw the stranger that had been emerging gradually through the evening. No—she saw her brother who had shared his life with her. As if by silent signal mutually received, conveyed, their hands rose slowly toward each other's. Palms facing, inches from the other's, the hands paused suddenly. Then as if pulled together by a magnet, the contact was made. Their fingers linked, a chain.

"Of course," Malissa said ambiguously.

Then Valerie pulled her hands away, turned her head: She faced: Lianne's suddenly violent face.

"Death is judgment!" Lianne pulled words from her shattered mind. Slowly she ascended the throne. She pulled out the knife she had buried there, and she dropped it to the floor.

Carefully Richard retrieved it. He inserted it again within the hollow stake.

Now Lianne sat on the throne. She closed her eyes. She leaned back rigidly. As if she were a corpse surrendering to its coffin.

"The dead queen," said Joja.

"Whom do you choose as your prince?" came Malissa's rapacious words at Lianne.

Mark stood before his mother.

Joja's body tensed with anger. And, she acknowledged, jealousy: Was she witnessing the breaking of their unspoken contract, hers and the boy's? Rejecting the sight —Mark erect before Lianne—Joja's eyes fell on the stake.

"Who is your prince, Mother?" Mark's startling words were soft, sensual.

"Richard," Lianne whispered.

Mark barely frowned.

"The only one who can resurrect the dead queen," Karen said aloud.

Bravo felt those words like knives.

Karen's words, Lianne's reaction—Tarah understood: They might thwart her confrontation of Richard fatally if they asserted that they had actually returned in a pilgrimage of gratitude to him. If so, she must prove that if he had "resurrected" them—if he could "resurrect" them—it was to emphasize the death of their souls, within the burning bodies. She prepared her rebuttal before the defense was stated.

Mark did not move from where he stood before his mother—not even when Richard bent over her, his hands on her shoulders.

Kissing her. . . .

Valerie touched her neck. Paul. Again the stranger. Paul. Like Richard. The blue moments. Valerie remembered Lianne's violent face. . . . Richard kissing the woman or— . . . The words flowed out of her mind: *Or sucking her blood!*

Like erect corpses, the mamaloi and the papaloi guarded the throne.

Finally Richard moved away from Lianne.

Still, Mark did not retreat.

A rivalry, yes! Malissa grasped. For Lianne?!

Lianne stood up. Her face was flushed. She stretched, she rubbed her shoulders, her breasts. And she yawned, as if awakening from a deep sleep. "I'm alive!" she said.

It was as if the words had come from her own lips—indeed, Joja mimed them silently: *I'm alive!* As if she had felt the contact, vicariously, between Lianne and Richard, her own body had responded.

Angrily, Bravo sensed Karen's own vicarious reaction.

"We killed death!" Lianne shouted triumphantly into the house. Her eyes, her mind—it was as if they had captured something of peace, an instant, no matter how fleeting.

"Kill death!" chanted the black man and woman.

Then Lianne whispered: "Richard, forgive me, please!"

Richard's face was inscrutable.

"For what!" Malissa pounced on Lianne's words. "Confessions!" she swung the game back.

Lianne pointed at Mark. "For him!" she screamed. "Richard knew!"

"What horrors did she witness?" the priest asked Richard.

"Horrors?" Lianne questioned. "I Escaped!"

"Into insanity," Valerie knew.

"It was *you* who pushed her there!" Tarah accused Richard, desperate because she knew her attack was being thwarted again. If she could use Lianne in her assault! "One of your demonic experiments—what was it, Richard?"

"He warned me!" Lianne flung.

"The accepted invitation to what?" the priest said aloud, the words of implied understanding surprising him—so jarring that he sought to obliterate them with anger: "This insane creature—your victim— . . ." he began accusing.

"At least for moments of peace she rules and controls her own world. *Do you?*" Richard demanded fiercely.

An odd defense. How to interpret it? Malissa wondered. Oh, was it possible? Had Richard indeed driven Lianne into insanity to allow her to . . . Escape? From what? Her obsession with death? From that? Or . . . from whom?

Mark stood on the stage looking at all of them. A smile was all but hidden in the dark, brooding face.

23

"More!" Malissa's rings flashed.

"That tattoo on your your ankle—what . . . ?" Lianne looked abruptly at Blue.

"Death," Blue said. "It's the pentagram of death."

"Of *Satan!*" Malissa corrected with a rubied arc of her hand.

"No," Blue insisted. "Without the ram's head— . . ."

"Death?" Lianne asked sadly. "Then we haven't killed it." She advanced swiftly toward Mark, and her hands rose as if to crush him. Quickly Mark's hands rose over hers.

"My . . . beloved . . . son." She retreated.

The priest addressed Richard: "Isn't this emotional carnage enough?"

"No!" Bravo said firmly. "Let the play continue!" She felt powerful.

Malissa glanced at Karen. Now! To strike at Bravo! But she must know that Richard was ready, too. Her hand rose toward him, lightly, weightlessly. He nodded. "Do you really think you can replace Richard for Karen?" she began her assault on Bravo.

"Yes!" Bravo answered. And then she felt the words ripped away from her: "Because I love her!" The word burned: Love? Desire? What did it matter which it was, or whether one was indeed the other—or whether one existed and the other did not? She had to win—over Malissa, Richard. And no matter how.

"Love!" Malissa laughed.

"Something you're frightened of!" Albert shouted unexpectedly at her.

"It may amuse me later to let *you* play the queen," Malissa ripped.

Hands knotted in fury, "I'll— . . . !" Albert started; but before it could blaze, the flickering courage was stifled by an impotent whimper.

Richard said: "Ascend the throne, Karen—you'll be the queen now."

The challenge! Malissa knew. She and Richard allies for now against Bravo.

"Yes, sit on the throne, Karen," Bravo said.

Like a somnambulist, her body cold, Karen ascended the throne.

Her voice incredibly soft and warm, gentle—incongruous: "Karen," Bravo pronounced the name. "Karen." At last she touched the woman's hair. Tenderly. "Karen."

"A prince?" mocked Malissa. "You'll choose this imitation *man* as your prince, Karen?" Why didn't Richard advance? Would he abandon her now? Was this his ambush? Without him, the scene might turn into her defeat, Bravo's victory.

Bravo's voice was a furry, intimate caress. "Karen, you don't need Richard. Remember, Karen?—that's why you came back; to prove it. He's made you believe you need him, just as he's made the others believe it."

Was she right? Had they been victims of a strong emotional trance? Joja wondered. Had he convinced them that they could not exist without him in order to chain them to him? Was *that* what created the emptiness? The pit, Joja thought. Richard. Mark. Had she allowed one victimization only to expose herself to another? . . . If Karen resisted! By turning from Richard

—to Bravo—indicating she no longer needed him! Then would it all be over? Richard's power rendered illusory? And would she too be free of him—and the pit? And Mark. That was the test.

Turn from Richard! Tarah's mind cried urgently to Karen. Choose Bravo—anyone! Reject Richard! A symbolic victory for them all, it would prepare the others to resist.

Bravo stroked Karen's hair. "Karen, his power over you is imaginary. Prove it! You don't need him, Karen!"

"The frail queen is on her throne courted by a very strange prince indeed!" Malissa rasped. Then she moved toward Richard, but not too closely: near, but still apart. Again her hand floated out toward him, in a reminder of the earlier signal. This time he did not answer it with a nod. Allies might turn on each other! she knew. "Look at Richard, Karen," Malissa goaded like an evil director. "Your true prince, not a substitute!"

Substitutes, Tarah thought bitterly. The countless bodies. Victims. The sexual war. A graveyard of sex.

Bravo's hands framed Karen's beautiful, livid face. Now they tightened about it, as if to squeeze Richard physically out of her mind. "Karen, I'll make you happy." She leaned over the throne, her face barely inches from Karen's lips. The intimate contact. Now?

Malissa's violet-shielded eyes: Shattering the chandeliered light, they blazed like purple burning mirrors. She saw Karen leaning toward Bravo. *Why didn't Richard move!* "Bravo's kiss—what could it be compared to Richard's?" she floundered angrily. Had Richard plotted to abandon her? Would he *allow* Bravo to win this crucial war?

Still, Richard did not move.

Now clearly Karen swayed toward Bravo.

Malissa moved desperately: "Karen! Remember the two women, locked in the darkness! Your mother and another woman, Karen! Remember!"

Bravo turned savagely toward Malissa.

Karen recoiled from Bravo.

"Don't you understand that, too?" Bravo yelled at Karen. "He wanted to sully everything, to render it dirty for you so he could seize control over you! And he did, Karen, brutally! *But he has no power over you now unless you allow it!*"

Karen touched her neck.

Bravo understood: "The symbolic wound—his brand on you. On the others. Don't you see, Karen? It's part of his ability to suggest—nothing more. Not unless you believe it!"

Valerie touched her own neck. Had she merely clawed at it during the blue moments? Paul. Suddenly he looked so much like Mark.

Now! Bravo kissed Karen's lips.

Was Karen responding? No! Yes! Had Bravo won! Malissa, Joja, Tarah stared tensely.

"Father— . . . ?" Mark began to form a question.

Richard moved toward the throne.

Suddenly Karen tore her lips from Bravo's. She faced Richard. Looping, clutching, tearing, Malissa's insane fingers proclaimed victory.

Tarah closed her eyes.

Joja touched her body, as if, finally, to localize the whirling pit.

Richard brought his mouth to Karen's.

Mark's lips parted.

Karen's mouth opened hungrily.

Refusing to acknowledge defeat, determined even now to *force* victory, Bravo clutched Karen's shoulders roughly. Devouringly she kissed the back of Karen's neck. Karen strained toward Richard. Now more desperately, Bravo's hands explored the woman's body, her shoulders, back, thighs—her lips on her shoulders. But Karen's hands pulled Richard even more tightly to her.

Malissa turned away in repugnance from the sexual scene.

Abruptly Richard withdrew. Anger smeared his face. His words came like the sting of Bravo's whip: "You can have her, Bravo! I've prepared her for you!"

Closing her eyes to block the reality of the violent rejection, Karen fell back on the throne.

Bravo looked down at her. And so Richard had won. Malissa's laughter seemed to attack her physically. Holding the butt of her whip like a giant phallus, Bravo thrust it brutally toward Karen as if to plunge it between her legs.

Karen screamed.

At the very moment before the whip would have rent Karen's body, Bravo stopped the savage movement. She withdrew her hand, the whip. She faced Richard. Her voice was hoarse and terrible. "I don't want her any more. I despise you, Richard!"

Karen rose from the throne. Her face was a mask of hatred.

Aimed at Richard? At Bravo? Whichever it was, Karen was through as a witness against Richard, Tarah knew with resignation.

In the hollow stake, the knife waited.

Richard faced the empty throne, his back to his guests.

Defying the very violence he was evoking? Jeremy wondered. Was *that* why the stake was there?

Savannah saw the monstrous opponents, poised in the raging war. Who finally would claim her? She stared at the shadowy, apathetic servants.

Tor, Savannah, Karen, the others on the precipice of

slaughter. And him, Freddy evaluated. Mere entertainment: Practice for the major struggle for ultimate control. Certainly one of them could be goaded into striking. Rev?—the ready executioner? Himself?—la Duquesa had been gentle, Freddy would be fierce now. The priest!—with the power of exorcism! But would he join them? The others would be moving against him soon. Oh, Bravo, yes! Bravo in defeat would be their most powerful ally! . . . Freddy's eyes glided toward her.

Bravo: She stood, coiled, ready to strike.

At Richard? Malissa? Mark. The father as a child, Freddy thought. Duke as a boy.

"The play, father," Mark reminded Richard. The boy's eyes on her clearly chose Joja for the next role.

"The throne is empty, Joja," Richard said.

"You may be the queen now," Mark said softly to her.

The contract, its terms. Its fulfillment. *Or its ultimate rejection—by her!* So what if Karen had failed, *her* own need might prove to be illusory!

Mark's eyes, darkening into the black of Malissa's ring. The hair which touched the collar of his open shirt. His young, young, sensual body. Joja stared at it. And, beside him, Richard, the beautiful, ineffable presence.

"Whom will you choose?" Malissa asked the actress.

Joja moved toward the throne. Her mind repeated insistently, as if to make its choice: The fulfillment of the contract or its final rejection. The pit filled—even if only momentarily—or conquered. Which would it be?

"No, Joja!" Tarah called. Suddenly she felt that everything that was occurring was in preparation for one revelatory moment in her own life, and only the resistance of the others would thwart the diabolical pattern.

But Joja already sat on the throne. Again on a stage. Still in search of her life, the one identity; her *own* role.

Like a priest offering the host to a communicant, with grave ritualistic solemnity the mamaloi handed the actress a blind mask.

Joja looked at it. Her identity. She fastened it about her head. Her red hair framed the stark eyeless mask. It covered only the upper part of her face, rendering it dead, only her mouth alive.

"The empty queen," Malissa announced. "Who can fill her?"

Now at Richard's touch of the panel of buttons on the wall, a curtain—a veil—exhaling, enveloped the throne. This phase of the play would be scrimmed from the others, the players within it would be shadows.

In a vacuum of self-awareness, Valerie and Paul stood apart. Yet Valerie knew: They would be flung into the midst of the play.

Behind the mask, even the blackness dissolved. Joja heard only silence asserting itself loudly. Now someone was approaching the throne. The scar on her neck burned. Her mind imploded with images which she crushed, resurrected, replaced: Richard! Vanquish him! The pit! Richard's face on the screen of her closed vision! His face fading! Into another! No, not fading—superimposed on: Mark's. Mark and Richard! Vanquish him! Vanquish them! The pit!

If Joja surrendered, it would be she alone; Tarah prepared herself.

Aware of a presence within the scrimmed throne, Joja reached out to touch the figure before her. Her hands outlined broad, straight shoulders. Richard! Her fingers traced the open shirt—no, it was not Richard—and through it felt the smooth young skin. Mark. Yes, it was he, finally. Magnetized by the feel of the flesh, her fingers lingered on his chest. Then she felt his hands sliding softly over her breasts. And she knew: She would fulfill the terms of the contract with him—this was his payment for her extorted loyalty. And she knew that in surrendering to the son, she surrendered to the father. She had lost: But it did not matter—because she "saw" Mark and she felt the sensation of awakening, of resurrection. Mark would charge her with life, like Richard: even if only for precious moments. And she knew: She could not—did not want to—be free of them. "Mark!" she whispered.

Boldly her hands slid down the body before her: surrendering willingly before the others beyond the scrim. This scene—like the rest of her life—played on a stage. It did not matter. Just this!

Suddenly her hands withdrew in shock. The small legs! The bulging, hard crotch! She tore the mask from her face.

Topaze stood before her on a stool. Topaze! Not Mark!

Discovered, the midget shook with lurid laughter.

Joja let out a terrible cry which spiraled from the pit. Her hands parted the scrim. She saw Mark staring coldly at her from beyond the stage.

His tongue flitted over his lips, as if something of fulfillment had occurred.

24

"A great stage director!" Malissa lauded Richard. But this time her look included Mark.

"There's no director—just players," Richard said. His face reflected no victory.

"Bastard!" Joja shouted at him.

"*I'm* the one who didn't want you any more," Mark's

words tumbled. "My father didn't have anything to do with any of it."

Any of it! Had she been wrong? The day-long extortion—not on Richard's behalf then? Joja was staring at Mark with rage. And it was then that she realized that she was off the stage. Forever? Her roles all ended? And now what? One assertive act of her own will?

The stake. The knife buried within it.

Savannah and Tor gazed ahead, as if at a mirror which had disappeared.

Tarah: And so she was alone. Joja and Karen were through. She would have to restructure her attack. Alone.

Jeremy: He studied the fierce eyes of those around him. Who will strike against "them"? he thought feverishly, not resisting his thoughts of violence.

Apart, Bravo counted possible allies—she was not through. But she might have to attack indirectly. Through Freddy? Rev? Albert!—to release the pressure of years: an explosion that might consume Malissa. Tor. Joja? Tarah—she seemed to be plotting a lonely vengeance. Blue, waging his own fight—the outcome might render him a strong ally; he had witnessed murder. The priest, now a single faction. Paul, Valerie—the shape of their allegiance was still to emerge.

Malissa swept into the middle of the stage. "The play! Certainly it's just begun," she insisted insatiably. "Valerie!"

"Will you be the queen now?"

Although it was Mark who had asked the question, it seemed to Valerie suddenly that the words had come from her brother. Recurrently words uttered by one seemed formed by another. *La malaspina.* . . . Sweet, wafting, violet-touched fumes lifting her gently onto turbulent waves seemed to pull her to the velvet throne.

Though she did not move, Valerie "saw" herself on the throne embraced again by the blue haze.

Abruptly Richard stood before the girl, blocking the throne to her.

Behind the purple shields, Malissa's eyes were daggers. This time there was no doubt that Richard had deliberately thwarted an examination of the girl. Already he was turning toward the priest, as if offering him in substitution. Yes, through Valerie she would move against Richard, Malissa knew, vaguely, now. But she would allow a postponement, accept this substitute: "The beautiful young priest! Whose prince will he be?"

Looking at the velvet throne, Jeremy saw instead the parody of an altar. Black.

"Not Savannah's," Malissa ground on; "she would have violated your symbolic sanctuary, your own purity —is that correct, Father?" Glancing about the room, she intercepted a distinct reaction from Tarah. "Perhaps Tarah," she offered the priest.

Quickly Tarah faced Jeremy.

This time the priest did not turn away.

To seize their attention, Blue moved toward the gold-framed mirror on the stage. Before it, he gazed at his own image. He raised his hands to touch his reflection. Against it, he resembled the gold silhouettes captured in the panels along the walls. Recoiling, he reacted in shock to the cold, impassive surface.

"The flawed prince!" Malissa announced. "The gold mirror rejects him. Like the youngman Cam!" she twisted.

Blue turned with fury toward her.

"Even the mirror rejects him!" Malissa trampled on. "Inescapably it's— ..."

"Glass," finished Savannah.

Blue opened his mouth, facing them: "I want to confess!" he blurted, as if Malissa's cruel words had forced him into the mysterious sudden action; an arcane proof against rejection.

"The confessions are over—you've told us all there is to know," the priest said quickly.

"Has he?" Richard asked.

The dark smile touched Blue's face once, just lightly, and disappeared. "No," he said.

Lianne walked toward the tall blond youngman. "Confessions, spreading the blackness into harsh light," she said.

"And light into blackness!" Malissa inverted.

"That part of the game is over," Jeremy insisted.

"The game has no rules," Malissa reminded him.

"In the house where I live, the sun stabs the windows. Its blood—yellow—spatters on the floor," Lianne remembered. "What is the color of your blood!" she shouted at Paul.

Within the burgeoning disorientation that was seizing her, Valerie wondered whether *she* had shouted the words.

Paul turned to Richard as if for a reaction, but Richard was staring at Valerie.

Then as soundlessly as a shadow Blue moved away from them. Out of the room. Into the domed hall. Through the white arches. Outside. Into the island.

"He wants you to hear his real confession," Richard said to the priest.

Suddenly the priest realized he was walking away too. Away from them! he told himself.

"Will you run away again?" Malissa tossed at him.

"Escape!" Mark coaxed mockingly.

"Escape, Escape!" Topaze echoed deliriously.

The priest had not realized he had moved so swiftly until, over him, he saw the accusing glass dome filtering the falling night. He looked down at the swirling black and white floor. Its vortex contained their confessions.

"Run away to save yourself!" Malissa yelled at him from the other room.

"No," Richard said to Malissa as he watched the priest leave the house. "He isn't running away."

Outside, the flowers were black. Icy stars shone desperately. The gray moon was as beautiful as a simulated pearl. Distant lightning trembled softly on the rim of the horizon. In the alcove where he and Jeremy had spoken before, Blue waited among mute statues. Mantled in the night's amber-lit darkness, they seemed to listen.

Moments later the priest stood before Blue. "I didn't know you were here," he pronounced the automatic words he must say.

"Yes, you did, man; you righteous did," Blue said.

Jeremy's voice entered the room where the others listened inside the giant house: "I didn't know you were here." And then Blue's answer: "Yes, you did, man; you righteous did."

"This is a terrible outrage!" Tarah said to Richard. "You've wired the alcove in order to listen— . . ."

"The play has merely shifted scene," Richard said.

"It's to *us* they have to confess," Malissa understood excitedly. "Inspired, Richard!" she complimented. "Is all the island wired—and the house? . . . Listen!"

The speakers carried Blue's voice: "You came out here, man, because you know you have to listen to my confession; like I'm the only one who can absolve *you* of the righteous sin of running away."

The priest sighed.

The speakers conveyed Blue's voice: "This is what I want to confess."

Then: Empty silence.

"The microphones, Richard!" Malissa said impatiently. "They've gone dead!"

"No," said Richard. "Some confessions are wordless."

"But what's occurring?" Malissa asked impatiently.

"They'll tell us," Mark assured.

Valerie felt imprisoned within the long ensuing silence. She thought: Paul. And the name assumed a form which melted quickly into: A fleeing black bird! She *felt* her brother's eyes on her; like the shape of her thoughts, his gaze was physical. And although she saw him standing apart from her, she *felt* his mouth on her neck. To save him! Those words became colors: Red! Tinted over by dark blue into: Purple! Deepening to: *Black!* Suddenly she felt herself scream—only felt it, because she heard no sound and no one reacted; it was a silent scream as she faced Lianne's insane smile as if she were staring into a mirror.

Outside: Blue removed his shirt.

His voice came through the speakers: "Forgive me, Father, for I have sinned. This is my sin."

Again: Silence.

Blue's tall body stood naked before the priest. In the hidden amber lights of the grotto it was tarnished gold. Now Blue's hands rested on the other's shoulders. The priest did not react. Blue's fingers removed the priest's collar, which fell, curled, to the ground.

Understanding the sounds which punctuated the electrified silence, "A quiet confession indeed!" Malissa said delightedly.

Blue's lips touched the priest's, which did not open; they merely allowed the contact. There was no reaction; the priest's body might as easily be preparing for violent rage, wound tightly, to uncoil, as for the release of bound passion. Now Blue's hands removed the priest's coat, the shirt. Flesh against flesh.

Blue's voice entered the listening house: "With Cam —that night, man; it bum-tripped me, and I haven't been hard since— ..."

In the black grotto, he opened the priest's pants. Now he stared at the priest's naked thighs. "And I knew it had to be like someone special and beautiful and pure, man. You, man." Now he took the priest's hand, guiding it downward along his own body. His other hand explored the priest's flesh—but not his groin. (The fear, remembered: *"You're not hard!"*) And there was still no reaction from the priest. Anger? Passion? Blue's hand did not yet dare commit itself to the answer. If the priest wasn't aroused— ...

La malaspina! The priest grasped for a reason for this scene in which he was a player.

"So I had to kill him," Blue said easily. The words emerged like flotsam finally surfacing from a deep ocean.

Malissa's fingers seemed to attempt to pull the sounds from the speakers.

Blue's body pressed against the other's. "My confession, man—listen. I killed Mr Stuart."

"It wasn't Cam," the priest said. Not even his voice contained a hint of what his reaction would finally be.

"It was me. I planted Mr Stuart's money on Cam; the jewels. I knew he'd run away. I threatened the Blue Woman if she didn't testify for me." His lips brushed the priest's face, the eyes, the cheeks; his tongue licked the other's mouth.

La malaspina.... "All because he didn't desire you," the priest said. "But you said that later you and Cam— ..."

Blue held the priest's hand, still guiding it. "That we made it on the blood? I lied, man," Blue said. "That, uh—it never happened. We just *fought* on the blood. Cam never wanted me, he never got hard." Now the movement of his hand narrowed about the priest's groin. ("*You're not hard!*" the remembered, terrifying memory bludgeoned him.)

"And you sent him to prison—and he could have got death—only because he didn't desire you," the priest understood.

"Yes," Blue's voice came coldly through the speakers. "Because he didn't desire me."

"And why didn't you kill Cam? You still desired him?" the priest asked.

The dark-blue eyes expressed rage, as if a secret had been exposed; but the steel-cold voice said: "No! I wanted his punishment extended, through the bust, the trial, the sentence. I wanted it to be righteous long."

A murderer! A powerful ally! Bravo thought.

In the alcove Blue's hand led the priest's to his cock, which was aroused, hard for the first time since the rejection by Cam. He said quickly: "I'll give you absolution from your sin of fleeing life." And his other hand finally committed itself to the fatal discovery: It touched the priest's groin. The priest was hard too.

In the house they heard Blue's sigh of triumph.

Suddenly the priest withdrew from Blue. He was aware that the hard organ against his was enclosed by a rubber. The blue rubber with the pentagram.

Blue's arms clung to the priest, containing his resistance. "You *are* hard!" he said victoriously.

The priest wrenched away. "And that's *all* you wanted to prove, that you could do it!"

"And I did, man!" Blue said.

"You substituted me for Cam," the priest said slowly. "And if you hadn't . . . won . . . would you have killed me too?" Even in the darkness he could see the demonic smile on the angel's face before him. The priest adjusted his clothes hurriedly, as if to dispel the reality of what had occurred between them—all, all made possible by Richard, the atmosphere of hallucination, the careful traps, the drug.... Now he looked evenly at Blue. "The face!" the priest struck in sudden retaliation, like an expert killer.

"What face?" Terror clutched Blue.

"The leering face you saw in that mirror long ago— it's back!" the priest continued his counterattack.

"No!" Blue shouted, covering his face. "That face, man—it's ugly!"

"It's back!" the priest moved relentlessly.

Touching his face anxiously, "You're lying!" Blue shouted at Jeremy. "Liar, liar!"

The priest abandoned him to the darkness.

"Motherfuckers!" Blue shouted at the enclosing shadows.

The priest entered the sudden vacuum of silence in the house. Through the speakers, still connected, he heard Blue's desperate voice: "Liar, liar, liar! It *isn't* back!" And the priest knew they had all listened, to everything. He felt rage like a sudden overwhelming fever. But he could not verbalize his ferocious accusation. Any words he uttered would release their judgments—and what form would that finally take?

The priest, a powerful ally, Bravo knew.

A blond shadow—dressed again, again barefoot— Blue entered the room. Anger was etched deeply into his face.

A murderer! An invaluable ally, Bravo evaluated again. But his victory over the priest had turned into rage against him; if it could be redirected against Richard, and Richard's faction included Malissa. Bravo moved quickly: "You look different," she accosted Blue suddenly.

"What, man—uh, why; what? The face!" Blue reacted.

"Yes, your face, your features—they're distorted," Bravo used the priest's assault for her own purpose.

The reaction she sought: Blue touched his face, again in panic. The leering face of long ago! The externalization of the horror within him? Was it possible that both the priest and Bravo were lying?

Bravo swept on: "A distortion— . . ."

Blue turned toward the mirror. He stopped suddenly. With a moan, he turned from it without looking into it. If the face was back! He did not dare find out.

"Richard brought it back!" Bravo redirected the rage.

"You did!" Blue said to Richard. "It was you who prodded and pushed!" He turned to the priest: "Help me, man! You're the only one who can!" he shouted, wiping his face as if to wipe away the despised, remembered, accusing visage.

The priest turned from him. His own life had been a search for a pure crystalline symmetry. "They" had not allowed it. And Blue had been their instrument.

The stake.

The knife.

Blue knew: Murder was easy.

The priest felt Blue's presence like an iron shadow.

The stake.

Blue saw: Blood. The automatic smile which hid, with the glow of an angel, the features of a killer, kissed his face.

The stake. The knife.

"A new queen, Richard!" Malissa moved. "A pure one!" She pointed her black-jeweled finger like an uttered curse at Valerie.

Richard blocked Malissa's path as she advanced toward the girl.

"Oh?" Malissa's purple gaze attempted to direct to Mark the significance of Richard's overt move. "Why don't you want her to play the pure queen, Richard?" she struck, her look on Mark emphasizing for him the significance of what was occurring. She began to understand— ...

"The pure queen!" Mark seemed to insist.

In defiance of his father? The wedge? Malissa stood abruptly between father and son.

Richard.

Malissa.

Mark.

A triangle.

"Let her ascend the throne, Richard!" Malissa's words cut.

The melting figures disappeared from Valerie's mind. There was a diamond clarity. She stood before the throne.

Beside her, the mamaloi and the papaloi were like attendants at a dark wedding.

25

Tarah knew she must thwart this scene. In testing Valerie they would test Paul—and Paul must not be tested. In a monstrous way—she knew it—Paul had been Richard's substitute for Gable. Or—her mind dashed furiously—was this only part of the ultimate, shattering experiment to be revealed? "There's nothing to be tested in this girl," Tarah said. "A test implies a doubt."

"Precisely!" Malissa countered. "And so why should she hesitate to play the role?"

"Leave them alone, Malissa," Tarah warned.

"Them?" Malissa seized. "We're testing only Valerie—and you'd deprive us of the pure queen?" she said to Tarah, but she looked at Richard. "Why, perhaps she might cleanse us all," she mocked. "Give her the mask!" she ordered Topaze peremptorily.

Clutching the eye-mask, Topaze leapt toward Valerie.

Richard's lips parted.

To protest?

Mark turned quickly toward him.

A challenge to his father? Malissa wondered eagerly.

Mark. Richard. A silent exchange between them.

Suddenly: "I'll be the blind queen!" Tarah offered herself in substitution. She snatched the mask from Topaze. She fastened it quickly over her eyes.

Valerie retreated from the throne. The black man and woman still guarded her.

And so again the girl's scene had been thwarted. Yes, the twins were the focal point of the evening's games! Malissa understood progressively more clearly, though there were still important deductions to be drawn. She felt no disappointment that Valerie had been substituted. For now. Just another postponement. Now it would be Tarah, and certainly that indicated enormous entertainment. Malissa began immediately: "But what prince can purify Tarah?" she asked derisively. "She's confessed that she's tried everything—and everyone! What *special* prince?"

"Perhaps none," said Richard. "Perhaps one."

Behind the scrim veiling the throne again—this scene too would be played by shadows—Tarah questioned herself feverishly: Why did I submit, like the others? And the rapid answer: To stop the assault on Valerie! Valerie? Paul. But why? Because Paul must remain unassailable—as she had wanted the priest to remain. But for what reason? Gable— . . . ! Another reason! Because my body is craving! (And desire immediately clouded anger. . . . The building sensuality of this tense day! The beautiful youngmen surrounding her. Images of naked bodies— . . .) No! Another reason! *Because this is how I'll prepare to kill Richard!* I'll force him to confront me! But how by surrendering to a role in his play? To discover how!

As if he were aware of the clashing doubts, "You do want to play the blind queen, Tarah?" Richard asked.

His voice—the remembered imitation of kindness—she resisted it. "Yes!" she said.

"You're sure, Tarah?" he questioned.

"Yes!" she asserted, to him, to herself. The reasons! Remember the reasons!

Jeremy thought: The acceptance of the invitation. And suddenly he looked at Richard in disorienting surprise.

Lianne uttered: "Richard warned me!"

Mark cocked his head as if to listen more attentively. But that was all Lianne said.

"Who'll be the prince?" Malissa had ended the prologue.

Not Mark! As if a knife had been twisted in her, Joja thought: Would Richard allow it? Then she remembered Mark's words: "My father didn't have anything to do with any of it." Would Mark dare? A further, hideous rejection of her?

Bravo counted Joja as an ally. An actress, she could be assigned any role she might be needed to play.

Karen's eyes followed Bravo like a jungle animal's awaiting the exact moment to strike. It seemed to Karen that her life had been a preparation for the invasion of fury; surrounding her, waiting to be allowed in. Now she allowed it. But as if the savage images of violence hammering at her mind were consuming her energy, she felt a numbing, draining weakness.

Rev.

Albert.

Topaze.

Freddy.

All caught in currents of loathing clashing in the room.

Blue: The mirror. He still did not dare face it. Deprived, then, of his sustenance by the possible presence of the leering, depraved, horrifying face. Was that the sinister presence he felt suddenly in the house? Or . . . Cam! . . . Cam and the priest! *I* am Lord Susej! The thought shaped suddenly on the black lake of his mind.

Richard's back was to them, again; he faced Tarah on the throne.

Taunting them? the priest wondered. Knowing—Richard—that none of them would strike against him? Could they? All that was required was a slight movement—and the easy plunging of the knife into flesh.

Spreading their hands out, arms like wings, as if to collect the waves of hatred roaring in this room, the mamaloi and the papaloi stretched their bodies.

Just once—an echo—softly this time, hardly a whisper, her eyes captured by the black man and black woman, Lianne sighed: "Kill . . . death." And this time almost delicately, she mimed the act of exorcism.

Behind the blind mask and the veiled scrim, Tarah waited on the velvet throne. Footsteps! Words! In rehearsal for this play? If it would test her life, it would also summarize the evil love— . . . encounter, she corrected herself. And still grasping for the iron reason for her presence on the throne (it existed, that reason, she had only to shape it), she found it: Of course: The insatiable sexual appetite which Richard had released again after taming it—the awareness of that—would trigger the murderous anger against him: She had "submitted" to conquer.

The veiled scrim parted; she heard it. A hand touched her breasts lightly. The mere contact engulfed her in desire. Who? The priest?—released finally by the encounter with Blue? But something was lost in her particular desire for him—he was no longer . . . pure. . . . Was it Blue then before her? The blond body. Eagerly she reached out. A bare chest, smooth, hairless. A muscular chest. Tor. The gleaming hard body. (Her mind spewed images quickly: Naked! The rock-hard body mounting her! Strong legs spreading her thighs!)

"A body," Tor's voice offered his tattered identity to her.

"Tarah! Do you choose him?" Malissa's voice shattered the black silence behind the mask like lightning tearing the dark sky.

Contain desire! Frustrate it! Tarah urged herself. Allow it to simmer! Channel it into rage! Rage catapulting murder! "No," she answered Malissa firmly.

Disoriented by the blind, masked eyes—eyes that did not stare—the muscular body removed itself from before the woman; and it retreated against the scrim as if needing to assert its presence, if only the body's outline, to the unmasked eyes beyond it.

Again, the rustle of the curtains, parting. Now without reticence, Tarah reached out. A slender torso. This time the mysterious blond youngman? Blue. A gorgeous depraved angel. Blue? Rev? The tight wiry body. Yes, it was Rev, she knew; he was not tall. (The flaming images scorched her mind: Imagining: The hard tattooed cock, the tattooed hands parting her legs for its entry, and simultaneously the muscular body of Tor, and hungry lips, mouth to mouth, tongue to tongue, twisting bodies, hands on flesh, organs exploring front, back, mouth.)

His radiating violence—he had to say no word—that was Rev's silent promise.

"Is *he* your prince?" Malissa's voice attacked beyond the scrim.

Feeding the growing rage, banking it, "No!" Tarah rejected.

"If you choose me," came Rev's hoarse urgent whisper —and he was determined not to fail in what was a test for him too, "you can count on me against them, and I'll— . . ."

Deliberately, Tarah evoked the memory of endless nights of hunting since Richard: feeding the resolve to murder. "No," she rejected Rev.

Rev heard the midget's choked laughter. From behind the scrim the knife buried in the stake seemed almost fragile.

The curtains parted again. Still within the scrimmed area of the throne, Rev had moved to one side, Tarah knew. She heard short steps. Now other hands touched her shoulders and moved down boldly. The beautiful midget, she knew. The sexual miniature. (The swollen cock, the hugeness exploding, even then growing within her, her scream turning into a sigh, a fierce heat spreading, the expert pumping rhythm, the withdrawing only to thrust again more fully, and Rev's arched body, and Tor's muscles straining, orifices filled, Tor, Rev, Topaze, changing positions, naked bodies, on her, in her!) Yet even if she surrendered, she would crave more. More bodies. And more, she reminded herself. Even as they emptied themselves in her, she would feel empty. Only Richard had brought surcease—and then he had withdrawn: Testing her, challenging her with the two men in that dark, distant room. Remember the terrible insatiability! she told herself. Avenge it!

"And him?" Malissa questioned.

The midget whispered to Tarah—but loud enough for Rev to hear as an implied challenge: "I'll go into you farther than anyone— . . . I'll— . . ."

"No!" Tarah said. Purposely her anger drowned the sexual images. Two twisting funnels—one ruled by desire, the other by hatred—were fusing into the inevitable action.

"Have you found your prince?" Malissa hurled again at the veiled throne. She knew: This was a prelude in the field of emotional crossfire.

"No!" Tarah breathed.

"I'll ball you like you've— . . ." Rev's whispered voice insisted.

"He's a coward!" Topaze said in a low voice. "But I can— . . ."

Legs, bodies, mouths! "No!" Tarah rejected. And it was happening: The deliberately frustrated desire ignited her fury.

"And so this blind queen has found no prince." A statement, it was also Malissa's question to Richard. Other than nodding at Tor, Rev, Topaze—allowing them to proceed toward the throne—he had merely let the scene glide aimlessly, or so it seemed. There had appeared to be no discernible strategy—and yet he knew of Tarah's building attack against him.

Mark too seemed to await a reaction from his father: the uncontested assertion of Tarah's need of him? When there was none, the boy looked coolly at the scrimmed throne, as if he would advance there himself. Instead, his eyes wandered about the room, as if to memorize expressions.

Paul. He watched the scrimmed throne intently.

Mark, studying them. Mark, the inheritor, the priest thought.

The stake.

"The insatiable, hungry queen hasn't found the one—or the ones—who can satisfy her," Malissa repeated, to force Richard to move. Something was wrong. Certainly this was not the end of this scene. Richard must vanquish Tarah's rebellion by proving that she would succumb willingly to him again. Or would this scene have a different ending?

"They're all shadows, like the others. Nothing more," came Tarah's voice. In the few moments on the throne she had relived the horrible emptiness that had driven her life outside of the time with Richard; she could strike coldly in vengeance.

"There's still another possible choice, Tarah," Richard spoke.

The real scene! Malissa understood in relief.

"Will you accept it?" Richard's words were slow. "Will you, Tarah?"

Again the extended invitation, Jeremy thought.

Instantly Tarah's mind was invaded by a shapeless brightness. Now it was the glimmering outline of a face which formed before the blind mask. She breathed deeply of the lilac-scented odor which seemed to cloak her protectively. "Yes!" she said.

"You're sure, Tarah?" Richard's words insisted.

Anger—there was anger on Richard's face. But what was its object? Jeremy frowned.

"Yes!" Tarah repeated. More emptiness! Her resolve would be strengthened even more.... Now she was alone again behind the scrim—footsteps had moved away from her as if responding to a mute signal beyond the throne. Now: Voices. In surprise? Movement. Directed. Other footsteps: Advancing. The veil surrounding the throne breathed, opened. Another presence with her. Richard! Her mind had not been able to block the name quickly enough. Richard! her heart screamed. His face! His body! Only him! But she knew: No, it was not Richard. And was it that knowledge that dredged up the savage fury? She crushed the unwelcome thought. The proof that she no longer needed him was this rehearsal, the preparation for murder. Then who was breathing so near her? Mark. Mark! No! Her mind veered dangerously away from anger and toward desire. Mark's beautiful young body—Richard's son. She remembered Mark clad only in the brief trunks. Suddenly: Paul! Oh, God, no! It was him she wanted to save. Save?! From what! For what! And why? . . . Her hands reached out. A face. Also masked above the lips, which she touched, outlining the mouth gently with her fingers: And his outlined hers. Now her fingers explored the exposed part of his face, his hair—and his discovered hers. Then abruptly her fingers froze. Suddenly his own stopped their movements. Tarah's mind blazed with a brightness which assumed a definite shape. Now her hands resumed their movements. She touched his neck, the bare flesh of his torso. And his hands floated over her breasts. Their lips met, opened, devoured. Desire flowered in Tarah; desire which was luminous, beautiful, glorious, fulfilling: a perfect dream finally realized. She stood. The two bodies locked tightly. Quickly she removed the mask from her eyes.

With a cry—flinging herself back on the throne as if it would ensnare her, Tarah twisted her head away from the masked beautiful face before her.

The shirtless youngman tore at his own mask. Moaning, he moved back in shock from the throne. "Oh, God! No!" he uttered.

Her head thrashing wildly on the throne, Tarah could

still discern the horror on her son's face staring down at her. Suddenly she pushed open the encircling curtains, as if to reveal the trap.

Gable recoiled from her.

Malissa hissed: "Your prince—your son!"

Quickly: "I didn't know!" Tarah protested hysterically.

"You knew, Tarah," Richard said, his words like iron.

"No!" she insisted. "Did *he?* Did Gable know?" her broken voice sobbed.

"Ask him," Richard said.

But Tarah could not face her son.

"Did you know?" Mark asked his half brother. "When my father invited you here, did you know?" His voice was even, soft, controlled—commanding: an assertion, not a question.

Gable stared at his mother. Then without answering Mark, he covered his face with his hands.

"He knew," Richard said.

"Liar!" Gable recovered. "I didn't even know you were my father!"

"Not when I first contacted you. But then I told you, Gable," Richard said.

"But not that it would be she! Just that I would be in your play—masked!"

"Yes, yes, we were masked, we didn't know!" Tarah asserted.

Malissa hovered about them like a vulture over violated carrion. "Of course you knew, both of you! You explored each other's features. The remembered shape of forbidden dreams. You knew!"

"This is what she tried to shelter you for," Richard said to Gable. "For herself. But you didn't have the courage, did you, Tarah?—until now. All it required was the subterfuge of a mask."

"No, no, no, no!" Tarah yelled. She pulled savagely at the scrimmed curtains about the throne. They fell about her, like her world.

"Your pure prince!" Malissa said. "Where was *he* when you went on your 'secret' escapades!" Her rubied fingers ground the words.

Tarah's eyes were green fire. "I'll still kill you, you bastard!" she yelled at Richard.

Richard said softly, almost a whisper: "For allowing you to experience what you've longed to experience?" His eyes made an arc about the room; it included Joja, Karen, the others.

"This is the most monstrous of this hell of horrors!" the priest shouted. He had felt judged by Richard's words.

"Monstrous?" Richard turned angrily toward the priest. "For seeing through to your monstrosities?"

"My father invited you here," Mark said.

"Yes, and that's your defense, Richard; and you've taught it to your son," the priest said. "You found the emptiness, you didn't create it—you found the horror, and you exposed it. But each of the women here has told us that she wasn't aware of the emptiness until you— . . ."

"Filled it," Joja finished. "He exposed our loneliness—in exchange for one instant of life."

"And that instant, was it worth it? Was it?" Richard demanded.

"To feel alive—for a moment; to carry the memory of it forever—yes! it was worth it!" Joja said finally. And this time there was no contract of extortion to fulfill. No lines of a role to read. It was her self which had spoken.

"Victim, victimizer—the line fades," Richard

breathed; a deduction drawn. He turned to Tarah, Joja, Karen: *"You* determined the length of those moments; *you* destroyed them; *you* destroyed yourselves. *You* failed *me!"*

How had *she* failed him, Joja wondered. She looked at Mark. But he was only a child then. Only eight years old. And when I held him, it was like— . . . Oh, God, she knew. *Even then!* This day's dark extortion had begun . . . years ago! *And was it over?!*

The stake. The buried knife.

"Oh, yes! Confessions!" Malissa seized. "Our host has joined the game! Confess!"

"Confess?" Richard said with amusement. Then his face became sinister. "I confess to disgust," he said.

Disgust.

Silence was like a violent whirlpool. Disgust. The word spun within the motionless funnel of silence.

"Because we accepted your invitations, your elaborate challenges and experiments, your roles to play," Tarah understood—but with anger. "Not once, but recurrently. Even after the confessions." She stood apart, alone. Was Gable looking at her? Could he face her?

He was a silhouette against the windowed wall.

And beyond the glass, the island's trees were grotesque lurking shadows.

The mutual contract to play his game—that was what Tarah's words had implied. "Yet you stirred the poison!" the priest's accusation rejected what he saw as Richard's judgment. He remembered: The tarantulas in the desert. "It would have remained dormant without you!" To resist the inexplicable flickering of a sudden feeling of closeness with Richard: "You drugged us into all this!" the priest thrust at him. "You used the drug to force our confessions, then to accept roles in your fantastic play! Yes, that's all it was!—the strange scent we've been breathing since we entered this— ... asylum!—this ... hell!"

"There was no drug," Richard said.

"*La malaspina!*" Valerie said urgently.

"A sweet fragrance, like incense," Richard said to Jeremy. "It has no power at all. All that occurred happened willingly. Did you have to think otherwise? Then you provided your own excuse."

Valerie heard a silent scream within her mind.

26

"The play isn't over yet!" Malissa moved for the denouement. The black-pearled ring sought Valerie.

"No, Malissa," Richard said.

Malissa looked at Mark.

Mark's eyes narrowed on his father.

"The experiment is still not completed!" Malissa went on. She began to understand fully—all the seasonal games!

"It's over, Malissa," Richard said.

"*Is* it, Mark?" Malissa advanced to create the split.

Mark's eyes did not release his father.

"The culmination of your experiments, Richard!" Malissa went on. Yes, now was the time! "You've plotted this drama with infinite care—and now you seem to be retreating from its ultimate conclusion. Surely I'm wrong?"

Mark watched his father relentlessly.

"Let's see the result! Now!" Malissa insisted. "Oh, it's not possible! Oh, you're not afraid, Richard?—that in just one day what it took years to prepare— ...

Not *you*, Richard!" She inhaled deeply in preparation for her next words, which her barbaric hands were already shaping: She said: "All your experiments have failed up to now, haven't they, Richard?"

"Succeeded," Mark corrected her.

"No—failed," Malissa insisted. "You were in search of the one who could—would—resist, weren't you, Richard? *And you still are!*"

"The one who would decline your invitation, your own deadly evil," Tarah said.

A wing of anger glided over Mark's face.

"Each time you seemingly won, actually you lost!" Malissa directed the words at Richard, but also at Mark for the impact of their meaning.

Mark's coldly fierce eyes on Richard demanded he reject her accusation.

Richard only smiled.

Malissa accused at last: "Your experiments—your obsessive search for purity! And you suspect it will fail you now too!"

Suddenly Mark moved toward his father. He stood before him. He opened his lips: "Father!" he said.

And then he kissed Richard fully on the lips. For long, long moments, their lips remained, open, on each other's.

"What you said isn't true, Malissa!" Mark turned quickly to the woman, as if within the contact with his father he had found silent reassurance.

"Then let the play proceed!" Malissa challenged.

"It's over," Richard said.

Mark wiped his lips violently as if to tear away the imprint of the kiss.

"You'd deprive us of the most elaborate drama?" Malissa's hands were thrust toward Valerie as if to rip her soul. "*There's* the pure queen!"

"The play is over," Richard repeated more firmly.

"Mark, your father—what's happening to him?" Eagerly Malissa traced the result of her words on Mark's darkening face.

Mark's eyes hammered their gaze at his father.

"Perhaps you're totally wrong, Malissa," Tarah heard herself speak. "Perhaps Richard is afraid his evil *will* finally be resisted." Earlier she had seen a glimmer of Richard's possible motivations—and they had found her guilty. She must erase that.

Richard said only: "The play has ended."

Malissa struck: "You're afraid of the result of your most elaborate experiment—for whatever reason: The one Tarah has offered or the one I suspect! Which one is it, Richard!"

"Was it all then because of your disgust, Richard?" Jeremy said suddenly to Richard. "Did you want to see your own evil resisted? Or are you afraid it will be?"

Then Mark said clearly to Richard: "The play can't be over yet, Father."

Richard moved away from Valerie's path, finally allowing the scene to proceed. "Ascend the throne!" he ordered Valerie. And now his voice was the commanding voice of before.

Tarah moved quickly toward Valerie. Now Karen joined her and Joja. Lianne floated toward the three. They stared at Valerie.

Valerie moved toward the throne. The mamaloi and the papaloi followed her slowly.

"No!" Tarah yelled at Richard. "God damn you!" she shouted. "Leave us all the possibility of doubt—that someone can, finally, resist the hungry evil!"

"That's what we'll see!" said Malissa.

"Ascend the throne, Valerie," Richard commanded.

"I won't allow it!" Tarah yelled. Swiftly she pulled

the knife from the hollow stake, and she lunged toward Richard.

Richard did not move.

"Kill death!" Lianne shouted.

Tarah stood with the bared knife before her former husband, and she was equally aware of Gable, still an inscrutable outline against the window.

Richard was staring at her without expression.

"Is *this* the game, Richard!" Bravo laughed.

With a cry, Tarah turned from Richard. She had glanced at Gable, and desire had flooded her body. In killing Richard, what did she want to kill? The knowledge of herself he had provided?

"Kill him!" came Freddy's voice.

Tarah placed the knife in Freddy's hand. Freddy grasped it quickly.

Rev! The savage tattoos!

Malissa! The shielded eyes! The evil hands!

Richard, Mark: One! Duke!

"Strike, Freddy!" he heard Bravo's voice.

Freddy! Echoes of his whimpered life. He turned away from Richard. From Duke. From all the unapproachable beautiful men. The knife fell before Joja.

Easily the actress retrieved it.

Mark! The black smile shadowed his face. Richard stood beside him.

Joja raised the knife. Then she shook her head wearily. Father. Son. Richard— . . . Mark. . . . The clearly conveyed promise, even now, of his sensuality. The continuing extortion. Forever? Her hand dropped.

Karen took the knife from her. She tried to stand firmly.

Bravo. The brutal whip.

Richard.

But it was as if even that much of action had drained

her strength. Karen released the knife as if it were something very heavy.

The mere ceremony of rebellion! Was it all to thwart the girl's ascent to the fatal throne? Was she a symbol now of their survival? ... Can anyone strike! Is Richard allowing all this! Jeremy saw the knife on the floor.

Rev seized it. Strike! At whom?

Malissa!

Topaze!

Bravo!

Richard.

"Kill her!" It was Albert, choosing Rev as the executioner of his tormentor. "Kill Malissa!"

Malissa moved quickly toward Richard. The beautiful violence—its reflection lighted her face. Her left hand like a sword, the black-pearled finger its sharp point, she outlined a circle which enclosed her, Mark, Richard: as if its invisible boundaries would barricade them against the others: rendering them unassailable within it—except by each other. Raising her hands insanely, the rings blinking like tiny maddened eyes in the light, she shouted at the others: "Don't cross into the circle, or— . . ." She allowed the threat to hover unshaped over them.

Topaze somersaulted against Rev, knocking the knife away from him with his feet. The knife slid on the floor. The midget rushed after it. It would be the key, his entry, to the magic circle which included Malissa. "I'll get it for you, Miss Malissa!" he shouted. But before he could lift it, he looked up at Albert, who held the knife in his hand, pointing it downward at the midget.

"Kill *her*, Albert!" Freddy shouted. He knew that one act of murder might stir another. Then *he* could strike. At Duke!—at Richard! he thought fiercely. "Kill Malissa for all the torture!"

Albert's body trembled. Suddenly his eyes filled with—...

"Tears! He's crying," Bravo said in disgust. "He really does love her."

Topaze seized the abandoned knife. He rushed toward the invisible circle, to enter it. "Here's the knife, Miss Malissa!" he yelled.

"Don't cross!" Malissa warned. If the midget penetrated the boundary she had established, the impact of her deliberate action would be destroyed.

Topaze stood like a tiny statue. He looked quizzically at Malissa. Would she allow him even another season? And if so, after that what! He would plot, learn from her—match her! He looked down at the knife in his small hands. Perhaps one day he might use it against her.

Contemptuously, Bravo took the knife from Topaze.

Head cocked, Topaze stared at her.

Neither Richard nor Mark moved.

Bravo's stare: On Malissa.

Malissa: The black-ringed finger among the rubied drops of gelid blood.

The knife: In Bravo's hand. The whip: In the other.

"We'll see if your crazy magic circle is impenetrable, Malissa! You and your supernatural bullshit!" Bravo's booted feet advanced toward the invisible circle.

"I warn you: Don't come closer!" Malissa shouted.

Suddenly Bravo stopped. A greater victory was possible, she knew: She would split the powerful alliance. She slid the knife on the floor toward Malissa, and she rasped a savage command: "Kill Richard, Malissa! You hate him as much as we do! You envy his power!"

Automatically Malissa spun about to face Richard.

Then she smiled. She saw Bravo's tactic clearly. For these moments she and Richard must remain allies. Canceling Bravo's strategic move, she laughed. To show her contempt, she pushed the knife away with her foot.

"She broke the righteous circle herself," Blue uttered. "She cut it with the knife. Now it's open."

Savannah and Tor looked apathetically at the knife as if for them there was nothing further to vindicate. Even at this moment of poised violence—as if the victor would claim her—Savannah wondered: What will happen to me now? The shadowy servants seemed to stare at her as if in answer.

Gable bent over the knife.

"Kill him!" Tarah shouted at her son. "For what he did to you! To us!" Yes, it would be this way! Yes, it must be Gable who would kill Richard! Mysteriously, without her conscious knowledge, she must have known that it must be like this.

Holding the knife, Gable advanced toward Richard.

Infinite moments.

"Kill him!" Tarah yelled.

"Her!" Mark said. That was all.

Gable turned away from Richard and toward his mother. He uttered only one word at her:

"Whore," he said.

Tarah's head lashed to one side as if struck.

Gable dropped the knife.

Blue studied it carefully before lifting it. Murder was so easy, flesh did not resist, it would melt at the point of a knife. Like wax. But first: Finally he would face the mirror. The knife in his hand, he stood before it. The demonic face was not there. Only the face of the sensual dark angel. "You lied, Bravo," he said.

"Yes!" Karen cried out at him. "She lied—because

she wanted to torture you. Like Cam!" she attempted to turn his murderous rage against Bravo.

Cam! Blue's eyes narrowed on Bravo. Then he transfered the dark-blue stare to the priest. He walked toward him as if pulled there. He stood before the priest.

Suddenly, in an insane, frantic gesture, Blue ripped at his own ankle with the knife.

"He's trying to erase the inverted pentagram!" Joja said.

"No," Malissa contradicted. "He's trying to carve the missing ram's head of Satan!"

Blue's ankle blossomed with blood.

"Don't!" the priest stopped him.

Now Blue straightened his long body. He raised the knife before the priest. Jeremy did not wince. Then Blue handed the knife gently to the priest and turned his back.

"Exorcise the evil," Blue said finally, looking down at his feet. Blood had erased the tattoo.

And did he mean to exorcise the evil in Richard? Or his own, Blue's? *Or my own!* Jeremy thought, and he held the knife.

"Kill him, Father!" Karen cried.

And she meant Richard, the priest knew. Blue still stood with his back to him. But now Jeremy faced Richard.

Stretched, hands as if ready to clutch the night, the bodies of the mamaloi and the papaloi prepared to welcome violent death when it struck.

Completely calm, Richard had made no move.

His confident coldness, did it warn that if they destroyed him, they destroyed the excuse, the blame—
. . . For what! Jeremy's mind demanded. Was it possible that they could indeed not live without him?

The priest dropped the knife.

And slowly, he nodded at Richard, understanding. Like enemies discovering, finally, that, all along, they were allies.

In a flash of white, Lianne glided with the knife toward Mark. In one swift threatening movement she raised it before him with both hands.

Calmly but firmly, "Give it to *her*, Mother," Mark said; and he indicated Valerie. Now there was not even a trace of the shadowy smile on the boy's face.

"Richard . . . warned . . . me . . . before . . . you . . . were . . . born!" Lianne struggled to form the words. She still held the knife before Mark.

"Give it to *her*, Mother," Mark repeated more firmly.

Lianne brought the knife down violently into the air. Then, obeying, she walked with it toward Valerie.

Valerie still stood before the throne with her brother. Lianne held the knife cuddled in her arms, like an offering to Valerie.

Valerie took it.

"Kill him!" came Freddy's voice. Then at last Tor's: "Kill him!" Karen's again. Savannah's, released. Albert's! Tarah's! Bravo's! Rev's! Topaze's! "Kill him!" "Kill her!" And now it was an exhortation directed at no one; it had no definable object—someone in their past, someone in their present—perhaps themselves:

"Kill him!" "Kill her!"
  "Kill him!"
"Kill her!"
  "Kill him!" Kill him!"
"Kill her!"
  "Kill him!"
    "Kill him!"

And then Malissa saw this: Mark stepped out of the invisible circle which she herself had torn with the rejected knife—separating himself from his father, from her, from the others. Soundlessly, as if in rehearsal of lines soon to be spoken aloud, the boy's lips formed the words—distinctly, coldly:

Kill ... him. ...

And whom did he mean! What victim had *he* chosen! Was it possible he had meant his father? Or what other victim? And for whom had he chosen that ambiguous victim? ... Malissa raised her head exultantly.

Valerie heard voices without discernible origin. Kill him, save him, kill him, save him, kill him, save him, kill, save, kill, save, save, save, save! Save!

The knife was cold in her hand, but she felt it scorching her.

She saw: Faces staring at her! Masks! Mouths! The bruise on her neck burned. Now she saw only Richard. And then Mark. Mark and Richard! Their eyes were red. Paul. Paul's face! Her brother's face was a mask like theirs! And his lips were smeared with— ... No!

Suddenly she rushed from the throne, running away from the leering maskfaces, away from this room, this fatal stage, into the hall trapped by the gaping dome exposing a dark heaven, up the stairs, along corridors, past mirrors, past the gold panels on the walls. Mirrors! Panels! Mirrors! Panels! Mirrors! They caught her fleeing image, tossed it into others; and momentarily it seemed to join, even in motion, the waiting figures frozen in silhouettes within the framed panels. Then: Mirrors! And her screaming, rushing image! She held the knife before her as if to destroy the very air in the house. Voices left behind her—downstairs! But someone was following her! Running after her!

Inside her room, she was enveloped instantly by the blue mist.

Breathless, she lay on the bed. She waited. She knew.

Already she saw the shadow at the open door, framed by the light from the hall.

"Paul," she said.

Downstairs, Malissa confronted Richard. "The speakers! Connect the speakers in her room!"

"No," Richard refused.

"You're afraid!" Malissa lashed.

This time it was Mark who touched the panel of buttons on the wall.

"Valerie," the speakers carried Paul's voice from the bedroom.

"Now we'll know the fruition of the carefully nurtured purity!" Malissa said.

Paul sat on the bed, beside his sister.

The speakers magnified Valerie's whispered words: "You did come to me earlier, Paul. You touched my neck with your lips, you drew— . . . blood."

"You imagined it," said Paul's voice.

"You had been with Richard first," she said. Then this thought occurred to her, for the first time: "Or with Mark."

"No, Valerie," he said. "You imagined it all."

"The bruise," she said, touching her neck.

"You tore at your own flesh, you had a dream, a nightmare," Paul said. And he touched her shoulders, softly. Now his hand brushed the bruise on her neck.

She closed her eyes. She felt his breath, his face only inches from hers. And now her hands rose.

"Valerie, Valerie. . . ."

Malissa held her breath. Then there was silence from the speakers. "*There* is your purity, Richard!" she announced the mock epitaph. "Incest!"

Richard sighed.

In defeat, Tarah knew. That sigh. She understood,

unequivocally and painfully: Yes, he had wanted each of his own experiments to fail.

And Malissa knew too. Her deadly fingers slaughtered: "It's over for you, Richard!" she pronounced.

Softly, "Yes, it's over," Mark said to his father.

Malissa's mind clashed: Before the season was over would Mark attempt to seize total control! Would it be Mark she would ultimately confront? This season? Next?

Then they heard the scream flooding the speakers.

Lianne echoed it.

Pulled by it, they rushed upstairs.

Paul staggered away from his sister. The knife buried between his shoulders, he fell face down to the floor.

Raging, Valerie stood over him.

Her scream erupted throughout the house.

Valerie knelt over her brother's body. She pulled out the knife she had thrust into his astonished flesh. His scream of terror blended with hers. Twisting his body in one final flailing, he faced her from the floor. Then she raised the knife, and she plunged it again into his body as if driving a stake into his heart. *To exorcise the evil!* Blood poured out like a red orchid. She plunged again. His scream rushed at her like a savage black bird, fused with hers, as if he too were slaughtering her. Now only her scream remained.

Faces suddenly at the door.

Voices surrounded her: *Is this the game no God nobody plays games like that an exorcism playing at God no Satan no no your terrible experiment exorcised is this the game?*

Valerie stood up. She saw the others now in the room, the maskfaces gathering about her and her brother. And she saw their lips dripping with blood. Quickly she looked down at her brother. His chest was covered with blood.

But there was no blood on his lips!

Then again suddenly she had the sensation of fire. She could hear it roaring! It would consume them all! She knew it was devouring the walls, the drapes, the furniture.

But she saw no flames, felt no heat.

Still, she knew they were all burning.

Even as she saw the house intact and the strange people gathering about her, even then she knew that the terrible house was on fire and they were all being consumed within the roaring holocaust of purification. She closed her eyes, and there was nothing but a pure, pure blackness.

At the door Malissa faced Mark.

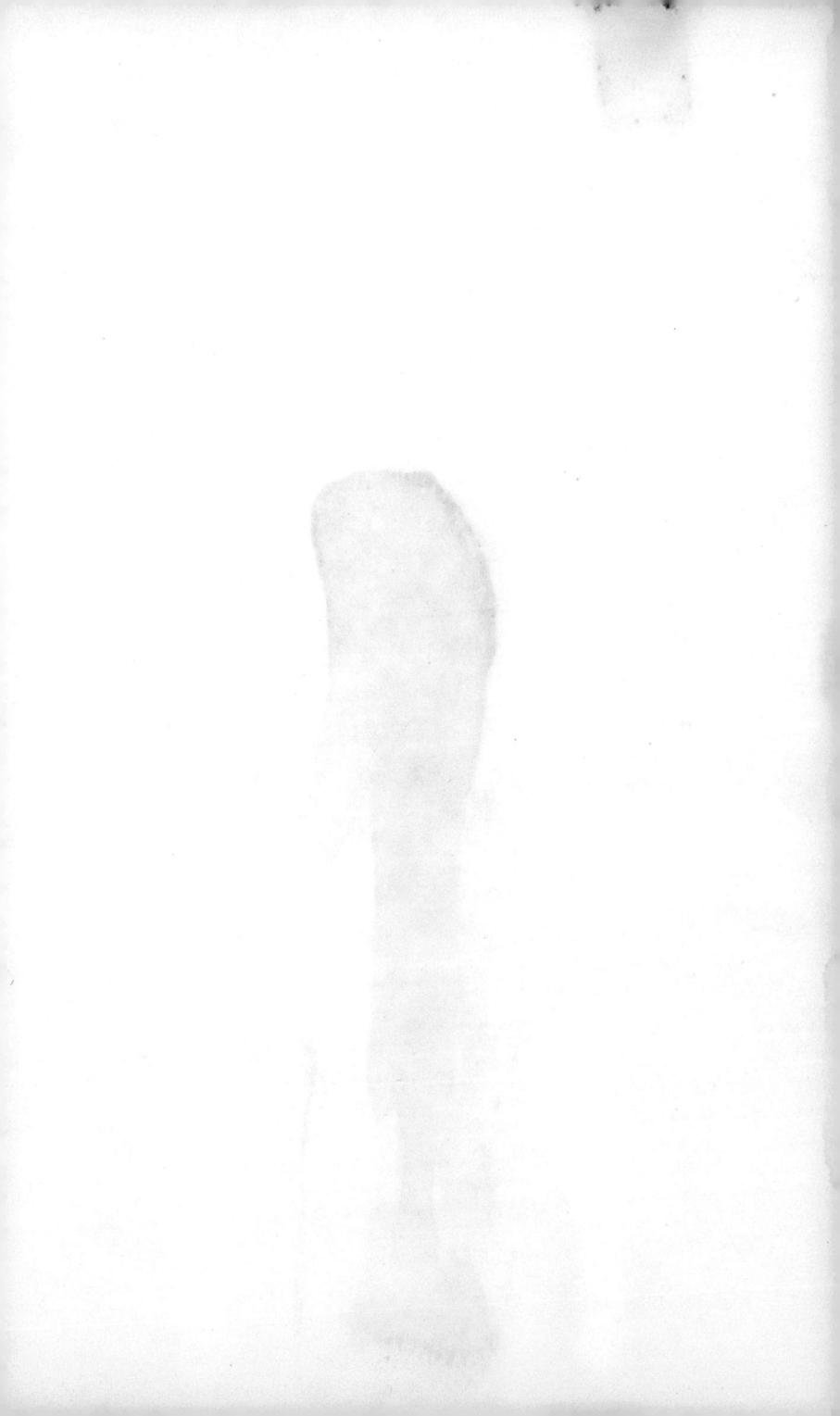